A NOTE ON THE AUTHOR

Abda Khan is an author and lawyer, and a passionate advocate for women's rights. She won the Noor Inayat Khan Muslim Woman of the Year Award 2019 and was highly commended in the 2017 NatWest Asian Women of Achievement Awards in the Arts & Culture category. Her first novel, *Stained*, was published in 2016.

With special thanks:
Afzal Majid
Suleman Mehboob
Salma Shah

Also by the Author
Stained

RAZIA

Abda Khan

30 Sept. 2020

Dedicated to the
families who are left
behind picking up the pieces
from other's actions.
    Much love,

unbound

First published in Great Britain 2019

Unbound
6th Floor Mutual House, 70 Conduit Street,
London W1S 2GF

www.unbound.com

Text Design by Ellipsis, Glasgow

A CIP record for this book is available from the British Library

ISBN 978-1-78352-704-5 (trade pbk)
ISBN 978-1-78352-706-9 (ebook)
ISBN 978-1-78352-705-2 (limited edition)

Printed in Great Britain by CPI (UK) Ltd

To the five lights of my life,
May you always shine brightly
Love you always,
Mum

1

LONDON

Farah Jilani walked out of Knightsbridge tube station, and stopped briefly to gaze up at the sky. She observed that there was still a vast blanket of grey covering London. It was a well-settled, clouded canopy which hadn't shifted for nearly a week.

She glanced over the road at the window display of the spring collection at Harvey Nichols; the mannequins were kitted out in the new season's colours of soft sherbet pink, creamy lemon and duck-egg blue. They stood and posed invitingly, trying their best to entice her over with their silent gaze. She was tempted to take on the busy traffic, and hop across the road for a quick browse, but a few seconds of hesitation was enough for Farah to talk herself out of it.

Farah felt the cool air sweep over her, so she buttoned up her long black coat, turned to her right, walked past the newspaper stand and headed up Sloane Street.

Although she was familiar with Knightsbridge, Farah had never visited Hans Place before. It was about as exclusive a postcode as one could get in London, being only a stone's throw away from Harrods, and all things high-end and unaffordable for most. Unless you were someone akin to a Russian oligarch or an Arab prince, owning or renting in Hans Place was well out of your reach. Farah didn't for a moment doubt that the apartment she was going to visit tonight would be palatial compared to the one-bedroom box that she rented.

As she ambled along Sloane Street, she glanced at her watch, and realised that she was going to be early. She did not want to be the first one to arrive. Time enough for a quick cup of coffee, she thought to herself, and stopped off at the next coffee shop she came to.

The shop was a small, rustic-looking outfit; the flooring was all old-fashioned, speckled oak boards, and the place was scattered with solid wooden tables and mismatched antique chairs. Farah looked up at the chalkboard menu behind the counter, and saw that it served all manner of organic and fair-trade hot drinks, as well as exotic-sounding smoothies and juices. A pale, gaunt young woman behind the counter came over to serve Farah. She spoke with a strong Eastern European accent. She seemed very keen for Farah to sample 'a super-detox clean green juice'. No? Then maybe 'an energy-boosting super-charged smoothie'? Perhaps there were floppy sticks of celery or overly spotty bananas which she had been told needed to be shifted. Farah wasn't about to find out, and so she politely declined. The girl's face crinkled. What would she like then? Farah opted instead for a large Americano, and the girl quietly obliged.

Farah went over and sat on a shabby but pretty dusky pink armchair by the window, and waited for her coffee to cool. It had just gone 6.30 on a Friday evening, and the coffee shop was quiet. There were only a couple of other people in there, both loners like herself.

As she settled into the armchair and placed her hands on the frayed armrests on either side, she wondered how much this chair had seen and heard over the years. The careful whispers of lovers at the height of their clandestine affair, when they caught a few stolen moments together? Or perhaps the shrieks and gasps of best friends spiritedly sharing and dissecting the latest gossip? Maybe a loved one offering consolation after bad news. Unlike humans, however, this chair would never give up its secrets, never betray the confidence of anyone who had sought sanctuary in its sunken softness. It wouldn't make false promises. It wouldn't pretend to be anything other than it was. It would just be there.

She gazed out of the window and noticed how the scene thronged with cars, taxis and buses that were all crawling along, trying, but failing, to make haste with their journeys. In contrast, all the pedestrians were dashing around hurriedly; most of them periodically looked up from their mobile phones, as they scurried about in a serious rush to be somewhere. Nothing and no one within her eye gaze was stood or sat still. She wondered if, after having been in London for over ten years, she was now tired of it all. She briefly closed her eyes and savoured her first sip of the coffee. Perhaps, she thought, it wasn't London the city that she was fed up with. In her heart, London was the best place in the world, for many reasons. The view of the River Thames on a misty morning often took her breath away. There were modern feats of architecture that sat happily alongside the resplendent heritage of bygone years. The museums and galleries allowed you to quite happily lose yourself for an entire day without a care in the world. No matter which corner of which street you turned, be it an old cobbled side road with tiny eateries and open-air market stalls, or Buckingham Palace Road or the Strand, you were never alone in London, for there was always life and vibrancy in every inch of this city. Perhaps, she mulled, as she quietly drank her coffee, and continued to stare out of the window, it was indeed not London, but some of its people that she'd had enough of.

Farah wasn't looking forward to the dinner party. Even though it was a Friday evening, her bosses had requested, or rather expected, her attendance. As work colleagues, they rarely met out of the office, and she hadn't seen Tahir Ghani (the junior partner at the firm) socially since their relationship had ended just over six months ago. Having to pretend to enjoy herself was going to be an enormous drag. She had, in fact, planned on going up to her parents' house this very evening, but had postponed this to the next morning. An invite from Zaheer Mansur to his apartment for dinner was too big a deal for Drake's Solicitors to ignore, because he had practically saved the firm from certain bankruptcy.

Paul Drake, the senior partner, and Tahir were more than grateful to Zaheer for his help. Farah, however, was never 100 per cent happy with their 'arrangement', for she was sure that the partners were not declaring to the Law Society the referral fees that they were paying to Zaheer. Zaheer and Paul's association went back a long way. They had studied together in London over twenty years ago, and as soon as Zaheer had been posted as the Deputy High Commissioner at the High Commission for Pakistan in London, they had reached a deal, and work had started flowing the firm's way.

The Pakistani High Commission was always busy, with all manner of people walking through the door, and said people were quite often in need of legal help. A man in Zaheer's position was more than respected; his advice as to who they should consult for their visa application, or to prepare that power of attorney, or to deal with a property transaction, or to represent them at court, was usually followed without question. Drake's had steadily become busier as a result, and of course new clients once referred became a continued source of income minus the need to pay referral fees; this new business had meant the saving of over twenty jobs. Tonight's dinner was to celebrate a year since the start of this mutually fruitful arrangement.

Farah and the two partners were the only ones attending this celebratory meal. She had originally been a little surprised that they had asked her to come, but once she had thought about it, she knew why. She was head of the immigration department, and a large chunk of the work sent to the firm ended up with her team; however, that wasn't it – the real reason that she had been invited was because she was a woman of Pakistani origin, and spoke decent Urdu, and therefore her bosses expected that she would provide ideal company for Zaheer's wife, Aneela. They had suggested she wear traditional dress, so Aneela would feel more comfortable, for Aneela herself would be sure to be dressed in a traditional *salwar kameez*. However, whilst Farah was just about agreeable to attending the dinner for the sake of the firm, she was not going to be ordered around about what she should wear, and so she blatantly ignored this request; she wore a purple silk blouse and high-waisted black evening trousers instead. She had made some effort; black heels, glitzy earrings and an immaculately made-up face. She had even styled her usually straight long black hair into soft gentle waves that cascaded down past her shoulders.

After her brief refreshment break, Farah proceeded to continue her walk to her destination. When she surveyed it upon arrival, it dawned on her that Hans Place was even grander than she had imagined. Dating back to the late 1700s, it contained imposing multi-storey buildings which were set around a fine-looking square, which was occupied by handsome, mature chestnut and lime trees. Farah had read that Jane Austen had resided at 23 Hans Place during her stay in London with her brother. Farah walked across to the tree-laden garden in the middle; she fancied having a wander about inside, but sadly, the gate was locked. After a short stroll around the square, she found the door; the entrance to the building was an ornate black door, surrounded by stone columns on either side, and a well-crafted stone arch overhead. Then she walked around to the side of the building, where she found that there was a round, royal blue plaque, which announced in simple print:

JANE AUSTEN

NOVELIST

STAYED WITH HER BROTHER HENRY

IN A HOUSE ON THIS SITE

1814–1815

Farah stood and gazed at the plaque for a few moments, and she imagined that perhaps Jane Austen used to sit in that charming garden and scribble away. Then she glanced at her watch and realised that she was now in fact late, having totally lost track of time. She dragged herself away, and walked round to find the Mansur residence.

2

Farah rang the bell, and after a short wait outside the large door, she was welcomed in by Aneela, who had indeed donned a zari-embroidered *salwar kameez* of stunning deep red chiffon and georgette. She had tied her auburn hair up in a high bun, and wore a vivid red lipstick to complete the red-themed look. Her eyes were heavy with black kajal that was shaped into fine flicks at either end; they looked almost like the arresting eyes of a sweet little deer, timid and eager to please. She showed Farah through to the lounge, where Zaheer, Paul and Tahir were already having drinks and chatting away.

The lounge was a large, impressive room, perfectly square in shape. It was impeccably decorated in every respect. All the set pieces, from the intricately patterned Persian rug, to the fine china vases, were pristinely arranged, and co-ordinated to convey exactly the impression that they were meant to: this was a room which oozed luxury and money.

They all exchanged pleasantries, and Zaheer went off to

pour Farah an orange and lemonade. Farah sat down, and Aneela disappeared from the room. The men then resumed their business talk, and Farah let out a silent sigh. She wondered if this was how the whole evening would progress: Aneela toing and froing from the kitchen, and the guys talking shop.

'You look lovely,' remarked Tahir, after he came and sat beside her on the tan two-seater chesterfield sofa. He looked closely at Farah as he leaned in towards her.

'Thanks,' was all Farah could muster in response to the compliment. She felt a little unnerved by his proximity. She wasn't over it yet. Not in a heartbroken, missing-him sort of way, but rather in an angry 'how could he have treated me like that' sort of way.

Aneela came back into the room.

'Dinner is ready,' she announced, with a theatrical, high-pitched, Pakistani accent-laced voice that denoted a sense of urgency. It made Farah wince a little. 'Please, everyone, come through to the dining room.'

Aneela led the way, and they all followed her. They walked across the large, high-ceilinged hallway into the room directly opposite. The apartment was situated on the ground floor of the listed building, which retained many of its original features, such as the old oak panelling that decked the lower half of the walls in the dining room, and the delicately crafted coving and ceiling roses.

The large oval table was carefully laid with white fine china crockery, glistening crystal glassware and heavy, gleaming silver cutlery. The centre was lit with a dramatic five-arm golden candelabrum, and all of this sat on top of a creamy rose jacquard-print tablecloth.

The appetisers were already in place: *papri chana chaat*, drizzled with a tangy tamarind sauce, with mini pakoras and samosas, and a wild rocket and cherry tomato salad. It was exceptionally delicious, as was evident from the fact that not a scrap was left on anyone's plate. Aneela looked very satisfied with herself when she saw that the food had gone down so well. Whilst her husband was oblivious to such finer details and only cared that his guests appeared to be happy to be in his company, who ate what and enjoyed it was clearly very important to Aneela. She smiled as she collected the empty dishes on a tray, and declared she was off to the kitchen to check on the next course.

The guests talked shop with their host, and exchanged a few funny stories about some of the clients. Paul made a particular effort to ensure that Farah was drawn into the conversation; his easy, familiar banter, which she always enjoyed, allowed her to loosen up a bit. Despite her reservations, Farah was starting to relax, and beginning to enjoy the evening. She joined in with the chit-chat, and now felt bad that she had been so reluctant to come in the first place. Zaheer was all charm and politeness; he spoke with a great sense of conviction about everything he touched upon, and Farah could appreciate why he and Paul were such good friends. And his wife was a very pleasant woman; she couldn't do enough, as she fussed and flitted around her guests, seeing to their every need, making sure everyone was well attended to at all times. They seemed a little bit mismatched as a couple; he was quite simple-looking, albeit smart in his manner of dress, but not terribly memorable, whilst she was beauty and glamour itself. She looked younger than him, although it was hard to say exactly how much younger, for the amount of make-up she wore made it difficult to discern her age with any precision. Farah was left wondering how he had managed to bag such a beauty. However, despite their outwardly mismatched appearance, they seemed very much at ease with one another; they were not only happy with each other, but they innately understood one another. They seemed to be able to communicate with just a glance at times; no words were necessary.

'Aneela has been gone quite a while. Excuse me whilst I go check if she needs a hand with anything,' said Zaheer, and then he disappeared out of the dining room.

Farah was now wishing she hadn't stopped off for that coffee, and found it necessary to disturb the two remaining gentlemen's conversation to confess that she needed to visit the little girls' room, only neither of the hosts was around to show her where it was. However, Paul had visited before, and was able to offer her directions.

'Go back out into the hallway, and as you look to your

left, there are two doors straight ahead, it's the one on the left, I think.'

Farah got up and went down the hallway. She carefully opened the door on the left-hand side, just as she had been directed. She searched for a light switch, which she located on the wall to her left, but as soon as the somewhat dim light came on, she realised that this wasn't the washroom at all. Rather, she had walked into some sort of a large pantry or utility room. It was a very good size, and it was well fitted with wooden cupboards and worktops which most people would be proud to have in their actual kitchen, and all around her were boxed and unboxed dinner sets, pots, pans and various kitchen gadgets. She was about to turn back when she heard shouting and muffled crying. There was another door on the other side of the room. The noise seemed to be coming from there. Farah walked over and stood by the door, and could just about make out the conversation, if she could call it that. It was a strange mix of English, Urdu and Punjabi.

Farah leaned against the door to listen.

'*Haram zaadi*, how dare you ruin the food, can't you do anything right, you little bitch!'

Farah was astonished, for she was certain that it was Zaheer that was yelling. She would never have believed that he could talk to his wife in this way, if she hadn't heard it with her own ears.

She gently pulled the handle to open the door ever so slightly, mindful not to make any sound, and through the tiny gap she could now just about see into the kitchen; from her somewhat limited view she was able to see that it was a large, well-proportioned showroom-type kitchen, with glossy oyster-coloured fitted units, lustrous black granite worktops and state-of-the-art fitted appliances. Zaheer had his back to Farah, and his wife was stood next to him, also with her back to her. They were both looking down. Farah carefully opened the door a tiny bit more, and a sensation of shock flooded through her entire body.

For there, in the far corner, sat next to the range cooker, visible between the gap between Zaheer and Aneela, cowering on the cold stone-tiled floor, was a young woman. She was dressed in traditional *salwar kameez*, both of which were a dirty brown in colour, covered with stains, and pretty much creased from top to bottom. Her mismatched scruffy-looking black *chaddar* was draped around her head, shoulders and chest, and she was wearing tatty plastic green sandals. Her hair was scraped back off her face, and mostly hidden under the *chaddar*. Her complexion was dark brown in tone, and completely plain, lacking any make-up; tears were running down her cheeks. She couldn't have been more than sixteen or seventeen years old.

'Please, *Sahib*!' she mumbled, in a tiny voice, in a dialect of Punjabi that was not Farah's mother tongue of Potwari Punjabi. She seemed to be begging, with both her hands clasped together in front of her, like a prayer pose. 'Everything else is fine; it's just the *murgh musallam*, I'm not sure what happened, but I think I became confused with the timer, and I must have set it wrong. I am still finding these electrical things difficult to understand. Please forgive me, Master!'

She sobbed quietly, but her brown eyes were painfully strained; they exuded fear. The scene unfolding before Farah seemed to be happening in some sort of cruel slow motion. The girl reminded her of a cornered, helpless animal. The girl's eyes darted continuously and desperately from Zaheer to Aneela and back, in an agonising search for some sort of a reprieve.

'*Kameeni*, how many times have I shown you how to set the timer properly, you can't get such a simple task right!' shrieked Aneela.

The girl let out muted sobs.

Zaheer raised his hand. The girl immediately untied her hands from the prayer pose, and spread them over her head. She hid her head in her lap, as if she was certain of the inevitable. However, before Zaheer could make contact, his wife yanked him back.

'Not now, Zaheer,' she urged him. Zaheer stood up tall, straight-backed. He looked down with sheer disdain.

The girl very slowly raised her head out of her lap, inch by inch, and looked up at the couple; her body trembled, and her tears continued to seep, but she didn't make a noise.

'We have guests, or have you forgotten,' continued Aneela, in a hushed tone. 'This is not the time. Leave her be. She will keep.'

Zaheer let out a grunt, as he screwed his hands into fists by his sides.

'She's just like the rest of them. They are always bloody good for nothing. I did say this from the start,' said Zaheer in an exasperated muffle. 'Once a slave, always a slave!'

Farah closed the door and stepped away from it. She moved into the corner of the room, and placed one hand firmly over her frantically beating chest, and the other over her mouth. She closed her eyes, and concentrated hard on trying to calm her uneven breath and stop her hands from shaking. She felt her heart pound. Slave . . . slave . . . she repeated in her mind. She had heard enough. She needed to get out of here. She took another long, deep inhalation, and headed back to the door from which she had entered. She stepped out of the room and into the hallway, and tried the door next to it, and found that this was in fact the bathroom. She quickly went in, and locked the door.

3

When Farah re-entered the dining room, Zaheer was already back in his seat at the head of the table. He was laughing and joking, and making small talk, just as any dinner host would be expected to do. He had just scared a young girl half to death, almost physically assaulted her, shouted abuse at her, reduced her to tears, called her a slave, and yet here he was the life and soul of the party. He was utterly carefree. How could he switch from evil and sinister one moment to happy chappy the next? What sort of a person could do that?

Just as Farah took her seat again, Aneela walked in with a large tray in her hands, which she placed on the table with great pomp and ceremony, as she announced, 'I hope you all like lamb *biryani*. And not only that; there is also chicken *shashlik*, *malai koftas*, and of course *dhal* and *sabzi*. And I will fetch the fresh *rotis* too, shortly. Nothing beats the taste of piping hot, home-made chapattis, especially *mine*; they are always soft and fluffy, just as they should be. It is after all, I think, the true taste of Pakistan, and the real touch of home

16

cooking, to serve home-prepared *rotis* with the meal. Of course, you can get them ready made from the shops nowadays, but the taste is nowhere near as good.'

She was exactly the same as her husband, thought Farah; such deceit!

The freshly prepared, piping hot food was served in elegant bowls and platters. It smelled divine, and was pleasingly presented, but eating was the last thing on Farah's mind. She was trying really hard not to look at either of them, but she was convinced that the more she tried, the more her eyes kept straying towards Zaheer, and then Aneela, and then back to him, in some sort of repetitive trance-like motion that she couldn't control.

'Is the food to your liking, Farah?' asked Aneela.

Farah looked up and met her deer-like eyes. 'Yes, it's delicious. But really, I don't know where you find the time to make all this fantastic food. I know from when my mum prepares feasts like this for dinner parties, or on Eid, that it takes a huge amount of time and effort to make. She normally ropes me plus one or two of the relatives into helping her. Did you prepare all these wonderful dishes by yourself?'

Her question, which was a deliberate pry, prompted a brief exchange of glances between the couple. Aneela suddenly appeared nervous, or at least that's how it seemed to Farah. Zaheer jumped in and answered for her.

'Seeing as you ask, we do actually have some domestic help; we employ a housekeeper who assists Aneela with the cooking and other household chores. This is a big apartment, and we do a lot of entertaining. All of this would simply be too much for Aneela to do all by herself.'

Aneela breathed out a tiny sigh. She gave a little smile to her husband, visibly relieved that he had taken charge. The two male guests, meanwhile, were completely oblivious to any tension there may have been during the exchange between Farah and the hosts. Farah wondered how Paul would feel if he knew about this side of his dear friend.

'Well, however and whoever made this food, it is absolutely delicious,' said Tahir, in between stuffing forkfuls into his mouth, and gawping at Farah.

Farah endeavoured with all her strength to appear relaxed. She tried very hard to portray an external façade of having a pleasant evening. But everything that Zaheer and Aneela now said pierced her ears, for she could only hear their earlier yelling. Any other conversation in the room seemed to dissipate into the background of her consciousness, like the subdued, slurred sound you hear when you swim underwater. Although she was troubled on the inside, she nevertheless continued to smile on the outside through the rest of the evening. Somehow.

Dinner was rounded off with several desserts which were, once again, like the other courses, made and presented to perfection. The dessert trolley was laden with hot rose-scented *gulab jamuns* served with cardamom *kulfi*, creamy white *badam kheer* and bright orange *gajar halwa* infused with the mellow flavour and aroma of saffron, as well as a selection of colourful *mitai*, and an exotic fruit salad. All of this was washed down with traditional cardamom tea. As they tucked into the sweet delights, the men congratulated themselves on the success of their business union, and declared: 'Long may it continue!' Farah felt nauseous, as she continued to think about the girl in the kitchen.

She couldn't head for the front door fast enough when Aneela confirmed that her taxi had arrived.

It was raining heavily when she stepped out onto the street, and Farah stood still for a second just to breathe. She then ran over to the taxi and jumped into the back as fast as she could.

'Terrible weather we're having for this time of the year,' remarked the cab driver in his cockney accent. It was a short while before she even realised that the driver was speaking to her. She looked towards him; he was looking back at her in the mirror, waiting for some sort of a response.

The driver adjusted his checked flat cap slightly, and his gaze darted from the road to Farah's face in the mirror.

'They're saying it's gonna be raining for another week yet.'

'Hmmm,' Farah said, still deep in thought.

'Are you all right, Miss?' asked the taxi driver, 'Only, you look like you've just seen a ghost.'

'That's one way of putting it,' Farah muttered.

'Eh?'

'Oh, sorry. I'm fine, really, thanks for asking,' said Farah.

But Farah was far from fine. She was anything but fine.

When she arrived at her flat, all Farah wanted to do was to get into her cosy bed and sleep. She wanted to stop thinking about that poor girl. But she had no such luck, for she tossed and turned for hours in her bed that night. Her brain was flooded with question after question. Who was this girl? Could Farah have done anything? Should she have gone into the kitchen and said something? Confronted Zaheer and Aneela? Or maybe she should have told Paul or Tahir? She kept churning over and over what she had seen and heard. And one word kept ringing in her ears. Slave, slave, slave . . .

4

Farah jumped off the tube and dashed past the crowds in a monumental effort not to miss her train. She even ran up the left-hand side of the steep escalators, and she was dismally out of breath by the time she finally reached the top. She ran over and hurriedly inserted her ticket into the machine at Marylebone train station. She darted through the barriers once they flung open. She ran as fast as she could, and only just managed by a whisker to jump on to the train before its 10.05 a.m. departure. She had meant to catch a much earlier train, but had slept through her alarm, and then she had wasted a lot of time looking for her stray earring. Before she had gone to bed last night, she had noticed that one earring was missing; they had been a birthday present from her parents three years ago, and she was mortified. She had been too tired and distressed to hunt for it last night and thought it would probably just turn up in the morning. Only it hadn't.

As if this weekend wasn't going to be stressful enough, she

thought to herself, as she sat at a table seat by the window, facing backwards, which she never liked to do, but the lack of empty seats left her with no choice. How could she have lost one half of her most treasured possession? And on top of that, she still couldn't stop thinking about that poor girl. It was all so terribly wrong, but what to do, she asked herself. Her thoughts flip-flopped back and forth between the missing earring, the nameless slave girl and the ghastly day ahead. Her tummy rumbled nervously. Although this could partially be attributed to the fact that she hadn't eaten any breakfast this morning, the rumbles were probably more likely due to the stress she was feeling about the second meeting today.

Farah was now thirty years old and was the only child of parents of Pakistani Muslim heritage. As she had now reached the dreaded number thirty, the issue of her marrying was becoming ever more urgent, especially in her parents' minds. But if she was truthful, it played on her own mind too. She didn't want to appear to be in a desperate rush to marry, but neither did she want to be 'left on the shelf', the woman who couldn't bag herself a decent husband, and was therefore resigned to being talked about endlessly. She wanted, eventually, to marry and have a family, but the task was proving much harder than she had anticipated. The biological clock was ticking, and she wanted to settle down now, but she couldn't move things along any faster than nature, common sense or good fortune would allow.

Recently, Farah had come to a very important decision. She felt that as she had clearly been unsuccessful in the matter herself, she had decided to delegate the important responsibility of seeking a husband solely to her parents. This ancient method of a truly arranged marriage, as opposed to the horrific practice of forced marriage, had worked successfully for centuries. She had made this resolution soon after she and Tahir had split up.

Despite Farah's pretty looks and successful career, she felt that she was in severe danger of not making it to matrimony, for, as she had heard it said many times, the good men will all be taken, and the rest will ask why she is still unmarried at her age if she's such a good catch. Also, to make matters worse, Farah was an only child, and not a son at that. She resented the fact that some people in the family and community had made her parents feel inadequate just for the fact that they hadn't managed to produce a son. Most of them never said anything directly, but somehow indirect insults always seemed worse. At least if people said something to their face, they could retaliate, have their say, but when an insult was pushed through the back door, when it was suggestive talk, when it was dressed up as something else, and said merely to poke and prod at their feelings, there didn't seem to be any way to address it.

When her aunts and uncles mentioned their children, and bragged about how their sons would be carrying on the family name and bloodline, and indeed the family businesses, and talked about how they (the parents) would live with their sons in their ripe old age, Farah knew that her parents felt it. They really felt it; especially her mum. Farah's paternal grandparents had always made her mum feel guilty, as though it was somehow her fault, that she hadn't given them a grandson. They had passed away now, but that didn't stop the other relatives from being hurtful, intentionally or otherwise. At times, Farah's mother would take offence, and let it be known, for unlike her father, who was a quiet and restrained sort of man, her mother could be very straight-talking. This sometimes led to fallings-out with relatives, although these were often short-lived, as there would be hasty reconciliations just before the next family event, if only to keep face, and present a united extended family front to the rest of the world.

It was all of this kind of talk spouted by the relatives, which ranged from mild, idle tittle-tattle, to outright toxic and mean rhetoric, that had spurred Farah to convince her parents, five years ago, to move out of Sparkhill in Birmingham, and relocate to the leafy suburbs of Solihull. She had taken out the mortgage jointly with her father, and after selling their terraced house in Sparkhill, they'd had just about enough money to move to the lofty heights of the very pricey Solihull, regularly referred to as one of the best places to live in the United Kingdom. Farah felt fortunate that her parents had decided to live in England, and not Pakistan; she couldn't even begin to imagine the disadvantages she would have suffered if they had settled in the Motherland.

Farah's father was a driving instructor, and had been one for the past twenty years. He was an easy-going, goodly sort of a man. His tall, slim frame and his gentle smile all added to the air of calmness that swept all around him. He had come to England in the seventies on a fiancé visa, and had married Farah's mother, his second cousin, who was already resident in the UK, soon after his arrival. He had worked in the Cadbury's factory in Bournville for many years, and he had enjoyed his time there, but had decided to become his own boss some years ago, when he passed the driving instructor tests, and started his own driving school. His calm composure and outlook served him well in this line of work. He never lost patience with his students. He was always composed and focused, and his business was a success as a result.

Farah's mother, on the other hand, possessed characteristics that could best be described as diametrically opposite to those of her husband. She was not an unkind or unpleasant person. In fact, she had an extremely good heart, and it was usually in the right place, but she was capable of being more than frank, and of displaying a fiery temperament at times. She did not take nonsense from anyone and was even known to swear given half a chance, which Farah found most unbecoming. Her mother dressed in traditional *salwar kameez* most of the time, which hid her large frame well, and she a wore headscarf whenever she left the house. However, her demure sense of dress didn't in any way cross over into her personality; here, she was anything but demure.

*

When Farah stepped off the train at Solihull train station, despite the nerves about the day ahead, she instantly felt happy to be home. Unlike the weather she had left behind in London, here the sun was shining. Being back here always lifted her mood, whatever the weather. She ran from the platform down the stairs, and out of the back entrance into the alleyway, and took the shortcut towards home.

As she wandered down the street and on to their cul-de-sac, she took in the artist's palette of colours around her: soft spongy green lawns, iridescent flower displays, rows of shiny yellow daffodils and intense red tulips standing tall, all overlooked by grand old oak trees and glittery tall silver birches. And of course, there were her favourite pink and white cherry blossom trees in full spring bloom, all the way down the road; to Farah it was all such a rich canvas compared to the sometimes immense, blank greyness of London.

When she neared her house, the elderly couple from next door smiled and waved to Farah from their car as they drove past, and she waved back.

Farah's father answered the door. A wide smile lit up on his face upon seeing her, and he planted an affectionate kiss on the crown of her head.

'Come in, my darling *beti*; how are you, my sunshine?' he asked.

Following not far behind her father, stomping down the stairs with great force and noise, was her mother, and before

Farah could answer her dad's question, her mum pushed past her husband and waded in.

'Where have you been? Why are you so late? Not a phone call or a text, young lady! And look at the state of you! Dressed in tatty jeans, and a hoodie! Go, *jaldi*, get ready quickly, we are supposed to be there in half an hour!' shouted her mum, even though Farah was stood right in front of her.

'Hello to you too, Mum,' muttered Farah, as she dumped her bags to one side in the hallway by the coat stand.

'Hello, *ki bachi*, upstairs, now!' was the reply.

5

Farah was going to meet Nadeem for the second time. Farah's mother had considered Nadeem an excellent match for her daughter right from the very start, when she had barely heard a whisper about him, let alone met him. He was the eldest of three siblings (so he was probably the most mature and sensible one), said siblings were all boys (which meant there were no evil sisters-in-law to deal with), he was a doctor by profession (obviously right at the top of the list of suitable professions for a potential son-in-law), he had his own house (this was an absolute bonus), he spoke good Urdu (highly impressive) and he was very respectful – in Farah's mother's words, 'What was there not to like?'

The first meeting, two weeks ago, had been one of the worst days of Farah's life. Her mum had told her in no uncertain terms that she was to 'dress up and look pretty', and then gracefully bring in the tray of tea, biscuits and samosas to the lounge where they would all be sat, eagerly waiting: Nadeem, his parents and her parents. Farah had tried to impress on her mum that it was no longer the 1970s; they did not live in a remote village in Pakistan; and that these things probably didn't even happen in rural Pakistan any more. She told her mum that she may have had to do such a thing when she met her father for the first time, but that was way back then, when their village in Pakistan didn't even have electricity or running water, and they had to go to the fields to do their business. Now these cultural anachronisms weren't necessary any more. In fact, Farah had told her mum that it was all very sexist and misogynistic to impose such rituals on young women in this day and age, and as they were a reasonably modern, progressive family (or so Farah liked to think), they should not be part of such a dreadful tradition. However, her protestations fell on deaf ears; her mother did not budge even an inch. Farah knew she couldn't win against her mum when she really had her mind set on something. She could win against most people – colleagues, fellow lawyers, toffee-nosed judges even – but she always admitted defeat against her mother – eventually.

Farah had found the whole episode demeaning and embarrassing; particularly the part where everyone stared at her when she made her entrance, wearing a bright pink, heavily embroidered *salwar kameez*, with a matching pink lipstick, and clattering bangles, as though she were some prize peacock at the Birmingham Botanical Gardens that the visitors had come to gawp at. She cringed every time she thought about it. Clink, clonk went her bangles; they had been such a distraction as she tried to make sure she didn't drop the damn tray.

Today was going to be different though. Nadeem and his parents would not be coming to the house. It had been agreed, at Farah's request, that as that dreaded first meeting was over, the couple should meet in a more relaxed and informal manner, so they could actually talk and get to know each other. Nadeem and his family had been very agreeable to this proposal. So, it was settled that they would all meet at Touchwood shopping centre, and the parents would go off to shop, or do whatever it was that parents did, and Farah and Nadeem would go for a coffee – to give them some time and privacy together. If things went well today, then there could possibly be a marriage proposal in the near future; at least that was Farah's mother's thinking. Farah didn't want to be so presumptuous; on paper it all looked good, but she was unsure yet as to how their interaction would be without the families around. She was certainly going to go with an open mind, and hope for a positive outcome.

Being an upmarket shopping and leisure venue, in an affluent town like Solihull, Touchwood attracted hordes of brand-name shoppers and coffee drinkers, cinema-goers and pizza lovers from far and wide, and today was as busy as ever. The teenagers wandered around in their little groups, clad in the latest fashion of ripped jeans and impossible-to-lace-up trainers, families walked about casually pushing the modern streamlined pushchairs laden with shopping bags, dragging their toddlers along, and classily clad women came armed and ready with their credit cards with the serious task of clothes and shoe shopping in mind.

The two sets of parents walked off together to have a browse in the department store, whilst Farah and Nadeem went and got coffee. They found a small table right in the middle of the coffee shop, which was brimming with shoppers taking a break. Farah grabbed a black hair bobble out of her jacket pocket and tied her loose hair up into a ponytail. Nadeem was dressed in a smart shirt which was paired with designer jeans. For the first time Farah realised how tall he was. They both sat tentatively waiting for the other to start the conversation.

'So, are you busy at work these days?' was Nadeem's rather uninspired attempt. Perhaps he was nervous, thought Farah.

'Yes, I am, as it happens. There simply aren't enough hours in the day. We were very quiet not so long ago, but things have really picked up in the last year or so. I'm getting more new instructions than I know what to do with. So, yes, I am very busy. How about you?'

Nadeem gave out a short, sharp cough to clear his throat before he answered. Farah waited. He scratched an imaginary mark on the table.

'Same,' he said, and took a sip of his coffee.

Same? What kind of an answer was that? Farah asked herself. She put her flat white down and took a good long look at him. He seemed distracted, edgy even; he was looking all around him, and then down at his coffee, and then scratching

31

the mark on the table that didn't exist. He most definitely seemed to be avoiding Farah's gaze. And then he looked at his watch! The cardinal sin. The guy was clearly not into her, that much was easy for her to conclude. She wasn't in the least bit upset, however, for there wasn't an iota of chemistry between them. In fact, she was relieved.

Nadeem started to clear his throat again, and then took a big gulp of coffee. His rather shiny face, with its neat, chiselled features, was now beginning to tense and screw up. After that, his colour started to change, and become paler. Farah was no doctor, but she sensed he might not be feeling too good.

'Are you all right?' she asked, a little concerned that he might keel over any second. She didn't fancy trying to pick up such a big, tall guy off the floor.

'Yes,' he replied blandly.

'It's just that you look a bit peaky. Shall I get you a bottle of water?' she asked, now more worried that he might throw up all over her. She preferred the fainting option.

'No, no, I'm fine, really.'

'Really?'

'No. I mean, yes, I am fine, only . . . I'm not.'

Farah blew out a little sigh, and tapped her fingers on the table.

'Make up your mind, which is it?' Farah now knew for certain that he was not the man for her, for she could never be married to anyone so indecisive.

'The thing is . . .' He looked down, unable to finish his sentence.

'Y-e-s?' asked Farah, trying to speak softly, in an effort to disguise her ever-increasing sense of impatience.

'The thing is . . . I can't marry you. There. I've said it.'

'Well, congratulations on that. But can I ask why, after just our second meeting, you have decided that I'm not good enough for you?'

He now looked up at her.

'Oh no, please, don't get me wrong. It's not that you're not good enough for me.'

'Are you seeing someone else? Like, do you have a girlfriend?'

'No, not exactly.'

'Not exactly? What does that mean? Either you do or you don't,' responded Farah, a little more loudly than she had meant to, prompting a few unwanted glares from the other customers.

'Shush! Keep your voice down,' Nadeem urged her, and he clung on to either side of the table as he spoke.

'I will keep my voice down, if you tell me what the flamin' heck you're talking about. Not that I'm complaining, but just out of interest, and courtesy, can you explain exactly why you not are prepared to consider me for marriage, huh? After all, I am a successful, beautiful young woman. Well?'

'Because . . .'

'Because, what?'

'Because . . . I'm engaged to someone else,' Nadeem whispered.

'You're w*hat*?' she shrieked, prompting even more stares. 'Oh my goodness! This just gets better and better. OK, so if you are already engaged to someone else, then why in the dickens are you seeing prospective young women, in other words *me*, with a view to marriage?'

'Duh? Because I haven't told my parents about her.'

Farah just stared at him in disbelief for a few seconds, open mouthed.

'Why on earth not? I mean, don't you think you should tell them, instead of messing girls like me around. How many girls have you seen before me exactly?'

'Erm . . . about five.'

'Five! That's ridiculous. Surely you should just tell them?'

'It's difficult,' he replied awkwardly.

'Why? What's so difficult about it?' Farah asked, her palms outstretched.

'It's difficult, because she's not Pakistani. She's not even Asian. Or Muslim. She's not even the same colour as us.'

'Oh . . . I see,' said Farah, dragging her words a little. 'So what? Just come clean,' she said more decisively, although a part of her knew that this wasn't an easy thing to do.

'Have you seen my dad? I mean, just look at the size of his beard. He's so strict. He's a five times a day *namazi*, and he even prays *Tahajjud.* Do you know anyone else who prays *Tahajjud*?'

Farah rolled her eyes up a little, thought about it for a few seconds, then shook her head.

'He's performed Hajj like ten times. He's the leader of our local mosque. He's about as strict and traditional a Muslim as you can get. He'll never agree to it.'

'That still doesn't mean you can't talk to him, and your mum.'

'You don't understand how difficult it is!' responded Nadeem.

Farah finally let go of the patient façade.

'Well, you can carry on seeing as many more girls as you like, but this one is just about to walk!' Farah grabbed her bag and turned to go, but twisted back around for a final word. 'For goodness' sake, grow a backbone, man, and tell your parents. They may take it better than you think.'

6

Later that evening, Farah and her parents spent some time together in the lounge. Her father got comfortable in his high-backed red armchair and eagerly watched the evening news bulletin, just as he did every evening on the same channel at the same time. Farah sat on the floor in front of her mum who was perched on the double seater sofa. She turned her back to her mum, who started to massage Farah's head and her long black hair with their favourite brand of almond oil; this was a ritual that her mother had performed since Farah was a little girl. And even now, aged thirty, every time Farah visited home, she pestered her mother into giving her the *tel malish*, although she didn't really need to pester her much, as her mum enjoyed the activity and the time they shared together just as much as Farah did. Farah's mother started with gentle strokes at the crown of her head, slowly building up the pressure, and then went on to massage the entire scalp with her fingertips, in sweeping, circular motions. The massage enveloped Farah's mind, and she fell into a complete trance of weightless relaxation, until the circular motions in her head ceased, and her mother moved on to tenderly stroke trickles of the oil into every strand of Farah's thick long hair.

The conversation after her head massage revolved around one subject, and one subject alone.

Farah walked in with a tray of tea and biscuits. There were three types of biscuit on the plate: plain digestives for her father, bourbon creams for Farah and ginger nuts for her mum. Evening tea and biscuits was another ritual that Farah remembered from whenever it was that her memory began. She had not been allowed to drink tea until she was a teenager; her mother had always told her that if she drank tea as a child she wouldn't grow and would remain a tiddler all her life, and so when she was younger her cup had always contained milk. Farah never knew if her mum had really believed this, or if it had been something she had said just to delay Farah getting a taste for tea, and consequently, caffeine, for as long as possible. Whatever the motivation, it had worked until she was thirteen years old.

As soon as Farah sat on the sofa next to her mother, the questions started to come thick and fast.

'But why aren't you interested in him?' asked Farah's mother. 'He seems like the ideal young man for you. What is wrong with you, girl?'

'Give the girl a break, will you?' intervened her dad. Her mum shot a sharp look towards him. Farah gave her father a warm smile. He always had her back when mother and daughter clashed, or at least he tried to, but on this occasion, as with most, his interruption was short-lived, as her mother responded with a razor-sharp reply.

'*Aap chup karein ji!*'

'Mum, don't tell Dad to be quiet, that's so rude!' Farah said.

'Me? Rude? You're saying I'm the rude one when it's you who doesn't have the decency to tell that me why you won't consider that poor boy—'

'Because that "poor boy" is already engaged!' Farah shouted back.

Both her parents just stared at her. Farah's mother put her mug of tea down. She asked in a hushed tone:

'Really? Are you sure?'

'Yes, I'm certain, he told me so himself. Only he's too scared to tell his parents because he is engaged to marry a *gori*. Or at least I think she is white. He said she was a different colour, but come to think of it, he didn't actually mention what colour she was, so I suppose she could be *kali*. Or yellow or green; I don't know. The point is that he doesn't think his parents will accept her.'

A few more seconds passed, and once it had sunk in, Farah's mother blew.

'*Hai* Allah! Engaged to a *gori*! *Tauba tauba!* And his parents were going around saying he's desperate to settle down with a nice *desi* girl, and have kids. And he even said to me that you

38

are lovely and he's looking forward to getting to know you. What a deception, why the little *pehnch—*'

'No swearing, Mum!' Farah implored her.

'OK. OK . . . the lying toerag, then,' she said, grimacing.

'That's a bit mean, Mum. I actually felt a little sorry for him, even if I didn't give him that impression at the time. He's obviously petrified of telling his mum and dad. But he must really want to marry this woman. He's so unhappy as things stand for him.'

Farah's mother grimaced for a little while longer, but before long her mood softened.

'Come here, my baby,' she said to Farah, and she gave her daughter a warm embrace.

'I love you, Mum; and you too, Dad.'

'We love you too,' said her father.

'We love you more than you could ever know,' added her mum. 'So, what now?' she asked her daughter.

'Well . . . if you will insist on my marrying, then you must keep hunting!' replied Farah cheekily.

'You know what, my darling daughter, it would be much easier if you found somebody yourself,' declared her mother.

'Well, I've tried, Mum, but to no avail! That's why I'm handing the baton to you.'

'I live in hope, *beti,* I live in hope, that one day you will say to me yourself, "Mum, I've found myself a nice Pakistani boy!"'

Farah laughed out loud at her mother's words.

'Well, as long as he isn't actually from Pakistan, I guess it's a possibility. He has to be British; born and bred. I don't want no *mangethar* or *pindu!*' Farah said.

'What? You mean like your father was?' Farah's mother responded, with a cheeky wink.

'What was that about me?' Farah's father asked, looking searchingly over at mother and daughter, who both let out a giggle.

7

Monday mornings were always a mad rush, but today was worse than a regular Monday morning as Farah was running unusually late. She had wasted yet more time looking for the stray earring, having turned her bedroom upside down. She'd then freaked out when she looked at her watch, and left her apartment looking like it had been burgled. In the midst of all that, the young girl she had seen at Zaheer's apartment had been uppermost in her thoughts. The image of her trembling in the corner of that kitchen – something that her colleagues had been fortunate enough not to witness – had continued to trouble Farah.

When she got to work she was cornered by the receptionist as soon as she entered the building, with a message for her from Tahir; he needed to see Farah as a matter of urgency, and could she go to his office as soon as she got in.

Great, she thought to herself, and tutted out loud. This was all she needed.

Farah considered ignoring his request and walking straight

past his office and on to her own, but then thought better of the idea. It wouldn't be very professional for starters, and perhaps it really was important. So she headed to his office, although she did so with a continuing sense of irritation: she was already behind schedule, she had a pile of stuff to see to, and she really didn't need this, whatever 'this' was.

Tahir was sat behind his desk, dressed in one of his favourite dark blue suits, with a crisp white shirt, and a red and blue geometric-pattern silk tie. His dark brown hair was swept back off his forehead, and the intense colour of his piercing green eyes was vivid against his pale skin, which was fairly typical of people of the Peshawar region of Pakistan, where his family originated.

'Right then. Here I am, as requested. What's up?' asked Farah abruptly, as she closed the door.

Tahir paused for a few seconds. He placed his black and gold Montblanc pen down on the desk and closed the file he had been looking at.

'Thanks for coming. Why don't you sit down, Farah? Can I get you a coffee?'

She shifted from one foot to the other, but stayed standing in the same spot, not far from the door.

'No thanks. I've got to leave for court in a few minutes, and I need to look over some papers beforehand. The message at reception was that you needed to see me urgently.'

Farah now had her arms crossed, and she waited quietly for a response.

'Well, it is urgent, sort of.'

'Go on then,' she said.

'Look, maybe now isn't a good time. You're busy; we both are. Can we meet up for lunch instead? We could go to your favourite, that pretty little Italian place around the corner?' Tahir asked hopefully.

Farah almost sniggered at him, but she reminded herself to keep things professional and maintain a calm composure, and she reined herself back.

'I don't think so, do you?' she replied simply.

'You don't? Why not?'

She looked at him with incredulity. She felt annoyed: annoyed that he had demanded to see her, annoyed that she had come running the second he had clicked his fingers and annoyed that there was nothing urgent after all. But she told herself once again that she must keep her cool.

'Well, for one, I'm not sure what time I'm going to be finished at court. I don't think I will make it back here for lunch. But that's beside the point; we don't need to meet up for lunch to talk. Whatever it is, just spit it out.' Her tone grew harsher with each word.

He stood up, and walked around his desk. He came close to her and looked her in the face. He was wearing the familiar deep, musky scent that had been her favourite; she had always bought it for him.

'I have been thinking about you a lot recently, ever since we broke up actually. But it was seeing you away from the office on Friday that really brought it home to me.' Tahir spoke softly, saying each word carefully, with a gentle purpose.

'Brought what home?'

'What a fool I've been to let you go. I was an idiot, pure and simple. Please, can we try again? Can we make a fresh start?'

Farah stared at him with complete bewilderment. She blinked hard, and looked away for a few seconds, then turned back to look at him with conviction.

'Are you for real? After what you did, do you think I'm going to go back there, and waste another three precious years of my life?'

Farah saw Tahir's face begin to tense up; he looked as though he was scratching around in his head trying desperately to find the right thing to say. He clearly wanted her back, and was making no effort to hide this.

'I was confused as to what I should do, that's all. I wasn't ready for it then, but I am now.'

'Confused? Is that the new word for dishonesty these days?'

'Oh, come on! You make it sound like I had an affair or something,' he protested.

'No, you didn't cheat on me, but you lied to me all the same, or at the very least, you misled me. When we met, when we fell in love, you gave me hope; hope of a future together.'

'I know I did; but you are well aware of the role that my family played in all of this. Consider how much of what happened was out of my hands,' Tahir responded.

'Yes, I know all that. But when we first got together, you said that all you needed was a bit more time to sort things out. And I gave you time; bucketloads of it. And then you pulled that stunt. How could you have hurt me in that way?'

'I never intended to hurt you!'

'Is that right? Well, that isn't how I see it. You behaved despicably. If you don't think that your actions were hurtful, then I dread to think what your definition of hurt is.'

Farah tried to keep her voice down, but the rage was now simmering inside her, and she feared it was going to boil over spectacularly any second.

Tahir rubbed the nape of his neck as he tried to assemble his thoughts.

'I just don't know what happened. I guess I caved in to all the pressure.'

Farah had heard enough.

'Then why the bloody hell weren't you honest with me from the start? Why string me along for over three years, let me make plans, allow me to dream about our happy ending, and *then* let me down in that way? Why did you break me in that way? Why did you build me up and then trample all over me? I was prepared to take my parents on for you. They were never going to be one hundred per cent happy, but I was happy to do it.'

The tears had now collected in Farah's eyes, despite her efforts to keep them at bay. Tahir slowly put his hands on her shoulders.

'We can still marry. I can still sort it all out, if that's what you want.'

Tahir gently rubbed his hands on her shoulders. He smiled, but Farah simply shook her head in amazement.

'You still don't get it, do you?' she said. 'It can't just be what *I* want, it's also got to be what *you* want! Anyway, it's too late. I'm done with it all. I'm done with you. I don't want to marry a man who is so cowardly he can't make such an important decision for himself. I don't want to be part of your life; not now, not ever.'

Farah took a deep breath.

'I think we're done here. It's over, Tahir. Move on. I intend to. Now, take your hands off me.'

Tahir was taken aback by this demand, but he kept his hands exactly where they were.

'What? Come on, please—'

'I said take your hands *off* me!' Farah spoke fiercely and left no room for doubt.

Tahir pulled his arms away, and she could sense that his pride had been hurt. Farah knew him well enough to understand what he had probably expected – most likely that she would at least give his proposal to start over some thought.

'I wouldn't be so hasty, Farah,' he said. 'For one thing, your possible upcoming promotion to partner of the firm will require my approval.'

Farah's mouth dropped open.

'So, now you're trying to *blackmail* me into getting back with you?'

Farah could see that he instantly regretted what he had just blurted out in anger; he looked ashamed of himself. But Farah's sense of shock was worse than his. The fact that he could use his position in this way to try and beat her down was the final straw.

'If I had any doubts before about my decision to dump you,' Farah declared, 'then I certainly don't have them any more. Have a good day.'

She left the room and slammed the door behind her.

8

It had been a long tiring Monday. Her exchange with Tahir first thing in the morning hadn't been the best way to start the week, but it went from bad to worse when her barrister at the appeal hearing spent more time trying to come on to Farah than focusing on the case; because of his general laissez-faire attitude and a lapse of concentration at a critical point in the hearing, the opposition barrister had walked all over him.

'Bad luck, eh,' said her barrister to Farah as they started to pack up.

'Luck doesn't come into it; I beat you fair and square. You were doomed from the start. You're losing your touch, mate,' joked the opposition barrister as he swung past them.

She turned to look at her own barrister. He studied her for a few seconds before he spoke again.

'You know the day doesn't have to be a total washout. We could go out for a nice meal. Just the two of us; what do you say?'

'I say, I don't do dinner with married men.'

Farah's icy cold response sent him packing, and she was left to pick up the scattered pieces. She tried her best to console a tearful client, who after having lost the appeal now had the prospect of giving birth to her first child alone in a month's time. Farah often had to witness the human cost of the stringent immigration laws which tore families apart; the ramifications that the lawmakers who sat comfortably in their ivory towers never had to see. She always made sure she carried plenty of tissues in her handbag, and tried her best to utter some reassuring words. Farah told her client not to worry, as the stress was not good for her or the baby, and that she could always try again, and perhaps she would be successful next time, and that she would support her in any way she could. But really, no measly offerings of sympathy, however genuinely meant, were going to cheer up a heavily pregnant woman who now had to face one of the most difficult times in her life without her spouse by her side.

After all that drama, Farah simply just wanted to go home and have a good long hot soak, with her new Dead Sea mineral and wild orchid bath foam; to close her eyes and sink in, and forget that this day had ever happened. However, this was not a possibility just yet. Despite all her efforts, she hadn't found her precious earring. She was now certain that she must have dropped it either at the Mansur residence at Hans Place, or when travelling to or from there. If she had dropped it in the cab or on the pavement, she could definitely kiss goodbye to it. But if it was lying in some pristine corner of Zaheer and

Aneela's flat, then there was a good chance she would be able to recover it. The earring was expensive, but its sentimental value, as a gift from her parents, was far more important, for it had been the present they had bought her when she had qualified as a solicitor. Straight after work, she headed over to Hans Place.

It was a clear evening, and it was a touch warmer than the last time she had come this way, so the walk from the tube station was a pleasant one. She headed into the square, past the wooded garden and towards the apartment. As she was thinking about the stray earring, her mind drifted to the girl she had seen at the dinner party, and she wondered if she would see her again today.

The door was indeed opened by the girl, almost as if Farah had willed it.

The young woman stood silently, in the same grubby clothes and shabby sandals that she had been wearing last Friday. Her *chaddar* was draped loosely around her head and shoulders. Her large, warm brown eyes looked at Farah, but she didn't utter a word. Was she scared? Farah wondered.

'Is it the grocery delivery, Razia?' shouted Aneela from somewhere in the apartment.

Farah looked past the girl's shoulder for any sign of Aneela, but there was none at present. She waited for the girl to say something . . . anything.

'No, *Malikin*,' was the girl's response, as she turned around to answer.

Upon hearing her reply, Aneela quickly appeared at the door. Farah registered the look of surprise on Aneela's face on seeing her there. Aneela quickly turned this into a smile.

Aneela was dressed in a long, flowing floor-length kaftan-style dress. It was a vivid pink silk, floral piece. Her hair was loose around her shoulders, and her nails were perfectly French manicured; everything about her oozed luxury and style, in contrast to Farah, who was in a basic two-piece black trouser suit with her hair up in a ponytail. Farah thought she must surely look as tired and fed up as she felt.

'Oh, hello, Farah, this is an unexpected pleasure. Is everything all right?' asked Aneela.

Farah felt the unexpected part was spot on, but the pleasure part was a blatant lie. Aneela wasn't in the least bit happy that Farah had turned up unannounced, even though she tried her best to hide it.

'Oh, yes, everything is fine. I just needed a quick word with you. May I come in?'

'Yes, of course, how rude of me,' Aneela replied. The words were accompanied by a phoney smile. She told the girl to go to the kitchen and continue with her chores, and showed Farah into the hallway. 'What can I do for you?' she asked.

'I think I may have dropped an earring here on Friday.' Farah opened her handbag and took the other earring out of the zipped inside pocket to show it to Aneela.

'It's very pretty,' remarked Aneela, as she took it into her hands and looked over it carefully. She handed it back to

Farah. 'I can't say I've seen it around, for I surely would have noticed it. I have an eye for things like that, you know. But give me a couple of minutes and I will check the lounge and dining room, just in case. If you just wait here, I won't be very long.'

Farah couldn't help herself. As soon as Aneela disappeared out of sight to embark upon her mission to hunt down the missing earring, she quietly wandered off and found her way to the kitchen. Farah only knew that she had to talk to this girl, even if she didn't know what she was going to say or how the girl would react.

When she walked in, she found Razia on the floor on bent knees, crouching with her head in the oven, scrubbing hard.

She took her head out, and seemed startled at seeing Farah. With the cleaning rag still in her bare hands, she slowly stood up, but didn't say anything. She looked more than startled; she seemed frightened. Her face tensed up, and she hunched her shoulders.

'It's OK. Don't worry,' Farah said to her, and took a couple of small, gentle steps towards her. 'My name is Farah. You must be Razia?'

The girl continued to stare at Farah. She stood completely still, and remained silent. She made no attempt to speak. Her fear seemed to increase with each moment that passed.

'Are you OK?' Farah asked.

The girl was beginning to shake. Farah herself now felt a sense of unease, as she wondered what on earth she should say, or do next. Should she stay? Or perhaps she should leave?

Aneela strolled into the kitchen and looked aghast to see Farah stood by the girl. Her face turned a strange shade of pink.

'May I ask what you are doing in here?'

'Oh, sure, yes, erm, I thought I heard something fall, but I think it must have been the noise of this young lady cleaning the oven. Anyway, I thought I should come and see if everything was OK, in case there had been any kind of an accident. So, here I am!' said Farah, using all of her lawyer's bluffing skills.

'Oh, I see,' Aneela replied sternly.

'Well, aren't you going to introduce me to your housekeeper?' Farah asked.

Aneela let out a short, sharp cough.

'This is Razia,' Aneela said begrudgingly.

'Pleased to meet you, Razia,' said Farah, and then held out her hand towards Razia.

Razia looked at Aneela, who gave a slightly indignant nod of the head, and upon receiving the signal, Razia held out her hand to meet Farah's, and when their hands touched, Farah discreetly passed one of her business cards to her; it was folded up, so as to fit neatly into Razia's palm.

'I'm sorry, but I can't find your earring anywhere,' said Aneela, walking towards the kitchen door. She didn't even offer Farah any tea or coffee; she clearly just wanted rid of her.

'That's fine. Thanks for looking,' said Farah, and then she handed Aneela one of her business cards, an unfolded one this time. 'But if it does turn up, please do telephone me as soon as possible,' she added, looking towards Razia for a second.

Aneela quickly showed Farah to the door.

Farah stood on the doorstep outside for a few seconds, trying to make sense of this bizarre exchange. It was unheard of to visit any Pakistani family or household and not be offered *at least* a cup of tea. And you weren't *asked* if you wanted tea; it was seen as offensive to ask. The tea was usually made without any discussion about it, and you were just given it, along with *badam* biscuits, cake rusks, Bombay mix, *boondi,* nuts, pakoras, samosas and a selection of soft drinks, in addition to the tea. In fact, whatever you had in the house, or whatever you could prepare quickly, was dished up for visitors. Even unexpected guests were fed most of the kitchen-cupboard contents. The very fact that Aneela did not even offer a cup of tea went against every Pakistani hospitality tradition there was.

Aneela had just wanted her out of the house, and the reason for this must be Razia.

9

Three long days had passed, and Farah had heard nothing from Razia. She had been careful to check her phone as often as it was possible – after her meetings, after her court appearances, at random points throughout the day – but there was nothing. That was until she was just about to leave her flat on the fourth day, when she heard her phone buzz in her handbag. She frantically searched around in the red leather slouch bag. When she whipped out her phone, she saw that it was a London landline number.

'Hello,' Farah answered quickly.

There was no response, only silence.

'Is that Razia?'

Still nothing.

'Do you want to speak in Urdu, or Punjabi instead?' Farah asked in Urdu.

'Punjabi, *Bibi Ji*, or Urdu; only little English,' was the reply.

'*Baat karo*,' Farah invited her to speak, but she was met only by silence once again.

'Tell me about yourself. I know you are called Razia, but where are you from? How have you ended up where you are now, staying with Zaheer and Aneela?'

'I am from Pakistan, from just outside Lahore. They brought me here. To work for them.'

Farah had never visited Pakistan but had heard much about Lahore, known for its history and its food.

'I overheard Mr and Mrs Mansur shouting and swearing at you on Friday evening, in the kitchen, because of some food that hadn't been cooked properly. What happened? Are you OK?'

'Oh, that. I'm fine. They are always like that. I am used to it.'

Farah could barely believe her ears. This girl was used to being abused and actually thought it was OK.

'They have no right to do that to you. We have laws in this country about this sort of thing. If this happens to you, then that is completely wrong.'

'I am their servant after all. They can speak to me as they want. But one thing I do know is that if they find out I am speaking to you, I will be in a lot of trouble. I can't speak long, *Malikin* will be out of the shower soon.'

'Aren't you allowed to use the phone when they are there?'

'No, *Bibi Ji*.'

'Please, call me Farah.'

'I'm not supposed to use the telephone at all. Now, I really must go,' continued Razia.

'Please, don't go yet. Tell me, is Aneela going to go out at all today?' asked Farah.

'I think so. She said that she needed to go to a big store to buy some new shoes. She says she needs new red ones, for an event she is attending soon, to match her new red clothes.'

'Well, in that case, if you're worried about speaking to me now, when she is in the house, then why don't you phone me back when she has gone out. Then we can talk properly.'

There was a brief silence.

'I can't do that,' said Razia.

'Why not? Don't be scared, she won't know.'

'No, I really can't telephone you, because I won't be able to.'

'What do you mean? Why won't you be able to?' Farah asked.

'Because . . .' Razia lowered her voice a little as she finished her sentence. 'Because she and Master lock me up when they go out.'

A cold, prickly feeling took hold of Farah. She felt goose-bumps like she had never felt before, as though the temperature had suddenly plunged to below freezing.

'They actually lock you up?' she asked.

'Yes, in the small room, where I do all the ironing, and where I also sleep. I have a mattress on the floor, and I'm allowed to take a bottle of water in with me. Although sometimes that is not such a good idea if she is out too long, as then I need the washroom and cannot go.'

'Oh my God,' was all Farah could say.

'I—'

And then there was nothing, apart from the long continuous high-pitched tone to indicate that the call had been cut.

Farah waited patiently with the phone in her hand, still standing by her front door, her thoughts whirling around in her head in a cloud of disbelief. The girl was being kept a slave and a prisoner. This was happening right here, in London, on her doorstep, and the culprits were the supposed best friends of her boss.

Two minutes later the phone rang again.

'Sorry, Farah *ji*, I thought I heard *Malikin*, but it is OK, she is still in the shower.'

'Why are you staying there if they treat you so badly? Why don't you just leave?'

For the first time in the conversation Razia became emotional; Farah could hear her voice beginning to crackle, and she could imagine the girl's struggle to fight back the tears.

'I can't leave.'

'Yes, you can. You have every right to leave.'

'No! I really can't. I don't think you understand. They have rights over me.'

'Rights? What rights?'

'They own me, or rather, they own all of us – in Pakistan – me and my family. I had to come here; I didn't have a choice. And even if I had the courage to do it, I can't leave. I don't even know where my passport is. In fact, I never saw my passport; they had it made and have always kept it. Even if I left, where would I go? Where would I live? Who would look after me? I don't have anywhere else to go to in this country. And I don't have any money; they don't pay me. And what about the repercussions for my family? I want to go back to Pakistan; I miss my mother so much, but they will not let me.'

'Hold on. Rewind a bit. What do you mean they own you? How can they *own* you?' Farah asked, feeling utterly bewildered.

'Because we are indebted to them, and we must serve them until the debt is paid.'

'OK. I'm really not sure I understand, to be honest. But coming back to you. You say you want to leave?'

'Yes. I do. But—'

'But nothing. If you want to get out of there, then I will help you, if you want me to. We can deal with all this family and debt stuff later. Do you want me to help you?'

'Yes . . . but I am scared. If they find out and you are not able to help me, then I will be in the most terrible trouble. I will be beaten . . .'

'No, I won't let that happen. I promise you. You have my word. You just sit tight. I'm going to speak to a few people and then get you out of there.'

Razia's crying was now audible to Farah, who remained as calm as she could in the circumstances. Farah knew that no matter how much sadness she felt for this girl, she must keep it together, as Razia was now relying on Farah her to get her out of that hellhole of an apartment.

'Thank you, Farah *ji*, may Allah bless you.'

10

When Farah got in to work, she headed straight past her own office to the other end of the corridor and knocked loudly on Paul Drake's door. She heard his muffled 'come in' and after taking a short, sharp breath, she walked in. She felt like a schoolgirl at the headmaster's door, not completely sure of what the reaction from the other side of the door would be, but she entered in the hope that there would be a fair hearing, followed by the right decision.

He was sat at his desk, which was as messy as ever; it was laden with piles of files, books, Post-it notes, telephone messages, receipts, loose bits of paper. His office was cluttered in any direction and corner you looked; there were countless files on the floor by his desk, and on top of the filing cabinets, and they just continued to grow as though they had a life of their own. Unlike the state of his desk and room, however, Paul always took great pride in his own appearance; today he was wearing a fine bespoke Savile Row three-piece pale grey suit with a striped dark grey and red tie. His mostly silvery head of hair was now receding, and had been shaped into a short, tidy cut. He closed the file that he had been going through, took his reading glasses off, carefully folded them and placed them on top of the file.

'Good morning, Farah, come on in, sit down. I don't normally have the pleasure of your presence very often, and rarely first thing in the morning. Is everything OK?'

Farah sat on one of the smart black and chrome chairs on the other side of the desk.

'I'm not sure,' she replied cautiously. She placed her handbag on the floor, and sat back in the chair.

'Oh?'

'I wanted to ask you about Zaheer, and Aneela.'

Paul raised his eyebrows slightly; Farah knew this had thrown him. She usually only popped her head through his door when she wanted to pick his brains about one of her more complex cases, or seek his opinion on a particular barrister she was thinking of hiring for one of her hearings. Or perhaps to ask for some extra time off. Perhaps he was expecting a conversation about when she might be promoted to partner status. Probably the last thing he had anticipated was that she would want to talk about his friend and his friend's wife.

'What about them?' asked Paul.

'How well do you know them?'

Paul raised his eyebrows even further.

'I know them reasonably well; I've known Zaheer since we

studied together at King's. Now that's going back a bit. Not that either of us look that old, eh? Why do you ask?'

Farah was hesitant. She hadn't really thought this through. She knew what she wanted to say, but wasn't exactly certain about *how* she should convey it. She may as well come out with it, she thought to herself.

'Do you know someone called Razia?'

Paul scrunched his face a little and thought about the question for a moment or two.

'No, I can't say I do,' he replied eventually.

'She is their so-called housekeeper.'

'Oh, so that's what she's called. I know they've got a young lady who helps with the housework. It's a big apartment though, so that's hardly surprising. Well, what of her? And why do you say "so-called"?'

Farah cleared her throat.

'When we were at their house last Friday, they said they had a housekeeper. And she was the one who had prepared all that lovely food. But the thing is, I don't think she's a housekeeper at all.'

'What else would you call her? Domestic help, perhaps? Housemaid? I mean, what difference does it make what label you stick on her?'

'No, Paul. The label does matter, because I'm afraid to say that I think she's a domestic slave.'

Paul's face slowly unwrinkled. He donned a graver look and tone of voice.

'Now, just hold on a minute. You can't go around making accusations like that.'

'I'm telling you the truth. She's being treated like a slave. No, sorry, that's wrong. The fact is that she *is* a slave,' responded Farah.

'How the hell would you know?' Paul asked, beginning to sound agitated.

'Because I spoke to her, and she told me as much. I wanted to ask if you would come with me to their house and see if we can rescue this girl.'

Paul let out a quiet laugh.

'Have you heard yourself? "Rescue" her? Rescue her from what, exactly? She works for them. Who they employ, and on what terms, has got nothing to do with you, or me. We can't just go around there, poking our noses in without rhyme or reason.'

Farah scrunched her hair in her hands above her head, and pulled it backwards. She was infuriated that Paul wasn't taking her seriously, incensed that he was simply trying to dismiss her as some silly little girl with an overzealous imagination. She really hadn't expected this lack of co-operation from him.

'Look,' she said, tapping her index finger on the spare bit of desk that she could find. 'I came to you as a matter of courtesy, seeing as Zaheer is your friend. I didn't want to go behind your back. But, if you won't help me, then I'm left with no choice.'

'Meaning?'

'Meaning I'm going to go to the police. I'm going to tell

them everything I know, and let them investigate it. I dare say they will be a damn sight more interested than you are!'

Paul suddenly became serious.

'That's ridiculous, Farah, go to the police and say what? You have no evidence; for all you know, this girl could be telling you a pack of lies.'

'Why? Why would she lie to me? I'm a complete stranger. She has nothing to gain by doing that.'

Paul let out a loud sigh, and rolled his eyes. He placed his hand on his chin and thought about it for a few seconds.

'I don't know. I can't make head nor tail of this. Just – don't go to the police; I will talk to Zaheer over the weekend, and I will discuss it with you on Monday. In the meantime, don't do anything you may later regret. Leave it with me for now.'

Farah had hoped for a better reaction than the one she had just received from Paul, but his assurance, in the end, to raise the matter with Zaheer was at least something. All she could do now was wait and see.

11

'Hello, Paul,' said Zaheer, as he answered his mobile phone on what he was hoping would be a lazy Saturday morning.

Zaheer was sat in the lounge in his recliner leather chair, and he took the call whilst he drank his coffee and flicked through the *Daily Jang* newspaper; there was a story about the surge in the popularity of the opposition party in Pakistan that had particularly caught his eye. He looked through the pictures of the latest rallies with hundreds of thousands of people having gathered to show support for change. Even though he was in London, he liked to keep abreast of everything that was happening back in Pakistan, especially matters of a political nature. It was essential. He, and his family, neither liked nor wanted change. The system as it stood had served them handsomely for many generations, and these mass movements did not bode well. They were potentially very harmful and therefore had to be thwarted as early as possible. He would continue to keep a keen eye on this story.

'Hi, I'm sorry to bother you on a Saturday morning, mate. Have you got a few minutes to spare?'

'Of course, Paul. I've always got time for you, my friend; you know that. Fire away.' Zaheer replied absent-mindedly, as his focus was still very much on the newspaper article. He had always fancied running himself one day. He knew he had enough contacts inside and outside the political world that would ensure his success should he ever wish to stand. He had the means and the influence, although he lacked the motivation at this point in his life. Perhaps in the future he would give it some serious thought.

'It's a bit awkward, actually. Farah came and had a chat with me yesterday, and I promised her that I would speak to you.'

'Speak to me? What about?' he replied, putting his cup of coffee down on the dark mahogany side table, but continuing to look over the headlines on the next page of the newspaper. 'New Trade Deal with China' caught his eye, and there was a section on how the Gwadar Port development project was progressing.

'She said you have a young lady called Razia working for you.'

Zaheer wondered how Farah knew her name.

'Yes, we do. What of it?'

'Well, it sounds preposterous really, but she has got it into her head that you . . . that she . . .'

Zaheer put his newspaper down and sat up straight.

'Yes? Go on.'

'That . . . she is your slave.'

There was a split-second silence from Zaheer; just long enough for him to grab his thoughts, and arrange them in line for a rapid-fire response.

'Slave? Goodness me, where did she get such a hideous notion?'

Zaheer faked the outrage well. Paul fell silent. Zaheer deliberately allowed the uncomfortable silence to fester for a little while.

'She said she spoke to her, and this Razia girl told her herself,' said Paul.

Zaheer was at a loss as to how Farah had even managed to have a conversation with Razia, unless of course Aneela had allowed it somehow, knowingly or unknowingly; it didn't make a difference, it was Aneela's job to keep day-to-day control of Razia. He could only wonder what on earth this interfering busybody of a lawyer had said to Razia.

'Look, I don't blame Farah for falling for it. I have to be honest with you. Razia has done this sort of thing before.'

'What do you mean?'

'She is the daughter of some very poor people that we know in Pakistan. My older brother asked me, as a favour, if I would bring this girl over as a housemaid, more to help her family out really. He told me that she was an excellent worker, and a very good cook; and so she is, you tasted her food when you came to dinner. However, he also warned me that she has a tendency to moan and exaggerate, and has been known to make stories up just for a bit of attention. I suspect that is all it was. Tell Farah I'm sorry that Razia bothered her in this way, and gave her any cause for concern.'

Zaheer took a moment to draw breath, before he continued.

'Rest assured, Aneela and I will both make sure she doesn't do it again.'

'Oh, that's OK. I will let Farah know. She was talking about going to the police and everything, but I convinced her to hang fire.'

Zaheer paused for a few seconds, and rubbed his forehead with his hand. Blasted women! Zaheer knew he had to nip this in the bud. And quickly.

'In that case, why don't you text Farah's number to me. I will reassure her myself, just as soon as I've had a word with Razia.'

Zaheer cut the call, put his phone on the table and walked slowly out of the lounge and into the hallway. He drew a deep, calm breath.

'Razia!' he called out. There was no answer, and he repeated her name.

Aneela came out of the kitchen having heard her husband. As she entered the hallway her pale green georgette *dupatta* fell to the floor. She bent down to pick it up, wrapped it back around her neck, and then walked up to her husband, who was stood just outside the lounge. Zaheer was quite calm, still waiting for Razia to emerge.

'What's the matter? Why do you need to speak to Razia?' Aneela asked.

'Actually, perhaps I need to speak to you first?'

'Oh? Why?' Aneela asked.

'Razia has been speaking to that busybody Farah. Do you want to tell me how that happened?'

'I forgot to say. She popped over to ask if she had dropped her earring here when she came over for dinner. I found her in the kitchen with Razia, but they can only have been together for a minute or two.'

'A minute or two is all it takes.'

He called Razia's name once again.

'Where is that *kuthi*?' he asked his wife.

'She's cleaning the bathroom,' said Aneela.

Zaheer headed for the bathroom door.

Razia was already screaming.

12

It was a tediously boring Sunday evening. Farah had not planned to do anything, or to see any of her friends. It was one of those loose-ended, nothing-to-do, whiling-away-the-day sort of Sundays. And to add to that, Farah couldn't help but wonder if Paul had managed to speak to Zaheer; she had been tempted to phone Paul for an update, but then thought better of it. She would know the outcome in any event when she got back into the office tomorrow.

Farah's old-fashioned little cobbled street was prettily situated in Westminster, in the heart of London. Her first-floor apartment within a row of terraced houses was part of a period restoration. The flat was tiny, just a small open-plan living room and kitchen-diner, a bedroom and a bathroom. Her rent was on the high side compared to equivalent properties in other areas, but the location, in her opinion, was worth it; at least that was what she had told herself when she had signed the lease. That said, the lack of space was suffocating at times, especially when she compared it to her spacious and airy detached family home back in Solihull.

Farah lay lazily on the sofa, with her feet dangling playfully off one end, past the armrest. She wriggled her dark plum-painted toes, and let out a lingering yawn. The living room was simply decorated; Farah was not one for clutter or knick-knacks; the walls were painted a plain straw colour, there were a few cherished ornaments dotted around, and her beloved print of Monet's *Purple Poppies* hung on the largest wall. A small bookshelf housed the eclectic mix of her favourite novels.

Farah lay on the cosy two-seater sofa thinking of nothing much, although her mind did wander towards Razia from time to time. She hugged a soft lilac-coloured cushion, and as she did so, she thought about Razia locked up in her little room; no comforts, no food, no freedom.

Farah grabbed the remote control. She switched the television on and flicked through the channels, but she could not find anything even a tad interesting to watch. She turned the television off, and got up off the sofa. She popped on her trainers, picked up her coat and bag and headed out for a walk.

Sometimes Farah would go grab a coffee down by the London Eye and just watch the world in all its technicolour glory drift by; tourists queuing for the attractions, or enjoying river cruises, or snapping photos with Big Ben behind them.

Quite often, and especially on evenings like this when she had time on her hands, she loved to sit in Parliament Square.

This place was special to her. She felt as though she were surrounded by the influences and institutions that denoted democracy, fairness and justice; all matters that were dear to her heart. She liked to sit still in the square for as long as was needed to allow her to ponder life, and all the stuff that it was made of. She usually did her best thinking here.

Farah ambled over to a bench in Parliament Square, which looked towards Westminster Abbey. It was now past seven o'clock in the evening, and the square and surrounding area were no longer heaving, as the tourists headed away, perhaps to catch a West End show, or to go to dinner.

She loved to sit and observe London in all of its peculiar quirkiness. Westminster was her favourite haunt. She had seen it all around here: elaborately orchestrated royal processions; slick politicians posing for the cameras on the lawn, trying to look important as they gave their interviews to the news channels; schoolchildren and tourists queueing for the tour of the Houses of Parliament; people waiting impatiently for their turn to board the London Eye; children dropping their ice creams whilst being pulled along from one tourist hotspot to another; sightseers stopping by the roadside sellers for those all-important but completely useless souvenirs to take back home to their loved ones, or posing before the street artists to have their faces sketched into an image that looked nothing like them. Farah herself was often stopped by strangers, who asked her in varying degrees of comprehensible English if she could give them directions, or if she would be kind enough to take a group photo.

As Farah sat on the bench, she thought about her freedom to wander about and enjoy her surroundings as she wished, whenever she wanted. In so doing, her thoughts turned towards Razia. Paul's idea that perhaps the girl was lying did allow a small niggle of doubt to appear in Farah's mind, but only very briefly, for a whisper that emerged from somewhere deep within Farah's conscience told her that the girl was not a liar.

Farah sat on the bench and thought deeply about freedom; her freedom to be where she was, the tourists' freedom to roam the streets of London, the media's freedom to report on whatever it wished. Yet again, her thoughts drifted back towards the curtailment, or rather prohibition, of Razia's freedom. She was anxious to know the outcome of Paul's conversation with Zaheer. After an hour on the bench, she came to the conclusion that she had deliberated for long enough, and headed back home.

As Farah let herself into her apartment, she heard her phone ring in her bag. She thought it would probably be her mum; she often phoned at this time in the evening. Farah was half expecting her mum to contact her about a new potential suitor, in which case it would turn into a long conversation all about him, his job, his family, his height, and so on and so on. She shuffled her purse and bits of paper around, and pulled the phone out from the bottom of her handbag. It wasn't a telephone number that she recognised.

'Hello.'

'Oh, hello. Is that Farah?' enquired the polite, well-spoken male voice on the other end.

'Yes, it is. Who is this?' Farah asked.

'It's Zaheer.'

'Oh. Hello.'

Farah was a little taken aback to hear from him, but nevertheless intrigued as to what he would say.

'I understand from Paul that our housekeeper has been talking some nonsense to you.'

Farah cleared her throat before she spoke. 'With all due respect, it didn't sound like nonsense. Razia seemed genuine enough to me.'

'Well, I assure you that whatever she said or implied, it was most likely a load of rubbish. She has a tendency to fabricate stories, does our Razia.'

'Really?' asked Farah.

'Yes, really. In fact, I would go as far as to say that she is a pathological liar. I don't blame her per se. She is the product of a poor, uneducated upbringing, and doesn't really know any better. A bit of a silly girl really.'

Farah's jaw dropped open at the audacity of this man. He obviously didn't think much of her if he thought she was going to swallow this so easily.

'I'm sorry, but I don't believe you. I spoke to her myself, and I believe *her*. She isn't a housekeeper at all. I know that you're treating her as your slave.'

Zaheer's tone remained civil, but he managed to change tactic within a matter of seconds.

'Miss Jilani, I would ask you to proceed with caution from this point onwards. And I say this for two reasons.'

Farah was more used to hearing this sort of spiel in a courtroom than in a telephone conversation.

'Firstly,' continued Zaheer, 'if you persist with this defamatory attack against me, then I may have to re-evaluate my position with your firm. I will not do business with people I don't trust, with people who are ready to malign my good character on the say-so of a prevaricator whose story they have not even verified. Paul and I may be good friends, but don't be fooled into thinking that would stop me.'

'Listen,' interjected Farah, 'your threats have no effect on me. There is always the option of reporting you to the police. I'm sure they will be very keen to hear all about how you are treating Razia.'

'Ah! That brings me to my second point. As you very well know, or at least you ought to know, for you are a supposedly intelligent and educated woman, reporting me to the police is pointless, for I have diplomatic immunity.'

Farah swallowed hard. She thought for a few seconds, and finally remembered a newspaper article she had read recently.

'I disagree,' she said. 'In fact, there is currently a case of a diplomat who is being sued for treating his maid as a modern-day slave—'

'Get real,' he jumped in. 'The only thing that will happen if you go to the police is that you will make a total fool of yourself! And think of your own position. How would this affect your credibility? Your professional standing? Your judgement is already questionable, given your rather tawdry affair with a married man, and not just any old man, but your work colleague. Major blurring of professional and private boundaries there, I would say. Take this course of action, and this could all go so spectacularly wrong for you.'

Without giving Farah the chance of a comeback, Zaheer cut off the call abruptly.

Farah was fuming. She cursed herself for the rest of the evening and into the small hours of the night as she ploughed through it all in her mind, again and again. She didn't enjoy being reminded by a man like Zaheer about her biggest mistake in life; she regretted the whole Tahir saga, from beginning to end, and was paying for it with uncomfortable daily reminders at the office. If she had learned one thing from the whole sorry mess, it was that she would never again make the mistake of entangling her personal and professional lives.

Moreover, she was beyond annoyed with herself for having handled the Razia problem so badly. She now felt that she had been a fool to go to Paul and blab about her suspicions, for all she had done in the process was to tip Zaheer off. After all the years of anti-money-laundering training, when it was instilled into her at every course she went to and on every online seminar that she had watched that a solicitor mustn't tip off clients in the process of reporting them to the authorities, she had gone and made a classic schoolgirl error. Zaheer was far craftier than she had given him credit for. And now she was stumped, she had absolutely no clue as to what she should do next. The man was a menace, and his personal attack on Farah gave her the idea that he was someone who was capable of going to any lengths to protect his position.

But Farah knew that she had to do *something*, for her persistent sixth sense cried to her repeatedly: that girl was in grave danger.

13

As soon as Farah stepped foot into the office on Monday morning, the receptionist told her that Paul wanted to see her.

She rushed along the corridor towards Paul's office. She was certain, judging by the conversation she'd had with Zaheer, that Paul must have been told a tall story. The question was, was he prepared to put aside his friendship in order to do the right thing by an innocent victim? Farah had always perceived Paul as not only a fair boss, but also a level-headed man, someone who would do the right thing when faced with a moral dilemma. Even on a professional level, the code of conduct required an incredibly high standard of ethics which didn't just sit inside the four walls of the practice; as solicitors they were duty bound to act so that they didn't bring their profession into disrepute.

Farah knocked on Paul's door, and entered far more slowly than she had hurtled down the corridor.

He was at the window with his back to her and both his hands in his pockets, when she walked in. He didn't have his suit jacket on. He had placed this carefully on the back of his chair at his desk. He was stood tall, his stance rigidly upright. He was looking down at the traffic crawling along Shepherd's Bush Road.

'You wanted to see me?' Farah asked him.

He turned around, softened his stance and leaned back against the windowsill, with his hands still in his pockets.

'You can guess what this is about, can't you?'

'Yes.'

'I had a chat with Zaheer, just as you asked me to.'

'He phoned me too,' she butted in.

'Ah, yes. He did mention that he might call you. Then you will understand, you really have got this all wrong, Farah. I think you have been led a bit of a merry dance by this Razia girl.'

Farah hesitated before answering. She needed a few moments to think about how best to proceed.

'I know.'

Paul cocked his head to one side, and scrunched his eyes a little.

'You do?' he asked. 'Only, you were pretty adamant the last time we spoke.'

'I know. But Zaheer explained everything to me. I'm sorry about the whole thing; it was all just one big misunderstanding. Thanks for your help. But you don't have to worry about it any more.'

Farah had walked in ready for a confrontation, but had quickly realised that there wouldn't be much point. As things stood, she had already spilled enough to Paul, and it hadn't done a scrap of good. She couldn't help wondering what the repercussions may have been for poor Razia. She shuddered to think. Farah knew that she had to deal with this on her own now, and what's more, she had to be a lot smarter about it.

'OK,' said Paul. The hint of surprise was still evident as he dragged the word from his mouth slowly. 'Let's hear no more about it, eh? I am saying this to you as a friend, as well as your boss.'

'Of course. Understood.'

Farah stood silently on the wide pavement outside and stared ahead at the grand building; the embassy was housed in a distinctive, Georgian period whitewashed property that looked like it had seen better days. It needed of a bit of a touch-up here and there, but it still looked very handsome nonetheless. There was a feature balcony on the first floor, where hung the British and Pakistani flags; there they were stationed, like two soldiers standing silently but decisively, on their guard. She hoped they would symbolise some sense of unity and partnership as she tried to find a way through the obstacle-ridden path on her journey to secure Razia's freedom. The flags danced lightly in the delicate spring breeze which drifted along ever so casually on this sunny Friday.

Farah walked in a little cautiously and saw that the waiting area was nigh on full; some people were seated, whilst others were just standing around. There was a baby in a pushchair crying profusely, despite the mother's best efforts to calm it down. She was hastily pushing the buggy back and forth, but the baby continued to bawl in a repetitive high-pitched screech, like a bird stuck in a cage begging to be let out. The baby's cries were competing with an argument that appeared to be in full swing in the far corner of the room. A tall, angry-looking Pakistani man with a large moustache was shouting at a distressed employee almost half his size. Farah couldn't actually make out what it was about, but tempers were frayed. She looked away and to her right she noticed that the reception counter was free. She strolled over, albeit with a little trepidation, going through in her mind what she would say.

'Can I help you?' asked the chubby lady sat behind the counter. She spoke with a strong Pakistani accent. She was chewing a piece of bright blue gum, and her large red glossy lips moved in an exaggerated manner with each circular chew. She had very curly, short, unnaturally coloured pale brown hair, fat round cheeks and a round nose. And to complete the look, she wore round glasses.

'Oh, yes, I wonder if you can. My name is Sara Khan, and I'm here to see Mr Amin.'

'The High Commissioner?' she asked, surprised. 'Mr Amin has been away all week, and he specifically asked me not to book any appointments.'

'Yes, I am aware of that. I phoned on Monday and was told he would be back today. I spoke to him personally earlier this morning. He did say he was not taking any appointments today, but when I explained it was a very urgent matter, he very kindly agreed to fit me in.'

'Hmmm,' she said, still looking doubtful. She phoned through and informed the person on the other end, nodded her head a few times, and then put the phone down.

'Mr Amin says he can see you now. I will show you the way. If you will follow me, please.'

Farah entered the large office with a few tentative steps, but she tried to focus her mind on the task ahead. It was traditionally furnished with solid wooden fittings and wooden chairs cushioned with burgundy velvet seats. On the wall behind the desk hung a large portrait of Pakistan's founding father, Mohammed Ali Jinnah, or Quaid-e-Azam, the title by which he was more fondly known to most Pakistanis. Her gaze lingered on the portrait for a second or two longer than she would have anticipated, perhaps because this was the first time she had seen such a large image of the founding father of her Motherland. She had never before given much thought to this man, but the portrait propelled her to think about him, even if for just a few seconds.

Mr Amin rose from his chair behind his desk.

'Please, come in, and take a seat,' he said, pointing at the chairs on the opposite side of his walnut desk.

Mr Amin was perhaps in his early sixties; he was clean shaven, and had a thick, impeccably combed and parted, mostly black head of hair, with the odd grey hair that had clearly been missed by the dye. He was dressed in a sharply tailored dark grey suit, a crisp white shirt, and his dark metallic grey tie was knotted to perfect symmetrical precision. When he sat back down he did so with a severely straight back, and held his head high. Everything about him suggested some sort of military meticulousness. Perhaps he was actually ex-military, thought Farah, which made her wonder what sort of a response would be forthcoming from this man after he had heard what she had to say.

'Thank you,' she replied, and slowly walked over and sat down.

'So, what can I do for you, Miss Khan?'

Farah opened her mouth, but then paused. She bit her bottom lip, as she often did when she was nervous. Mr Amin waited patiently. Farah knew she had to be upfront and honest from the off if she was going to have any hope of this man helping her.

'Firstly, my name isn't Sara Khan.'

'Oh?' he remarked, and twisted his head slightly to one side, breaking the symmetry of his posture.

'My name is actually Farah Jilani. I work at Drake's Solicitors. My boss, Paul Drake, is a good friend of your colleague Zaheer Mansur.'

'Ah, yes, I have heard Zaheer mention him occasionally. But then, I don't follow: why the cloak and dagger?'

'It's rather a sensitive matter.'

'Go on. I'm listening.'

Farah paused again for a moment or two, just to make sure she had his full attention. Mr Amin gestured with his hand for her to go on.

Farah recalled the event at Zaheer's house, and what Razia had told her, and the fact that she was convinced that Zaheer was lying, but he had managed to persuade Paul otherwise.

She took a deep breath once she had finished. Mr Amin had sat and listened quietly, without interruption. His face gave nothing away.

'So, do you think that despite my professional standing, and my years of legal training, that I could be still so gullible as to be duped by a so-called pathological liar?' Farah asked him.

'No, you seem like a rational young woman, although of course I've only just met you; I don't know you at all.'

'I appreciate that, but I have come to you because you are his boss, and you have a duty to investigate the allegations I have made against one of your senior members of staff, for whom you are responsible.'

Mr Amin slowly brought his right hand to his chin, which he stroked gently with his thumb and index finger whilst he thought about the matter for a few moments.

'Fine,' he said to Farah, 'I will go over to Zaheer and Aneela's house this evening, unannounced, and see if I can find out what is going on.'

Progress at last, thought Farah to herself.

'I'm coming with you,' Farah said.

'No; I think I should go alone.'

Farah was having none of it.

'Why? So you can go there and all be boys together, and he can convince you I'm wrong, by feeding you some cock and bull story, just like he did to Paul? In all fairness, I don't know *you* very well, do I, and I would feel much better about the whole thing if I went along too.'

'If you don't mind my saying, you do sound a tad paranoid.'

'With good reason. I trusted Paul and look what happened. And I have made a promise to that girl, which I have to see through. I'm coming with you. And I'm not taking no for an answer.'

Mr Amin gave out a short sigh.

'OK. Meet me outside their apartment at half past seven this evening.'

14

Farah reached Hans Place a little early, and stood by the tree-filled square, waiting for Mr Amin to arrive, assuming he would arrive at all. She looked towards the apartment and thought about Razia; she wondered how this evening would pan out for her. She had started to walk towards the apartment when she saw Mr Amin pull up in his black S-Class Mercedes.

They acknowledged each other with a quick nod of the head, and a reassuring glance, but said nothing. Mr Amin held out his arm in the direction of the front door, and declared, 'Shall we?' and Farah, having placed her trust in him, led the way to the apartment.

Zaheer opened the door, and Farah saw his face change instantly from a neutral expression to one of astonishment. He feigned a wide smile.

'Zaheer, may we come in?' asked Mr Amin.

'What an unexpected pleasure this is, Sir. Of course, yes, please do. Is everything all right?'

Zaheer threw a brief glance at Farah but did not acknowledge her directly. She was not surprised. She let the snub go and refrained from saying anything; she didn't want to give him any satisfaction.

Just then Aneela strolled into the hallway.

'Mr Amin *Sahib,* what a lovely pleasure. And Farah. How delightful to see you again,' said Aneela. Farah could sense that she was trying to diffuse the tension. 'Please do come in; would you like tea or coffee, or masala chai perhaps?'

'No, that won't be necessary,' replied Mr Amin.

'Is everything OK, Sir?' persisted Aneela.

'I don't know yet,' said Mr Amin, turning to Zaheer. 'I will tell you once I have spoken to your housekeeper.'

'My . . . my housekeeper?' he asked with another smile, although this time it was more forced.

'Yes, Razia is her name, I believe,' Mr Amin said, in a very matter-of-fact way. 'Can you fetch her, please?'

Zaheer's laboured smile began to evaporate.

'Mr Amin. With all due respect, Sir, this is highly irregular, and to be honest, quite absurd. You are my boss at work. Fine. But you have no right to come to my house and interfere in my domestic affairs. What on earth can you want with Razia? She has nothing to do with my job. This is an invasion of my privacy.'

Mr Amin cleared his throat.

'Either you go and get her immediately, or I telephone the police. Miss Jilani here has some information about your

87

domestic affairs, and I'm sure the authorities would be more than interested to hear all about it. So, which is it to be?'

Farah exhaled a quiet sigh of relief, feeling thankful that someone was finally taking her seriously.

Zaheer reluctantly went off to fetch Razia. Aneela threw a steely cold glance at Farah, which she held for a good few seconds, but she said nothing to her, nor to Mr Amin.

A few moments later, Razia came into the hallway, walking slowly behind Zaheer.

'You wait here, please,' Mr Amin instructed Farah, before he took Razia into the lounge. On this occasion, Farah did as she was told and waited in the hallway. Farah noticed Zaheer quietly disappear off towards the kitchen. Farah had half expected him to start questioning her, to start demanding answers about the intrusion, but he refrained from any kind of confrontation, unlike during the telephone conversation they'd had; she found this both surprising and a little unsettling. Perhaps he just wanted to ignore her to make a point, thought Farah, but she observed that he did seem to be very good at controlling his outward appearance and suppressing his emotions whenever he needed to, and she wondered how many different masks he wore.

Aneela drew closer to Farah. Her face was flushed, and she spoke to Farah in a hushed tone.

'What on earth are you doing?' Aneela asked her.

'What on earth am *I* doing? It's you and your husband who need to be asked this question.'

Aneela's eyes misted over, but she didn't blink or flinch in any way.

'Don't give me those doe eyes,' continued Farah. 'I heard and saw you *both* the evening of the dinner party, laying into Razia as she cowered on the floor. I know you both lock her up. I know you both throw abuse at her whenever the mood takes you. I know she is beaten. What sort of people do that?'

'Now listen to me, and listen carefully,' said Aneela. She moved closer to Farah, and lowered her voice even further. 'They've only been in there a minute. There is no real harm done yet. You can go in there and tell Mr Amin that you made a mistake and stop this whole thing right now.'

'And why on earth would I do that?' said Farah, as she stepped away from Aneela.

'You need to listen to me. If you don't put a stop to this you will regret it. Whatever vendetta you have against my husband, *let it go*. Now get in there before it's too late.'

'Not in a million years. Nice try to save your husband's skin, and indeed your own, but it's not working. I am staying right here, and there is nothing you can do about it.'

Aneela stared at Farah for a few seconds with an unwavering, strong gaze; she slowly opened her mouth to say something, but then seemed to think better of it. She headed off to the kitchen to join Zaheer. This encounter only filled Farah with a renewed sense of determination, and she was now certain that rescuing Razia was the right thing to do.

*

Razia stood in the middle of the large lounge; her head was down, and her eyes were fixed on the colours and patterns of the Persian rug. Her *chaddar* was wrapped around her head, arms and shoulders tightly. Her *salwar kameez* was a dark grey, shapeless outfit, and there were what appeared to be two large turmeric stains just above the front hem, underneath which her ragged sandals peeped out.

'Please, do sit down,' gestured Mr Amin.

She looked at him briefly, and then scanned the room around her, before seating herself on the rug.

'No!' said Mr Amin, almost shouting, although he hadn't meant to raise his voice at all. He quickly tempered his tone. 'No, no, *beti*, you must not sit on the floor, you must sit on the sofa,' he said softly.

Mr Amin walked a couple of steps towards her, and gestured again with this hand for her to sit down on the leather settee.

She still hesitated; her eyes darted uneasily from the door, and then towards the sofa.

'Please?' Mr Amin asked.

She stood up and made her way across to the sofa. She perched herself on the very edge. Her body was tense; her shoulders were hunched, and she crossed her arms beneath her *chaddar*. She carried on looking at the flowery, paisley patterns on the silk rug. She did not lift her gaze; she seemed to him to be sitting in a state of complete unease.

If he was honest with himself, Mr Amin had to acknowledge that there was probably no need to ask her anything. Just one look at this poor girl told him everything he could possibly need to know. She was painfully thin; she looked like a brittle, parched twig, as though she would break if one so much as touched her. Although her eyes were large and brown, from what he could see of them, for the girl barely looked up, they possessed a sallow sadness and lacked any life or vibrancy. Her cheeks were sunken and colourless. Mr Amin noticed that her face was devoid of any expression, other than perhaps fear; he could sense that she was fearful, even though he had not given her any cause to feel that way. This filled him with a deep feeling of sadness, and he wondered what this girl might have endured to be full of so much dread.

Razia unfolded her arms, and twirled one corner of her *chaddar* around her fingers; all the while she continued to look down and avoid eye contact. Her hands were bony; her nails were chipped, and her fingertips were dry and cracked like an old woman's. She was a stark physical, and no doubt equally disturbing mental, embodiment of her circumstances. In another situation, at another time, she may have looked beautiful, youthful, happy. Not here. Not now. She was a shadow of a girl.

Farah noted from her watch that they had been in the lounge for over forty minutes. She couldn't help but wonder what was being said in there; wonder how the conversation was progressing.

Zaheer reared his head back out from wherever he had disappeared to, and came to stand by Farah. Aneela was nowhere to be seen.

He put his face just a few inches from hers.

'You will bitterly regret this, Farah; both you and Razia. I will make sure you pay for this,' he said. Each word was spoken with a cold, sinister edge.

'I don't think you're in any position right now to make threats, do you?' she retaliated coolly.

But Farah wasn't feeling at all cool inside. She could feel an uncomfortable, sticky sensation behind her neck and ears.

'It isn't a threat, you stupid girl. It is an absolute *pukka* promise,' Zaheer said.

Farah could not look at him any longer, and turned her face away.

Just then, the door to the lounge opened.

As soon as they stepped out of the room, Razia quietly disappeared off down the hallway and Mr Amin came to stand opposite Zaheer.

'Look, I don't know what she's told you,' Zaheer said, before Mr Amin could speak, 'but like I have already explained to Farah, Razia is a serial liar—'

'Quiet!' roared Mr Amin, and Farah almost jumped out of her skin.

'I do not want to hear another word,' he said a little more gently. 'I cannot believe the way in which you have treated this young girl. It wasn't easy getting her to talk, I can tell you that much; but she did talk, eventually, and she has told me as much as I need to know. You have conducted yourself in a way that is not befitting for any human being, let alone a man of your position within our organisation. I think you can consider your career over!' Mr Amin stood with his arms unswervingly straight, down by his sides, and he had his fists clenched as he spoke. Otherwise, he made no show of emotion.

Farah's sense of relief was quite extraordinary. Seeing Mr Amin act in this way had restored her faith in humanity and went against the commonly held belief that all Pakistani men in positions of power were corrupt. Mr Amin, she surmised, was a good, honest human being, prepared to step up for the oppressed, and to do the right thing. How utterly refreshing, she thought to herself, and what a relief that she no longer felt alone in her pursuit of freedom for Razia.

'Right then,' said Mr Amin, 'One thing is certain, Razia cannot stay here a second longer. I could ring around some charities; perhaps there are some refuges that house women in her situation—'

'I will take her in,' announced Farah.

Both men looked at her.

'Are you sure?' Mr Amin asked.

'Yes, I am absolutely sure; she can come and stay with me.'

Farah didn't hesitate in taking on this responsibility; she had made a promise to Razia, and she wanted to see it through.

'Well, that would be very helpful. Thank you,' said Mr Amin.

'But what's the long-term plan?' asked Farah.

'She has asked to be sent back to her family in Pakistan, I understand that her family owes a debt to your brother,' Mr Amin said, as he looked at Zaheer, who did not say anything in response. He shifted his weight from one leg to the other. Mr Amin looked back at Farah. 'I believe he is the feudal landlord of the brick kiln where she and her family work, some thirty or forty miles outside of Lahore. Razia is very anxious about the fact that this debt will remain if she goes back to Pakistan, as the idea was that she would come to the UK and work for nothing to help to pay off at least some of the money that is owed.'

Mr Amin shook his head in disbelief, and then pointed his right index finger at Zaheer, although he spoke calmly and precisely.

'You had this poor girl at your beck and call, twenty-four hours a day, seven days a week. You kept her passport from her, which, by the way, you will now hand over. You haven't paid her a penny since the day she arrived. You haven't allowed her to make any contact with her family. She hasn't spoken to them since the day she left Pakistan, not even once. You haven't bought her any clothes or toiletries, and she eats only leftover food. You haven't taken her out since the day she set foot in this place; worse than that, you lock her up when you are out yourselves, shopping and partying and having a great time. You have treated this poor girl worse than an animal. And the beatings. Not to mention the obscene verbal abuse that she has had to put up with.'

Farah swallowed hard as she tried to digest these details, as she tried to comprehend just how much pain this girl had endured.

Zaheer opened his mouth, but Mr Amin put his palm in front of Zaheer's face.

'Coming back to this debt that her family supposedly owe,' continued Mr Amin, 'she doesn't even know how much it is. But, however much it is, we will take care of it, and I will arrange the flight back to Pakistan. As an organisation whose senior member of staff has treated someone so abhorrently, it's the least we can do. As soon as I leave here, I will make arrangements for someone to go out and speak to her family tomorrow, to start the ball rolling.'

Zaheer listened to all of this quietly, without moving, and without giving much away about what he was feeling. His head hung slightly; he had his arms crossed and he was silent throughout Mr Amin's speech.

Mr Amin directed one final comment towards Zaheer. 'Make sure you come to the office first thing tomorrow morning, when I can deal with you properly.'

Razia walked slowly towards the front door, carrying a small carrier bag that contained all her worldly belongings – one change of clothes and a spare *chaddar*.

'Come, ladies, I will give you a lift in my car to your destination,' said Mr Amin.

Farah and Mr Amin stepped out of the front door; they had walked a few steps before Farah noticed that Razia hadn't moved yet. Farah walked back towards her, and Mr Amin turned around and looked on.

Farah noticed Razia was a little shaky, and her eyes were bleary.

'It's OK; come on, we will look after you, I promise,' Farah reassured her, and then she held out her hand.

Razia grabbed hold of Farah's hand and took her first step, followed by the second, and a tear escaped her eye as she walked towards the car.

15

One Year Earlier

Razia, Karim and Javed were all squatting on the ground. They were just a few feet from each other as they continued the daily task of shaping the bricks in the rusty old moulds. They then patted them upside down, so they landed firmly on the ground with a solid thud, and left them to dry in the blazing sun.

Razia's *salwar kameez* were covered in dirty marks from all the brick-making work. She had her *chaddar* wrapped around her head and shoulders, but ensured her arms were free to carry out the tasks. Her neck hurt from the constant strain of drooping her head down, not only to get the work done but also to keep the ferocious sun out of her eyes.

Karim looked much older than his probable age of around fifty. He did not know his actual date of birth. Razia knew that years of working in the brick kiln for long hours in searing temperatures had taken their toll. His dark face was wrinkled like that of a man in his seventies. But what alarmed his daughter even more was the way in which the work had now affected his hands; as always, they were covered in the dirty gunge from which the bricks were shaped, but the disturbing part was the way in which his hands shook whilst he carried on with the work. Razia guessed that this was probably the onset of some unforgiving disease taking hold. But she didn't know any more than that; her father had not actually been seen by a doctor for any sort of official diagnosis. The medical fees were totally out of their reach. Each day, Razia observed her father living and working with the illness as best he could, for the requirement of the master to produce a thousand bricks a day meant there was no choice but to keep working, regardless of the heat or the increasing inability of his hands to work as fast as they used to.

Javed, who was now in his mid-twenties, had the benefit of youth, and the energy that came with it, and Razia was grateful that he was able to work with such speed and agility. Thankfully, he took responsibility for many of the jobs that involved heavy lifting and carrying, and he undertook the work involving the fire; these tasks were now beyond their father's physical capabilities and they were jobs Razia knew he would never expect her or their mother to do if he could help it.

Razia knew that today they would not meet the demand for a thousand bricks; far from it. Today, their mother Nusrat had not come to the brick kiln, for she was ill, and Razia was going to leave early. She had begged to have some time off; she had told her brother that she needed to help her friend prepare for her forthcoming wedding. Worse still, Javed himself had to leave earlier than usual for an errand that could not be avoided. In her heart, Razia was torn; she felt guilty for leaving early, and even guiltier for not being completely honest about why she needed some time off, but at the same time, she needed to seize these little opportunities to escape the gruelling labour, and snatch a few moments of happiness whenever possible.

Razia and her fellow bonded slaves worked fourteen hours, or more, each day, even though the severity of the work almost broke their backs, and the summer heat beat them down until they were barely ghosts of themselves by the end of the day. And the next day, it would begin all over again. There were no schools for the children. When Razia looked around the brick kiln, she saw that the babies lay forlorn on one side, and the toddlers played absent-mindedly in the dirt, never knowing what toys were. For their amusement they used oddly shaped stones, rough ones and smooth ones, and prickly sticks. As soon as Razia and her brother had been old enough, they had been set to task; she recalled how they had continually and diligently fetched and carried for their parents. Their hunger for a meal that evening meant they had both worked industriously, without fuss.

Razia knew that their life must differ in a million ways from the lives of children in other places that she had occasionally seen depicted in pictures in books, or from what she had observed when she had gone into town. Instead of walking to school every day, Razia and her brother had trudged to the brick kiln. Instead of carrying books, they had carried bricks. Instead of designing and making objects in the classroom, they had shaped bricks. They never had a childhood, or anything resembling an education, for these were not seen as an entitlement for such youngsters like Razia and her brother. Reaching the target number of bricks was all that mattered to their family: day in, day out. Nothing else existed. They made their bricks, they were paid a pittance and they barely survived.

It was now time for Razia to go, and as she left the brick kiln, she also left behind the negative thoughts and focused on what lay ahead.

Today, it was scorching hot; the mid-afternoon sun was relentless in its pursuit of spreading its brutal light across the land.

When Razia reached the edge of the stream, she took off her sandals and carried them in one hand, and with the other she gently lifted her *salwar* well above her ankles, and stepped nimbly across the blue grey stones so aptly placed along the shallowest crossing of the stream. The water twinkled as the sun's rays caressed its steady flow. Once she was across, she placed her feet back into her sandals and walked through the tall field of corn, until she reached the small round clearing in the middle. She was now out of sight from any prying eyes from her side of the village, and with the height of the long-eared corn on all sides of the clearing, she was in fact invisible from any angle. She felt safe, and she was excited to be back here again.

He stepped out of the tall corn, grabbed her arm from behind and pulled her towards him. She felt his arms wrap tightly around her waist. She turned around and returned the embrace; she circled her arms around him, and breathed into his neck. His familiar scent was hypnotic, and comforting.

Razia felt him move away from the embrace, and she looked at him inquisitively.

'It's been two weeks since I last saw you! Why didn't you come and see me the last three times?' Ahmed asked her, and then he pulled Razia back towards him; she could feel his mouth seeking hers, and longed to feel close to him, she longed to taste his kiss again.

'Javed is suspicious, I'm sure of it. He's been acting really strangely lately,' replied Razia, as she pulled away with a slight frown.

'When is your brother not acting strangely?' Ahmed teased. But Razia did not laugh in return.

'It's not funny, I'm scared. I think he may suspect something.' Razia went and sat on the small dry mound in the middle of the clearing. She screwed up her nose, annoyed that Ahmed was not taking her concerns seriously.

Ahmed came over and sat next to her. He held both her hands in his, and now talked softly.

'OK, OK. So, why are you so worried, my love? If anything

bothers my Heer, then it is cause for concern for her Ranjha. What has happened?'

'Nothing . . . really.'

'Has he said anything?'

'Not directly, no.'

'Then what is it?'

'He's just acting differently. He's asking me more questions about where I'm going. I can't seem to go to the well to fetch water, or to the neighbours to get milk, without him asking fifty questions. He scrutinises my every move. I hate lying about where I'm going. I told them all I was going to my friend's house today to help her prepare for her *nikah*. I only managed to get away from the brick kiln early today because he himself is out of the village this afternoon; he had to go into town to fetch medicine for *Amee*. Mother hasn't been well. Her asthma is very bad these days. I keep telling her to stop working so much at the brick kiln, but she doesn't listen. Then again, we all have to put in all the hours we can manage. Even so, after all these years, we haven't scratched the surface of the debt.'

'It's the same for us too,' remarked Ahmed, 'only there's more of us in our family, so it's easier to share the load, which you will find out, *Insha'Allah*, once we are married!'

Razia imagined such happiness; such fulfilment. Would they really be married soon? Could she ever really feel so complete? She wished and longed for this day to come. The day that she would be his bride.

'I want nothing more. But what about my brother? If he finds out about us, he will kill you!'

'I don't think so!' Ahmed snorted. 'I'm one of five brothers. And he's an only son. There's no competition. He wouldn't dare.'

'OK, so he will kill me then!' Razia said.

'I will never let that happen to my Heer! What would Ranjha do without you, my love?'

'Before it ever gets to that, why don't you speak to your father and get him to come over and ask for my *rishta*? Either you come and ask for my hand in marriage, or we stop seeing each other, and you can go and marry your stupid cousin!' Razia said. She really wanted him to take her seriously.

Ahmed gently stroked Razia's cheek.

'I have no intention of marrying anyone other than you, my love. Anyway, I have a plan.'

Razia quickly turned her head to look at him. She gazed into his eyes hopefully, and clasped her hands together in anticipation.

'Really? What's the plan?' she asked.

'I have to go away with my father to visit his eldest brother, as he is practically on his deathbed. He has a couple of days at the most; that's what his family have said. We leave first thing in the morning. Whilst I'm there, my other uncle will also be visiting. I will speak up and tell my father and uncle that I don't want to marry my uncle's daughter. They won't like it but I know that ultimately my father will back me. Anyway, there is another cousin that she could marry. Once that is sorted, I will be back, probably in a few days, and upon our return my father will come to your house and speak to your father.'

'But your uncle's village is so far away! You could be gone for ages!'

'Calm down, I will be away for a few days only, one week maximum. You know we both can't be away from the brick kiln for too long. I will return as quickly as I can, and the next time we meet, we will be betrothed. You have my word.'

Ahmed leaned over and they started to embrace. Their lips touched, and once again they fell into a passionate kiss. She knew that in the eyes of her family and community, and indeed in God's eyes, what she was doing was wrong. But when she was with him, all those thoughts left her mind, and all she could see was the man she loved deeply. And she believed with all her heart this was the man she was going to marry, and spend the rest of her life with.

Razia suddenly pulled away.

'Did you hear that?' Razia jumped up, and spun around in search of something, although she didn't know what.

'Hear what?' Ahmed asked. He stayed where he was, perched on the mound, and looked puzzled.

'That rustling – there was somebody or something here, listening to us, or worse still, watching us!' Razia's heart was racing, as she continued to wonder what the noise was.

'It was probably a snake, or some other creature. Relax. Stop being so paranoid. Come here.'

Razia didn't register his words instantly. But when she looked at him, she saw that his arms were wide open, and she went over to him, and sought sanctuary in his lingering embrace, and a soft, tender kiss.

'One week at the most, that's all, and then we will be at your house, asking for your hand in marriage,' Ahmed reassured Razia.

'One week? No longer?'

'Yes, one week. Nothing much will happen in one week. Just sit tight and wait for me to come.'

Razia's face softened, as she thought about the prospect, the idea that he would come with his family, *mitai* in hand, to ask for her hand in marriage. How jubilant she would feel on that day.

But it was now time for them to part. It was always so; they could not risk being missed by their families, so their meetings were always short. She now dared to hope that this would be their final clandestine meeting.

'One week. You're right; it's not long. Have a safe journey. I will wait impatiently for your return,' she said, trying to reassure herself; she was going to miss him terribly, but the pain of parting would all be worth it when he got back and came to seek the betrothal.

'*Insha'Allah.* And I will see you as soon as I get back.'

'May Allah protect you and bring you back safely to me.'

16

The village in which Razia and her family lived was very primitive, much like many of the other villages around Lahore, and indeed much of the Punjab. On paper, Punjab was the wealthiest province in Pakistan, but that wealth had not seeped into the lives of ordinary people. Most of the inhabitants of this and the surrounding villages consisted of the workforce which produced the bricks at the local kilns. Razia's village, the outlying land and the brick kiln were all owned by Choudhry Fazal Mansur, although he was always addressed by the workers as Choudhry *Sahib*, to denote his superior status.

The Mansur family had been feudal landowners for centuries, and Choudhry Fazal, being the elder of two sons, and now in his late fifties, had carried on with the system just as his father had left it when he had passed away over ten years ago. His younger brother had chosen to seek a formal education, and work outside of the ancestral undertaking, which the wealthy family could well afford. Zaheer was educated abroad and worked in the diplomatic service out of choice, not necessity. The family owned several houses, or rather mansions, in Pakistan, and overseas, although, Zaheer always regarded the large family *haveli* as his permanent home.

Razia's late grandfather had taken a loan from the Mansur family many years ago; he was an illiterate man, and had had no idea at the time of the details of the document that he signed. Nothing had been explained to him about the exorbitant interest rates and charges, which continued to pile up over the years. Over the decades, the family had been forced to take out more loans, mostly just to meet ordinary living expenses; for food, bills, medicines, and indeed any expenditure that was out of the ordinary. Now, years later, his son and grandchildren were saddled with the ever-increasing debt. After the landlord took what he was owed each week, there was barely enough for subsistence living, but until the loan was paid in full, Razia's family were tied to working in the brick kiln, having to produce over a thousand bricks a day just to have enough to eat.

Razia often wondered why they had been dealt such a bad hand in life. No matter how hard they worked, the ceaselessly turning wheel of debt continued to spin round. No end ever seemed to be in sight. Her only ray of light was her hope of marriage to Ahmed.

Razia's house, if one could call it that, was situated at the lower end of the village. The paths that led down towards it were narrow and uneven, and dirty water trickled along them as it drained out from each dwelling, and joined the scummy, polluted flow. Sometimes, the bumpiness of the path caused the smelly water to flow in different directions and gather in the holes. Razia skipped her way through the slender, crooked paths, and jumped nimbly over the wet patches as she made her way home.

Their house was a tiny, single storey construction, consisting of only two rooms and a small yard, which had a cooking area in one corner and a washing area directly opposite. The food was cooked over a wood fire, and the *rotis* in the tandoor. The washroom was extremely basic, with just a latrine, and a tiny space for bathing. The house was crumbling and decaying in patches; bits had fallen away from the walls to expose sporadic holes. But to Razia, this was home.

By the time Razia reached home, she had forgotten about all the negative thoughts that had charged through her mind not long ago, about what would become of her and Ahmed, and she smiled quietly to herself as she remembered his soft touch and hypnotic voice. In a few days, a week at the most, she thought to herself, Ahmed's family would come over and seek the betrothal. Hopefully, her father would be agreeable, and even if her brother wasn't keen, her father would have the final decision, and she was quietly confident that he would say yes; her family did not have anyone else in mind for her, and as long as Ahmed was able to break free from his current betrothal to his cousin, she could see no reason why her father would object. Then the sneaking around would all be over. She would marry the love of her life, and she would live in bliss. She was sure that she would be the happiest girl alive, for so very few women in these parts ever managed to marry for love. Most of the girls in her village were given away in matrimony as part of arranged or forced marriages. Their opinion was never considered to be worthy or even relevant enough to be sought, let alone their consent ever obtained; they were simply told who they were to be married to, and when. It was all a matter of quiet acceptance of whatever fate had in store for them, for every single aspect of their lives was mapped out by the men; firstly, by their fathers and brothers, and then, after their marriage, by their husbands and their fathers-in-law. Razia was grateful that the family that would be coming to seek her betrothal would be the family of the man that she loved fervently; she would be blessed indeed, as her love for Ahmed would naturally lead to a loving bond between her and his family.

When Razia stepped into the small courtyard, Nusrat was sat on the *peeri* by the stove. When she wasn't at the brick kiln, her mother could usually be found here, on the low handmade stool, preparing the next meal. However, today, she did not appear to be cooking. In fact, she had her face down in her *chaddar*. Her whole body was drooped forwards. Her shoulders moved up and down rhythmically. Her asthmatic wheeze was the only audible sound, like a soft intermittent whistle. This worried Razia; she wondered what was wrong.

As Razia walked closer, her mother sat up from her slouched position and uncovered her face. She silently stared at Razia. Her eyes were puffy and tender-looking; something was terribly wrong, thought Razia.

And then her mother began wailing, quietly yet melodically. She wailed in hushed tones, and the words were indistinct. It sounded as though she were singing the saddest lullaby in the world. Razia's initial assumption was that someone had died. She rushed over to console her mother, but stopped dead in her tracks before she quite got there. For just then, right at that second, Razia knew. She just knew. No one had died. But someone might as well have died. It would all amount to the same thing.

'*Amee*, what's wrong?' Razia asked feebly.

Her mother looked straight at her. The wailing had now stopped. Futile tears slid down her hot cheeks, but they could save no one and nothing. Though Razia had seen it day in, day out for her entire life, it was as though she was noticing her mother's wrinkled face for the first time; it was a face that depicted a lifetime of hardship. Razia knew that each deep line was a testament to injustice and strife: the loss of three children in their infancy, the endurance of four miscarriages, the never-ending servitude towards her husband and the toil of the brick kiln – each and every one of these adversities was embedded in the grooves in her face. They were permanent reminders of the difficulties that she had borne, and they were reminders which could not be smoothed away.

'*Amee*! Speak to me!' Razia implored her.

Her mother rubbed away a stray tear from her right cheek.

'What is there to say? I have no words. Or at least, I do not have any words that will be of comfort to you now. I am powerless, my child. Powerless.'

The gate swung open, and before she could twist around to see who it was, Razia was hit fiercely from behind. The sudden shock of the powerful blow to the back of her head sent her spinning off her feet, and she collapsed into a heap on the dusty ground. She cradled the back of her head with one hand, as she squinted and doubled over with pain, and then she looked up and saw that her brother was towering above her. Her father stood a couple of feet behind him.

'What's the matter? Why are you hitting me?' Razia sobbed.

Javed howled, 'Did you think that I wouldn't find out! Do you think I am such a fool?'

Razia felt a powerful sense of dread gush through her, causing her to feel dizzy.

'What do you mean?' she asked, fearing what his answer would be.

'I saw you with that Ahmed boy!' barked Javed. 'How could you play with our *izzat* in this way, and in broad daylight! Do you have no regard for this family's honour? We may be poor, and we may not have much, but the one thing we do have is our honour.'

Javed pulled Razia by the arm. She screamed and cried out for her mother and father to help her, but neither of them stepped forward. Javed dragged her along the ground with disdain, as though he were dragging a lifeless rag doll. Her clothes sucked up the dust from the ground as he carted her into the smaller room. And then he locked the door from the inside.

Razia's screams escaped from the small room of torture, and hurt Nusrat's ears. She placed her hands over her ears and closed her eyes, wishing she could not hear her daughter's cries: Razia begging her brother to stop, begging him for mercy.

'Please, that is enough. Go in there and tell him to stop!' Nusrat pleaded with her husband, as her tears flowed. But Karim was unmoved by her words, and stared into the space in front of him, as though he were temporarily paralysed; as though he was deaf and blind for as long as he deemed it necessary.

More excruciating, scream-ridden moments passed. Nusrat's heart raced uncontrollably; her body shook with fear.

'This is the way it has to be,' Karim finally said. 'This is the way it has always been. You know that. She cannot do what she has done, and there be no consequences. She was having a relationship with a man out of wedlock. Thank God, Javed spotted the problem in time. Imagine if someone else had seen them. I wouldn't have been able to show my face for miles around. And Javed would most likely have killed her. Be grateful that it is just a beating.'

Javed finally emerged from the room, after what had seemed like an eternity to Nusrat. He closed and locked the door from the outside, thus ensuring Razia's incarceration. His face was calm; Nusrat wondered how he could remain so serene.

'Stop crying, *Amee*,' he said, as he bent to sit on the *manji* next to his father, flipping the back of his light brown *kurtha* upwards behind him before he sat down. 'She had it coming. To be honest with you, I've let her off lightly. I could easily have broken every bone in her body for what she's done, but I didn't. Families have killed their girls for much less. She should consider herself fortunate.'

In the end, Nusrat was somewhat relieved. Her daughter would be sore, and upset, and miserable, but at least she was still alive. She knew full well it could have been much worse. She could console herself knowing that at least.

'But the question is, how do we make sure this doesn't happen again?' asked Karim. He rolled his thumbs around, and placed his crossed hands in his lap. 'I mean, we are at the brick kiln all day. Either she stays with us there, in which case she is likely to bump into that boy, or someone stays at home with her, but then we won't make our target. The girl has put us in an impossible position.'

Javed gently placed his left hand on his father's right shoulder. Karim turned to look at him.

'Don't worry, Father, I've sorted it,' Javed assured Karim. Nusrat remained silent throughout the exchanges between father and son; she listened to the conversation with one ear, but her mind was fixed on trying to listen for any sounds that might come from her daughter. But the small room was eerily quiet.

'I don't understand. How?' Karim asked.

'I was speaking to Munshi when he came around the other day to sort the books. He said that Choudhry *Sahib*'s brother, Zaheer *Sahib*, has been posted to work in London, and they are looking to take a maid with them from Pakistan. They need someone who will work hard at household chores, cook all the *desi* food and generally look after the needs of Madam. I suggested Razia, and he said that he would mention it to Choudhry. Anyway, he came back to me this morning and said that if we are agreeable then they will take Razia with them. She will live and stay with them at all times; they will provide her with sleeping arrangements, food and other necessities. He said they won't pay her directly, but instead they will take whatever she would have earned and put it towards the debt we owe. It seems like the best solution to me.'

'Best solution for who?' piped up Nusrat. 'What about me? She is my daughter, and you are thinking of sending her to some foreign land, thousands of miles away. When will I see her again?'

Nusrat wiped the tears from her face with the corner of her pale green *chaddar*. She couldn't imagine her life without Razia; her daughter had never been away from home, not even for a single day or night. Razia was her closest companion, the one she shared everything with; whenever she needed to air her hopes, her thoughts or her fears, Razia was the one she turned to.

'*Amee*! I can't believe you are talking like this. Look at what she has done! She has left us with no choice!' retorted Javed.

'He is right, Nusrat. Let it be. It has been decided,' added Karim.

Nusrat didn't say another word. She swallowed her tears in silence and grieved inwardly for her daughter, for her precious child, who was still so young and innocent, but who had now been catapulted into the world of self-important, angry men, who would try desperately to defend their so-called family honour, and do whatever it took to prevent it being tarnished in any way.

17

Razia struggled to drift out of her state of unconsciousness for some time. She didn't know if she was dreaming, or if she really could hear her mother muttering the words 'wake up my child'. The sounds and words seemed to be floating towards her from somewhere far away. When she finally did open her eyes, her mother was sat beside her in the room that was devoid of anything other than the one *manji* on which Razia lay, and a high wooden shelf that was sparsely decked with a few bits of mismatched crockery, and five tall, proud steel drinking glasses, which sparkled even in the dimness. They were her mother's finest possessions; she polished them regularly and not a speck of dust could be found on the inside nor the exterior of the shiny vessels. Their glimmer danced in Razia's eyes.

Nusrat was sat with a *chakor* in her lap; the round, basket-like object contained two chappatis, and atop was a small clay plate with some *masoor dhal* in it.

Razia's eyelashes flickered as she tried to come out of the slumber that had taken hold of her being.

'Wake up and eat something. You haven't eaten anything all day,' Nusrat said. Razia could feel the warmth of her mother's caress as she gently stroked Razia's hair away from her face.

'I don't want to eat anything. My arms and legs hurt. And my back hurts too. Everything hurts,' Razia said. She clutched at her back with both her hands. She clenched her teeth hard, although this did nothing to alleviate the pain that she was feeling. The physical soreness was the least of the trauma, for the emotional punches ran far deeper. To have been so brutally beaten by her own brother, and for her father to have just stood silently outside and not intervened, made Razia feel as though she had been cut slowly into pieces with the sharpest of daggers. She wondered if those pieces would ever mend back together again.

Nusrat hugged her daughter gently, and began to cry.

'I know, my beautiful one. I know. And I am sorry. I couldn't do anything to help you. I am helpless, my child. Simply helpless.'

Razia, with her eyes firmly clamped shut again, placed her aching and bruised arms around her mother. She didn't blame her mother. She never could. She savoured the warmth of her mother's embrace, and wished she could just stay here, and never have to move. This was the the one place where Razia felt safe.

'Nusrat, where are you?' shouted Karim from the yard outside.

Nusrat pulled away, and held her daughter's face in her hands for a minute.

'I have to go. Your father needs me. Eat the food, please,' Nusrat implored her daughter.

Nusrat placed the food next to Razia, who lay back down on her side. As her mother left the room, Razia felt all alone in the world, until the noise of the *azan* slowly seeped into her ears. It emanated from the mosque that was situated in the centre of the village. She opened one eye slightly; she had noticed from the momentary gap in the door as her mother left that it was not dark yet, so it must be *Maghrib* time, she thought to herself. The back end of the call to prayer recited melodiously by the muezzin continued to drift into Razia's ears:

> *Hayya 'ala-s-Salah, Hayya 'ala-s-Salah*
> *Hayya 'ala-l-Falah, Hayya 'ala-l-Falah*
> *Allahu Akbar, Allahu Akbar*
> *La ilaha illa Allah*

Hurry to the prayer, Hurry to success, God is Great, There is no god except Allah; Razia repeated the verse to herself as a whisper. Where was her God now? she thought to herself.

Nusrat carefully locked the door from the outside, under her husband's vigilant eye. She looked at him as he stared at her like a hawk, and despite her anger and exasperation she said nothing. Instead, she entered the other room and picked up her prayer mat, which she brought out into the courtyard, by which time her husband had already left for the mosque to say his prayers there. Nusrat lay her simple *janamaz* down in the corner, facing the direction of Mecca; the head of the red and green prayer rug had a large image of the Ka'ba. She began reciting her intention to pray, and commenced her *namaz*.

Razia lay still on the *manji*, and felt as though if she moved even an inch she might break. The muezzin's voice had now ceased, but the whispers of the *azan* continued in her head. Her eyes were sore, and her vision was bleary. Her head felt as heavy as a rock. She didn't touch the food that her mother had brought to her. She could not move, other than to curl up into a ball, and push away the cruel world by wrapping her *chaddar* over her entire head until she could see nothing.

18

LONDON

On the drive from Zaheer and Aneela's apartment to Farah's home, Razia sat quietly in the rear of Mr Amin's car, and thought back to how everything had been prepared for her departure without any knowledge or effort on her part. She had failed to pick up on the signs. Two weeks before she had been caught with Ahmed, at Javed's request she had accompanied him into town to have her photograph taken. He had told her it was in order for her national identification card to be prepared. Razia took him at his word. It was only after the beating that it had become evident that the photographs had been used for her passport. Her brother had been plotting this for some time. Javed must have been in talks about the possibility of Razia's going to London for a few weeks at least. Razia never saw the images, or the passport itself; this was always in the custody of Mr or Mrs Mansur. And knowing she would have to travel soon, her brother had been very careful during the beating not to mark her face; she could hardly believe this level of cold calculation on his part.

And now, Razia could barely believe that she was being driven to freedom. She had only ever known life as a bonded slave making bricks, or lately as a slave at the beck and call of the Mansurs, expected to fetch and carry, scrub and shine, cook and iron, at any hour of any day or night. But this passage of hers, this weaving of a tumultuous path for Razia into yet more servitude, only thousands of miles away from home, was one in which she'd had no hand, no say and no right to object to. She had begrudgingly but silently stepped into the unknown, and borne whatever it was that fate had held in store for her. And she had borne it alone, without the company of her mother, and with no knowledge of when she would see her beloved Ahmed again.

During that solitary week between the beating and leaving for England, Razia was locked away in the small room. Her mother visited her regularly, as only a mother could; to provide her with food, and water, and above all to give her some love and comfort. Her mother did her best to provide reassurances: London was not going to be forever, she would be back with her before long, and the work couldn't possibly be as difficult as working at the brick kiln. But Razia could find no reassurances about Ahmed; he was still away at present, but what would happen when he got back? Would Javed go after him? And how would Ahmed feel when he found out she had left the country?

Razia never blamed her mother for not being able to change anything, for she knew her mother was as much a victim in all of this as she was.

'Are you OK, Razia?' asked Farah, noticing that she was distracted. Mr Amin was focused on the road ahead.

'*Ji*,' replied Razia simply, and turned her head to stare back out of the window again.

She could vividly picture the day she had left home; Razia had stood in the yard with her mother. Nusrat's asthma had been so bad that day that she couldn't manage to walk the few minutes from their house to the lane on the edge of the village where the car sent by the Mansurs had parked up in readiness. Razia's father and brother had gone on ahead, and waited by the car.

Razia remembered sobbing wildly. She had rushed towards her mother and embraced her tightly. She had whispered into her mother's ear. She had wanted to try one last time to see if there was any way she could stay, even if deep down she had known that her mother was powerless to make such a wish come true.

'Please, *Amee ji*, please don't send me! I don't want to go! I'm frightened. I don't want to go on an aeroplane. And I don't want to go to London. I won't know anybody there. *Amee*, I will be all alone. I will miss you.'

She recollected how her mother had shed feeble, futile tears, as she had struggled, both physically, with her heavy, laboured breath, and emotionally; she had opened her mouth and tried to utter something to try and take the fear away, but Razia remembered her mother being unable to finish her sentence. All she could say was how sorry she was.

'*Meri bachi*, I am so sorry. Please forgive this useless mother of yours. I have no power. I have no control. I am of no use. If I could swap with you, if I could be in your shoes, and take your pain, I would do it in less time than it takes for my heart to beat and for my eye to blink. But I can do nothing for you, my child. Nothing. Except pray for you, and pray that I see you again soon, safe and sound.'

The banging of the gate had caused them both to tear away from their embrace.

'What are you still doing here?' Javed had shouted. 'Come on!'

She remembered him grabbing her by the arm to take her away.

The last vision Razia had of her mother was of her being glued to the spot. Her mother's tears had continued to trickle down her face, but she had been unable to move.

'Please, *Amee*. Please! I will miss you. Please don't make me go! Please don't let them take me. *Amee . . . Amee . . .*'

Razia remembered being dragged by her brother down the alleyway towards the lane; her home had started to disappear from her sight. After she had been bundled into the back of the car, Razia's village had then slowly disappeared from her vision. That was the last she remembered of her home in Pakistan.

Now, Mr Amin parked his car on the cobbled street outside Farah's apartment, and Razia looked up at the building through the window.

'Welcome to your new home,' said Farah.

Razia clasped her carrier bag close to her chest, and disembarked from the car.

19

The next morning, when Razia came out of the bathroom, she looked different. This was the first time Farah had seen her without her *chaddar* swathed around her. Her long, dark brown hair was still damp, and extended so much further down than Farah had imagined; it tumbled to below her hips, although the ends were split and scraggly. This was also the first time that Farah fully saw Razia's face, without obstruction. Farah observed that she was quite an unusually pretty girl. Her skin was a warm tone of brown, and perhaps in happier and healthier times it would exude a fresh, golden hue. Although her face was gaunt, it was nevertheless entirely free of any blemishes, aside from a vivid scar that lay to the right of her chin, on the jawline. Her eyes were not completely brown, but rather they appeared to be different shades of brown tinged with little flecks of grey. They seemed sad and tired-looking.

Farah asked Razia to come and join her for breakfast. Razia went over and sat on one of the two chairs at the small, round table.

'So, what shall we do today?' Farah asked her, placing a plate of toast and eggs before Razia, and then going to fetch two mugs of freshly brewed tea. This had only taken about ten seconds, but when she got back, she found Razia sobbing.

'Hey, what's the matter?' Farah asked. She quickly put the mugs down, went around the small table and placed an arm snugly around Razia. She gently rubbed her back.

'No one has ever made food for me before, except my mother of course. I miss my mother so much!'

Farah popped a tissue out of the box that was luckily at the centre of the table and passed it to Razia. The girl's sadness jolted Farah into thinking about how fortunate she was; she had to acknowledge that she often moaned about things without thinking, but they now seemed frivolous, and tedious. And far too often she took her parents for granted; she complacently assumed that they would just always be there.

'I understand,' said Farah. 'You must miss her terribly; my mum isn't even very far away, and she can be trying at the best of times, but I miss her too. Before long, you will be back home with your mum. I promise. Now come on, dry your tears and eat your breakfast. You have to eat. *Shabash*.'

Just as she was about to take her first sip of tea, Farah's mobile phone started to ring. She went over to the kitchen worktop to grab it, and saw it was a call from Mr Amin. She answered it straight away.

'Good morning, Miss Farah. How is Miss Razia doing?'

'Good morning, Sir. She's OK, I guess,' replied Farah, in a slightly muted tone. She looked over to see that Razia had now stopped crying and started to eat her breakfast. She didn't use her knife and fork. She tore bits of toast off with her hands and scooped pieces of the fried egg into the bread. She stared into space as she ate. 'I think perhaps she is a bit confused, and she is definitely pining for her mother.'

'Well, there is good news on that front; her ticket has been booked for tomorrow evening. She will be on a direct flight from Heathrow to Lahore. The flight leaves at six p.m., so we will send a car to your apartment for three p.m. The tickets have been emailed to you, along with the details of the travel agency that arranged the flight. Printed tickets will be given to Miss Razia when she is taken to the airport. I have given your telephone number to the travel agents as the point of contact, seeing as she is staying with you. I hope that's OK?'

'Yes, of course. That makes perfect sense,' replied Farah.

Farah was relieved to hear that the travel plans had been sorted. She thought back to Zaheer's acrid threats, the complete lack of co-operation from Paul and Aneela's efforts to get her to change her mind; but none of these things mattered now, as she had done it. She had freed Razia, and soon this young woman would be on her way back to her family, and away from Zaheer's grip.

'Also, we are making arrangements to settle the family's debt, and have them rehoused in the city of Lahore, close to their relatives. My people went out to see her father and brother; we have all the details now, and this should all be actioned within a few weeks of Miss Razia arriving back in Pakistan.'

Hearing this made Farah feel even more satisfied with the outcome of her intervention: freeing Razia would now mean freedom for her entire family. This was something Farah had never envisaged when she had first made the decision to help the girl; this news made the victory all the sweeter.

'And another thing,' added Mr Amin. 'I have Razia's passport. I will give it to the driver with strict instructions for him to hand it to Razia tomorrow.'

'OK. Thank you,' said Farah. She reflected on the fact that this was going to be the first time that Razia was going to hold her own passport; and not only hold it, she was now going to have the freedom to use it to get herself back home.

Farah put the phone down and went to the table to relay the information to Razia, and for the first time, Farah saw her smile; she had a beaming, effervescent smile and Farah thought it a terrible shame that, firstly, she had never seen her smile before, and secondly, she could only imagine that at least recently, she'd had so little cause to smile.

The rest of the day was spent in the only way that Farah could see fit – shopping. She had settled on taking Razia to Green Street. It was mild and sunny outside, and so they were provided with the perfect day for their walk from store to store up and down the road. Razia took in all the sights and sounds, pausing at shop windows to look at the mannequins, and turning her face away, bright red with embarrassment, when they stumbled across a mannequin with no clothes on. Farah's comment that Green Street was a bit chaotic didn't seem to resonate with Razia at all; she could only see and comment on the civility of this place, the orderliness and thoughtfulness of things such as traffic lights and pedestrian crossings, bus stops with shelters and seats and clear signs, large clean taxis that were not overloaded, and buses that did not have people perching on the tops of them or dangling perilously from the sides. Seeing her like this made Farah feel a little guilty about just how many of the comforts and freedoms of her life she took for granted, day in, day out. She had never come across a girl like Razia before. Although they shared a sense of mutual cultural heritage, there were not many similarities between them beyond the ties to the land that Razia lived in and that Farah's parents came from.

Razia told Farah that she rarely went shopping in Pakistan, for she, along with her family, worked long hours at the brick kiln, all day, every day. And if she wasn't at the brick kiln, she would be at home, preparing the food, or washing the clothes, or carrying out other household chores. She had certainly never been bought the sort of clothes that Farah insisted on buying for her. At first, Razia was extremely reluctant to agree to Farah paying, even though she could not have paid herself, but Farah managed to talk her round. Farah also insisted on buying Razia a handbag and a small suitcase that she could carry on the plane, and Farah filled the latter with clothes for Razia and her mother. These acts of generosity meant that there were sporadic moments of tearfulness on Razia's part, but also phases of fleeting joy, and Farah got the distinct impression that being happy was such a rarity for this girl that it was almost unnatural to her; it was so alien that she had to keep checking herself to see if it was real – yes, someone was talking to her kindly, yes, someone was taking her shopping, and yes, someone was buying her gifts. They settled on two pretty pastel-shaded floral lawn suits for Razia, along with one special occasion outfit in lilac georgette and silk, stitched with delicate pearl embroidery at the neck, hem and sleeves, and two matching pairs of sandals. To this Farah added for Razia's mother an unstitched creamy beige cotton/linen mix suit and a beautiful taupe and ivory coloured *jamawar chaddar*.

The afternoon was a great excuse for Farah, and consequently Razia, to enjoy a plate of spicy samosa *chaat* at a local eatery; it was one of those places that look very basic and unassuming, but where the food was so tasty it popped in your mouth with a song and a dance. There were a multitude of dusty, old-fashioned pictures on the walls, depicting rural village scenes, that looked like they had been there since the 1970s. There were framed newspaper cuttings of various articles that had been written about the place over the decades, awards that had been won in years gone by and snaps of local celebrities visiting the restaurant for their curry fix. The tables and chairs looked even more ancient than the pictures and photographs that clung to the walls. The glasses were the type that reminded Farah of the ones they had with their school dinners, and the paper napkins were literally paper thin. But this deceptively primitive little restaurant was one of those that served the best, most authentic food. Early on a Sunday morning, the queue was usually out of the door as people waited for the freshly stewed spicy *chana handi* served with sugary sweet *halwa* and, just out of the karahi, deep-fried puffy piping-hot *puris*. But today, the girls settled happily for plates of spicy tamarind-chutney-soaked samosa *chaats*. These dishes, with their tangy, chilli kick, were followed by the rose syrup indulgence of hot *gulab jamun* served with pistachio ice cream. And there was more, for all of this was washed down with a delicate cup of pink Kashmiri masala tea each.

They sat at the table in the corner towards the back of the restaurant, and waited for their tea to cool. A tall waiter walked towards their table; he smiled at Farah, and gave her a cheeky wink as he walked past. Farah rolled her eyes.

'You did not like the man winking at you?' Razia asked.

'No, I certainly did not. No man has the right to be so presumptuous; I would rather just come and eat my food in peace and quiet, and not be winked at.'

'But that is nothing compared to Pakistan.'

'Really? How do you mean?' asked Farah, as she continued to blow on her scalding hot tea.

'I don't get to go the bazaar very often, but when I do, I never return home without having been touched or pinched by the some of the men that I have to walk past.'

Farah's mouth dropped open.

'Really?'

'Yes, it is a regular occurrence.'

'Tell me one thing, how do they get away with it?' demanded Farah.

Razia thought about it for a second.

'The bazaar is a very busy place. Everyone is rushing past one another, and they just seize any opportunity they can get. Obviously not all men do that. Most do not. But a lot of them do.'

Farah listened in disbelief while Razia recalled one time when she had gone to the market with her mother. The bazaar was teeming with the usual stalls and carts selling all manner of goods and customers rushing around from stall to stall. She was walking behind her mother. One of the men coming from the opposite direction approached her, and when they were side by side, he quickly raised his left hand and cupped her left breast. She was only fourteen years old. It lasted just a moment, but it left her upset and angry. She was mortified that this man could invade her body in this way and there would be no repercussions. She couldn't tell her family; she didn't even know who the man was, nor was she able to remember what he looked like. She soon realised that this was one of the perils of being a young woman in a place where some men didn't think much of women at all.

'It happens, but you don't say anything, you just put up with it,' added Razia, looking down at her tea.

Farah was mortified to hear Razia talk about the level of overt physical sexual harassment that she and other women like her had to endure. Yes, there was sexual harassment in her world, but thankfully she had never experienced anything like this.

'I feel like I've eaten a week's worth of calories; but, oh my goodness, it has been so worth it,' Farah told Razia, changing the subject; she didn't want Razia to become upset again. Razia looked perplexed and then confessed that she didn't know what 'calories' were. Farah suddenly felt bad for speaking without thinking; of course, Razia and her family would never have to worry about counting calories, for they probably barely had enough to eat at all. There she was wittering on about food, and how full she was, when this girl had probably hardly ever had a square meal in her life. Yet another thing that she always took for granted, Farah thought to herself.

They stumbled into the apartment, placed the bags in the middle of the room, and then flopped, Farah on the sofa and Razia on the armchair. A few minutes later, while Farah put the kettle on, Razia opened her first ever brand-new little suitcase and laid it open on the living room floor. Soon scattered all around it lay the purchases of the day. Farah brought the tea over and then talked Razia through the best way to pack her items, and sort out her handbag.

Farah despised packing, but she could see that this was a thrilling experience for Razia, who placed each item carefully into the small suitcase. It was almost like an act of love, Farah observed, as Razia laid down each item with the utmost care and pride.

Farah's mobile phone rang with an unknown number.

'Hello, is this Farah?' asked the lady on the phone. She had a high-pitched voice, and a mild Pakistani accent.

'Yes.'

'I am from the travel company that arranged Razia Begum's flight to Pakistan. We were given your number as the point of contact.'

'Yes, that's correct. Is everything OK?'

'There has been a slight change of plan. Unfortunately, there has been an administrative oversight, and due to this, Razia does not have a seat on the flight to Lahore tomorrow.'

'I'm sorry, but that's not good enough. I was told she would be on that flight to Lahore,' said Farah.

'We can only apologise for this, but the request for the seat was made very last minute.'

'Yes, I know that, but I was informed by the High Commissioner himself that this had all been sorted. There must be something you can do?'

'As an alternative, we have managed to book Razia on the flight to Islamabad, which leaves at four-thirty p.m. From

Islamabad she will be placed on the next internal flight to Lahore. As this is a diplomatic issue, she will be looked after at all times by a member of airport staff, and will be assisted closely throughout the process. Is that OK? I am really very sorry, but this is the best we can do in the circumstances.'

'Just hold the line one moment,' said Farah, and placed her hand over the mouthpiece. She knew it wasn't ideal, but the fact that they had managed to arrange an alternative route for Razia was something.

Farah conveyed the gist of the conversation to Razia quickly. Razia didn't hesitate for even a second. She confirmed she was happy with the changes, if it meant she was able to leave for Pakistan tomorrow. She was grateful to Farah and Mr Amin for all their help, but she didn't want to stay in England even a day longer than she had to. She wanted to go back home, to her loved ones.

Farah went back on the phone and confirmed Razia's agreement to the revised travel plans.

It was a relief to Farah that Razia would soon be reunited with her family, and thanks to Mr Amin's help they would be leaving the brick kiln. But Farah knew she could not rest easy until Razia was on her way back home, and a long way away from the terrible clutches of Zaheer Mansur.

20

The car arrived promptly the following day, as the time came for Razia's departure. Although Mr Amin had told Farah that the driver would accompany Razia into the airport, help her to check in and see her through to the security point, Farah still explained to Razia what she should expect at the airport, and the procedure for catching a connecting flight once she got to Pakistan, although she had been assured by the travel company, and by way of another phone call from Mr Amin, that Razia would be looked after the second she set foot on Pakistani soil at Islamabad Airport.

Farah had offered to accompany Razia to the airport, but Razia had assured her that she would be fine, there was no need for her to go to any trouble, and that she had done enough already. In all honesty, Farah felt that she ought to go with her, but Razia's insistence on doing it alone made Farah think that this was probably the first time in her life that she was going to do anything independently, that never before had she had any freedom of movement, thought or decision making. Farah knew that she had to give Razia the chance to do this in her own way.

Farah helped Razia with her suitcase as they left the apartment. It was a pleasant, sunny day, with only the faintest streaks of cloud obscuring an otherwise vivid blue sky. Before she got into the back of the black Mercedes, Razia turned and gave Farah a great big hug, taking her quite by surprise, and almost knocking her off the pavement and into the road.

'Thank you, Miss Farah. I will never forget you, and everything you have done for me and my family. May Allah bless you with eternal happiness.'

'Thank you, but really, I haven't done anything, only what any reasonable person would do. Now you take care of yourself over there. Have a safe journey, and give my *salaams* to your family, especially your mother.'

'*Allah hafiz*,' said Razia.

'*Allah hafiz*,' replied Farah.

Farah closed the car door, and watched the car drive off. Although she felt certain that she would never see this girl again, Farah nevertheless felt a pang of sadness as she watched the car disappear around the corner. Her life had, for a short time, become unexpectedly entangled with Razia's; ever since she had seen her cowering in the kitchen that day, so much of Farah's existence had been consumed by the quest to free Razia. Moreover, the experience had brought into sharp focus for Farah the privileges of her own life, which she had before now taken for granted. Farah was content that she had done as much as she could have to help Razia out of her terrible situation. She hoped that this young woman's life would now change for the better.

21

The next morning, Farah sat on her sofa with a half-eaten slice of toast in one hand and a mug of tea in the other. She switched on the television to check the morning news. It was Monday, and ordinarily she would have just about been getting into the office around this time, but today she was not going into work. Whilst she was overjoyed at the eventual outcome of delivering Razia to safety, she was still seething. Paul obviously knew this, for in fact he had called her, and suggested she not only have today off work, but informed her she was welcome to have the week off. Farah didn't protest.

He clearly felt embarrassed about the whole thing, although he didn't say that in so many words. Farah had observed that apologies didn't come very easily to certain men, and he was one of them. He sounded uneasy about what had happened, but he couldn't quite bring himself to apologise to Farah for having dismissed her concerns with such flagrant disregard. Allowing Farah to have a week's paid leave was his way of trying to make it up to her, and it was a substitute for that elusive word 'sorry'.

'Anyway, as far as I know, he has been summoned back to Pakistan for some sort of disciplinary action,' Paul had told Farah when she had asked about Zaheer during their telephone conversation, 'and if he hasn't left already, I expect he will be leaving very shortly. So, I guess that is that. I just hope that we aren't going to be affected too badly at the office. He has passed a lot of work our way this last year.'

Typical, thought Farah. Poor Razia had suffered so terribly at the hands of his best friend, but all Paul could think about was the potential loss of business.

'But on the upside, the introductions have meant a steadily growing list of new clients, and we are getting a healthy amount of word of mouth referrals from the new clients themselves,' Paul continued insensitively. 'His departure will impact us, but I dare say we are in a much better position to cope with it now than we were a year ago, especially as the efficiencies we've made have now had an effect.'

Farah rolled her eyes but kept her mouth shut; she had little to say in response, and cut the conversation short.

She wasn't used to having days off work, and wondered what she should do with her time. There was only one thing that came to mind; go home to Solihull, and visit her parents. But she wasn't sure if she was in the right frame of mind for that, for it would mean the inevitable conversations about marriage, and finding a husband, and how she needed to hurry as time was ticking away, and she would miss the boat, and the longer she left it the harder it would become. Farah's recent experience with Razia had taken her mind off the issue completely, and whilst it was something that she was keen to turn her attention back to at some point, right now, she couldn't give it the same importance she had before; somehow it seemed trivial when she considered Razia's circumstances. She didn't want to go home and hear stories about all the latest betrothals and upcoming engagement parties and nuptials, or receive unwanted advice as to how she should go about finding a suitor, or hear all about how so-and-so up the road had managed to bag a real catch.

As she chewed over some other alternatives for the week – a quick last-minute booking for a holiday in the sun, or perhaps going up north and visiting her old university friends, whom she hadn't seen for some time – her mobile phone rang. There was no caller ID, so she guessed it would probably be someone promising her compensation for a car accident she'd never had, or wanting to talk about PPI she had never taken out, or a charity wanting her to sell raffle tickets. But she could never not answer in case it was important.

The line was fuzzy, but she could discern that it was a man on the other end of the line. He spoke in Punjabi, but it wasn't her mother tongue. It was a very strong dialect.

'*As-salamu alaykum*,' he said.

'*Wa alaykumu as-salam*,' replied Farah.

'My name is Karim. I am Razia's father. I was given two

numbers by the officials at the airport for people I could contact in the UK. And your number was the first one.'

'Oh, nice to speak to you, Uncle. How is Razia? Has she arrived safely? I did say to her she must ring or get someone else to phone me to let me know when she touched down.'

'No, *beti*. She has not arrived. We have not seen her. That's why I am telephoning you.'

'I don't understand. Why has she not arrived?'

'What can I tell you? A terrible thing has happened.'

The man's voice was shaky; he was finding the words difficult to spit out.

'What is it? Is Razia OK? What have you been told?'

Farah's heartbeat quickened. She couldn't imagine what 'terrible thing' might have occurred.

'Please, tell me from the beginning, as clearly as you can; what has actually happened?'

'We went to Lahore Airport to fetch my daughter. We were there on time. Me, my wife and my son. My wife especially was so very excited about seeing Razia again. She has longed for her to be back home since the day our daughter left. We were met by someone who had been sent by the government people. He waited with us. We all waited for a long time, and there was no sign of Razia. Everyone from the flight had come out, and still there was no trace of her. We asked around, and we were told by the officials, after they made a few enquiries, that Razia has been arrested in Islamabad and taken to the police station there, because they found drugs in her suitcase.'

Farah felt numb; she couldn't quite take in what she had just heard.

'I do not know what is happening, but I know for certain that my daughter does not know anything about drugs. We don't know what to do. The man who came said he is going to make some enquiries, but he gave us these telephone numbers if we want to contact people in the UK who might know something he didn't. Please can you help us?'

Farah was blown away. She felt her body waver a little, as though she might faint. She steadied herself, and blinked a few times as she tried to take it all in. What the hell was going on? Listening to Razia's father, and the simple manner in which he spoke, it was obvious to Farah that he would not be able to find much out, and she knew she had to take charge and try and discover exactly how and why Razia had ended up under arrest.

'Yes, of course, I will try and help. I am as shocked as you. I will make some enquiries and come back to you. I am just going to get a piece of paper and a pen, so I can take down your telephone number.'

Farah looked in her bag and found a blue biro and a scrap piece of paper.

'I am phoning from our village shop. I do not have a telephone at my house. When I have finished, I will hand the phone to the shopkeeper and he will tell you the number. If you phone this number, then he will get a message to me and I will come to the shop. Please, Madam, please help, we are in a desperate situation. We just want get our daughter back. My son is at the local police station here, but they are not giving him any information, and my wife is beside herself with worry. She hasn't stopped crying since they told us.'

'I understand. I will phone you back.'

Farah took down the number. She left her toast and tea on the coffee table, and ran to get changed. As she was getting ready, she remembered how carefully Razia had packed the little suitcase, and how she had watched her do it. She knew for a fact that there were no drugs in that suitcase when Razia left London. So the drugs had found their way in after Razia had landed in Pakistan.

Farah wondered where Zaheer was right now.

22

'Come in, Miss Farah. Take a seat,' said Mr Amin. His manners were all old-school charm; he stood up as Farah walked in, and he sat back down only after she was seated in one of the chairs opposite him.

'I can safely assume that I already know why you are here to see me.'

'I want some answers!' demanded Farah. She felt anxious and jumpy. She waited for a response; she hoped that Mr Amin would tell her that there had been some terrible mistake and that Razia was now safely with her family, but perhaps deep down she knew this was wishful thinking.

'I received a phone call from my people in Pakistan. I had asked them to contact me once the girl was safely reunited with her family. But our man, who was waiting with the family for Razia's arrival, was told by the police that she had been arrested in Islamabad.'

'Her father seems to think they found drugs in her luggage.'

Farah was keen to get to the bottom of what had happened as quickly as possible.

'They did; I have personally spoken with one of the senior police officers in the case, and he has told me that they found a substantial amount of heroin.'

Farah thought back to the packing of the suitcase. She could smell the foul play at work here.

'You know as well as I do that Razia wouldn't be able to tell heroin from icing sugar. She wouldn't know what it was if it was wafted right in front of her face. Furthermore, I helped her pack her bag, there was nothing untoward in it. She came to me with one small carrier bag of old clothes which weren't even worth keeping. We threw them out. Everything that she took with her was what I had bought for her. I watched her as she packed, the whole time.'

'And that may be true,' Mr Amin responded, 'but nevertheless heroin was found amongst her belongings when she tried to board the connecting flight to Lahore Airport. The sniffer dog picked it up. I have it on very good authority. There is no room for doubt as far as the facts go.'

'You know her flight was changed. The travel company said there was some administrative error. So, they put her on a flight to Islamabad, and then on to Lahore, rather than allowing her to fly directly. They said they would look after her. When she stopped off in Islamabad, when she was being "looked after" between the two flights, that's when they must have planted the drugs.'

Mr Amin shifted forward in his chair, and placed his hands on the desk, one on top of the other. Farah waited with patience for him to respond.

'This is a very serious accusation. Who exactly are "they"?' asked Mr Amin.

'"You will bitterly regret this", Farah muttered.

'I beg your pardon?' said Mr Amin.

'No, sorry, I didn't mean you. Those are the exact words uttered as a threat to me and Razia by Zaheer Mansur. He is the one behind this. How could I have been so foolish as to underestimate him? The real question is, however, what are you going to do about this?' asked Farah.

'Regardless of what he did or didn't say to you, the fact is that Zaheer is still in London. He and his wife are leaving tonight, so he wasn't even in Pakistan when all of this happened. Even if what you are saying is true, and right now I have no idea what the truth is, I cannot do anything unless I have concrete evidence. This is a police matter now. It's out of my hands.'

'But you must be able to do something! Make some phone calls, talk to some people . . .'

'Not without evidence.'

'Fine! Then I will have to get the evidence myself, won't I?'

'And how exactly are you going to do that?' asked Mr Amin.

Farah grabbed her handbag, pulled out her phone and opened a travel app.

'I'm going to start by catching the next flight out to Pakistan.'

Farah's parents were not very happy when they received the sudden news about her unexpected visit to Pakistan. Her father had last visited over five years ago, when his own father had passed away, his mother having died a few years before that. His parents had spent the last years of their lives enjoying retirement in Pakistan, aside from the annual summer visit to England when they stayed with their son and daughter-in-law. Farah's parents had always intended to take her to Pakistan themselves someday, but the timing was never right once she got past the age of about nine. From then onwards, she was forever preparing for or sitting exams: grammar school 11+ entrance exams, end-of-year exams, GCSEs, A levels, degree . . . and the years just rolled by. But there was another reason why they were never in a hurry to take her back to her roots: at the back of their minds there was always the threat of relatives chasing them about Farah's betrothal the second they set foot back in Pakistan. This prospect had always managed to make them put the visit off to another time, a time which never came.

Farah was deliberately sketchy with the details when she telephoned her mum. She knew that if she gave all the particulars they would worry incessantly, and probably try their very best to talk her out of going – which they attempted to do anyway.

'Why do you have to go? Surely someone else from your office could be sent instead? Can't you say no?' her mother asked.

'No, Mum. I can't say no; it's a work matter. It's my case, and I have to go over,' Farah replied. She did feel guilty about not telling her mum the whole truth, but she knew that if she said it was office related then her mother would make less of a fuss.

'But you have never had to go abroad for work before?'

'Well, there's always a first time, Mum. It's a really important case.'

'For how long?'

'I'm not sure at the moment,' Farah said. 'I will know more when I get there.'

'But did it have to be Pakistan?' Farah's mother moaned. 'Couldn't it have been Switzerland or Canada or New Zealand? Any one of those safe countries where there is no crime, and nothing ever happens. Why Pakistan? Where there are bomb blasts and murders and kidnappings and—'

Farah thought back to some of the most devastating terrorist attacks in recent years in Pakistan, reported on both the Asian Sky channels and in mainstream news reports. In the back of her mind, she had to acknowledge to herself that it wasn't the safest place to go to, but she would have to put those fears to one side if she was going to help Razia.

'Mum! You can't believe everything you hear. And it is my Motherland; it's probably about time that I saw it for myself.'

'OK, OK. But please, be very careful. Pakistan is not like England; everything is different, and nothing is straightforward. Even to cross the road you have to zigzag around the cars and the overloaded buses and motorbikes and donkeys and carts, and the *tangas*, whilst you continuously read your *Ayat-al-Kursi*, praying hard that you won't get knocked over. And absolutely no walking around on your own, young lady. Make sure you travel only by car with a trusted driver arranged by the hotel or the work people, from door to door. And also, make sure you phone us as soon as you get there, and every day after that.'

'Of course, Mum,' Farah assured her. 'I'll be back before you know it.'

'Wait, I haven't finished yet.'

Farah let out a stifled breath, but didn't say anything. She thought it best to let her mother get it all out of her system.

'Don't be too quick to give money to beggars, however sorry you feel for them. And only drink bottled water. Do not go out after dusk, and try and buy one of those vests with a pocket at the front to wear under your *kameez* or blouse, in which to hide your money. And avoid dressing too Western; they will spot you a mile off. If they know you are from abroad they will see you as an easy target.'

None of this was helping Farah in her mental preparation for the visit. She knew her mum meant well, but the warnings only served to heighten the nervousness that was grumbling away in her tummy.

'OK, Mum.'

'You promise?'

'*Pukka* promise, Mum.'

'OK, my darling. *Khuda hafiz*.'

'*Khuda hafiz*, Mum.'

23

The direct flight to Islamabad from Heathrow Airport the next evening was packed to bursting. When Farah had enquired about a first-class seat, the price tag had sent her into a dizzy orbit, so she settled for economy. She had booked a room at the Marriott, which was widely thought to be the finest hotel in Islamabad, but, more importantly, was known for having the best security around.

As she had never been to Pakistan before, she had never flown on the national carrier. But it couldn't be all that bad, could it? This was the question she had comforted herself with. Surely, those tales about the flights which she had heard from the aunty *ji*s, told in the most fervent and animated fashion, must have been highly exaggerated. Really, how awful could it be? she had asked herself.

As soon as she had sat in the window seat that she had been allocated, buckled her belt and got comfortable, she was approached by a rather mouthy teenage girl who asked her if she would move, and she didn't even say please. She was wearing a strange mix of clothes: a mid-length red and yellow stripy *kameez* with blue faded jeans, white Nike trainers and a headscarf which was stuck into place with a brooch pin that said 'FU'. She had a huge skyward swoop of liquid eyeliner on each eye; the wings were so long and upwardly mobile that they almost joined with the thickly pencilled eyebrows. She was crunching on what seemed like a few mints.

'So, will you move?' she asked. 'It's just that if you go sit in my seat, then I can sit here next to my grandma and gran-dad, innit?'

Farah looked at the grandparents. They were both stood in the aisle, staring at her meekly. The grandfather looked like he was well into his eighties. He wore a grey *kurtha* outfit, with a blue tank-top jumper, and had thick chunky brown-rimmed glasses. The grandmother looked a few years younger, but was small and frail-looking. She had a white *chaddar* gathered around herself. They looked so kind, and quiet, and timid. Especially when one compared them to the granddaughter. Farah obliged, and they swapped seats.

Farah went and sat in the middle seat of the middle row. The large plane was filling up with noise, chatter, shouting, babies crying. The staff were trying their best to instil some sense of order in the cabin, with carefully worded phrases and frantic arm gestures, but through no fault of their own, they were failing miserably.

Farah was sat next to an elderly Pakistani lady who appeared to be travelling on her own. She looked to be in her late sixties. She was on the chubby side, had silvery grey hair and was wearing a cream-coloured *salwar kameez* with a thick knitted camel-coloured cardigan that had huge pockets. She stopped a female flight attendant who was walking past to go help a passenger with the storage of her case. The flight attendant was wearing a uniform that looked as though it hadn't been updated since the seventies. But she was very attractive: her hair was up in an intricate bun, her face was made up beautifully, and her gel nails were striking.

'*Beti*, please can you get me some water?' the old lady asked the flight attendant.

The flight attendant smiled, and bent down to speak to the old lady.

'If you could wait a few moments please, Madam. The flight is very nearly ready to take off, and as soon as we are in flight we will be bringing around the refreshments.'

'But please, Miss, my throat is really very dry, and I am asthmatic.' The old woman then started to cough. It was a convincing enough cough. She was not going to give up.

'OK, just bear with me,' replied the flight attendant, and went off to fetch the water.

Farah watched the old lady; as soon as the flight attendant disappeared, so did the cough.

The flight attendant reappeared after a minute or so with a glass of water. The old lady smiled, and quickly grabbed it from the flight attendant's hands. She sipped it, and suddenly gasped. 'This water is icy cold. I only drink warm water. Cold water is not good for you, you know. It damages the organs, and upsets your stomach, and it is bad for digestion. And it is especially bad for someone as ill as me. The doctor has warned me about drinking cold water. In fact, he has forbidden me from drinking it.'

Nothing wrong with the voice though, Farah thought.

'I'm sorry, Madam, I will fetch you some warm water,' said the flight attendant with a smile that tried to disguise her gritted teeth.

The old lady sat back in her chair and waited.

The flight attendant promptly came back with a glass of warm water. The old lady had a gulp.

'No, *beti*, this is too hot!' the old lady shrieked.

The flight attendant looked at Farah, and Farah couldn't help but shake her head and roll her eyes. Unlike Farah, the flight attendant remained patient. She was just about to open her mouth to say something when the old lady got in there first.

'I tell you what,' said the old lady, 'just get me a can of cola instead.'

Farah's jaw dropped.

'All cabin crew to their seats, please, plane is ready for take-off,' came the announcement, which luckily for the flight attendant was a timely cue for her to leg it; she informed the old lady she would come back to her after the flight had taken off.

The rest of the flight followed in the same vein. The eight hours passed painfully slowly, and there was absolutely no chance of Farah sleeping. The in-flight entertainment system was on the blink, so there was no prospect of whiling away the time with a good movie. The fat bald guy next to Farah on the left snored raucously all night. Two guys a couple of rows up to the right of her decided it was OK to stand in the middle of the aisle and chat away in Pushto throughout a night flight. They were laughing and joking, and the worst of it was that Farah couldn't understand a word they were saying. Every time Farah turned towards them with an indignant look, instead of acknowledging the death stare and quietening down, they just carried straight on, and even worse, the older of the two men winked at her each time she looked their way, which infuriated her even more.

To add to all of this, there was something even worse than the noise coming from the fat bald guy and the Pushto dudes; the kid in the seat immediately in front of her decided to take her shoes and socks off, thereby baring the smelliest feet Farah had ever come across in her life. And to top it all, the smelly girl's kid brother in the seat next to her thought it was OK to mess around with the buttons on his seat all night, pressing it from upright to recline repeatedly. Farah felt like she was trapped in a nightmare. In the end, she stuck her earphones in, played one of her calming playlists from her phone and pretended to fall asleep; as she did so, her thoughts drifted towards Razia: Where was she now? How was she feeling?

Alone? Scared? And what about Zaheer? She wondered if he knew that she was on her way to Pakistan. She speculated about what lay in store for her once she got there. She was, after all, leaping into the unknown.

24

ISLAMABAD

Farah stood for what seemed like a gruelling eternity in the long, tedious passport queue, before she reached the desk at the front, and presented herself to the immigration officer, a tall, thin man of about forty years of age, with a neat beard and moustache. He carefully compared the image in the passport with her face (the photo was now eight years old) and checked the visa stamp which she had hurriedly had endorsed at the High Commission; having Mr Amin as a contact had proved very handy for this task.

'How are you today, Miss?' the officer asked her.

'I'm very well, thank you,' replied Farah.

'Are you travelling alone?'

'Yes, as you see.'

'For what purpose?'

'I'm here for work. I'm a lawyer.'

'You are from the UK, I see. Your parents?'

'They're from Pakistan, but I was born in the UK.'

'Very good, Miss. Now please look into the camera.'

'You're taking my photo?' Farah asked, without thinking.

'Standard procedure, Miss.'

Farah stood as she was told and looked into the obtrusive black camera that was directed towards her face.

The immigration officer stamped her passport and thanked her for her co-operation.

This was followed by an equally long wait for her suitcase. Farah couldn't help but feel nervous. There was a tiny chance that her suitcase might be checked, and while she knew she had nothing to hide, after what had happened to Razia she couldn't help but feel an inkling of distrust. Fortunately, she breezed through with her suitcase, and finally made her way out of Islamabad Airport, which was now officially known as Benazir Bhutto International Airport, after the late leader whom many in Pakistan regarded as a martyr. In light of the albeit limited knowledge Farah had regarding the position of women in Pakistan, she appreciated what a big deal it was for Benazir Bhutto to have become the first female prime minister of Pakistan; not only that, but she was the world's first female Muslim leader. Even given the political prominence of her family, that still could not have been easy for her in such a male-dominated society.

When she stepped out of the airport building, the heat whacked Farah's face with full force, and she could feel her make-up begin to melt right off. Farah now stood outside, and the first thing she noticed was the sun: it sat high in the sky and cast its dazzling bright light on everything.

The car park was straight ahead, on the other side of a wide pavement and service road, and beyond that there were large billboard posters advertising a well-known Western brand of fizzy drinks, instant baby formula milk, cigarettes and mobile phones. It dawned on Farah that this was the first time she had seen a billboard advert for cigarettes; she had never seen anything like it in England.

There were policemen and army officers crawling about everywhere, carrying large machine guns and keeping a watchful eye on all that surrounded them. Some were stationary in vehicles, but many were on foot, patrolling the whole area. She didn't know whether seeing such heavily armed men, ready to shoot to kill if necessary, made her feel safe or vulnerable. Once again, it was a sight she had never witnessed before.

Farah noticed a taxi booth straight ahead of her, just before the steps that led across to the car park, and she started to walk over to it. However, before she quite made it to the booth, a small boy, six or seven years old, approached her. He was dressed in a dirty grey *kurtha* and he was carrying a bunch of *thasbees* for sale. He looked up at her, and with his right hand raised high, dangled the prayer beads, which consisted of different coloured stones threaded through the pieces of string. There were rosy pinks, aqua blues, pearly whites and bottle greens. Farah couldn't help but reach into her bag, and she handed him some rupees. She told him she didn't need the prayer beads, but he could have the money. Before she knew it, she was surrounded by more beggars: one old, toothless woman, an old man who seemed to be blind, and a young man with a leg missing, all declaring their tales of woe and poverty. She reached into her bag for more rupees, and did what she could. The man at the taxi booth came over. He was a tall, burly, middle-aged man. He had a side parting, and his glossy grey-speckled black hair was neatly oiled into place. He had a heavy moustache, and a large nose that was dotted with indentations that looked like moon craters. He was just finishing smoking a cigarette.

'Excuse me, Miss, pardon the intrusion,' the taxi man said, 'but you need to put your money away. You keep doing this and you won't be able to see to the end of the queue of beggars that will be lined up in front of you.'

'Oh, I see,' replied Farah a little nervously. She didn't really enjoy the slight tone of chastisement in the man's voice, although if she was honest, this was pretty much what her mother had told her about the beggars.

'Do you need a taxi?'

'Yes, please.'

'Where to?'

'To the Marriott Hotel, please.'

'OK, come on.' The man took Farah's suitcase, and shooed the beggars away. Farah wasn't sure exactly what he said to them, but they disappeared quickly enough. A sense of uncertainty was beginning to creep into the back of her mind. She did her best to ignore it.

'Where have you come from?' asked the taxi man, brushing his large moustache with one hand.

'From the UK.'

'Alone?'

'Yes, well, sort of. I have travelled alone, but I will be seeing people here . . . I'm here for work.'

'No offence, but you don't seem like you know Pakistan very well.'

'I don't, really. My parents are both from Pakistan originally, but I was born in the UK and this is my first visit.'

The man put the suitcase in the boot of the cab, and came around and opened the back door for her.

'Be careful, Miss,' he said after Farah had got in. 'This is Pakistan, and anything goes. You must be watchful. A foreign-looking woman travelling alone . . .'

He looked Farah up and down, and she felt uncomfortable, although she couldn't quite say why. He wasn't really eyeing her up; she didn't get that feeling. He was just staring, and she didn't much like it.

'I see. Thank you for the advice,' she said to him. He closed the door and went and spoke to the driver.

The advice left Farah feeling even more uneasy as the taxi drove off; was she doing the right thing, she asked herself, or was she putting herself in a place where she was way out of her depth?

*

Islamabad wasn't at all as Farah had imagined it to be. She wasn't exactly sure where she had gathered her preconceived ideas about Pakistan from. Perhaps it was the tales she had heard told by her parents when she was little, or the stories that the aunty *ji*s had conveyed upon their return from their annual vacation. She had thought that the roads would be a little more archaic, and that they would be littered with creaky donkey carts, and hordes of beggars, and there would be piles of overflowing litter, and incessant noise and smog, and fumes. But Islamabad turned out to be quite the opposite. It was squeaky clean, and had a tranquil and yet welcoming vibe; there were generously proportioned wide roads and avenues, flanked neatly with tall evergreens and an abundance of native trees, and the houses ranged from basic dwellings to modern apartment blocks, to houses-cum-palaces that exuded grandeur and luxury. There were modern shopping areas, and huge, impressive-looking malls. But there was one sight that outdid all the others – the view of the magnificent Margalla Hills, a vast expanse of land that was draped in a blanket of emerald pine trees, all of which sat at the foot of the majestic Himalayas.

The five-star hotel where she had booked her room lay on the famous Aga Khan Road, and had the enviable advantage of being situated so as to overlook Margalla Hills in all its glory.

Although she was aware that this hotel was extremely well guarded, Farah had still not anticipated that there would be three strong layers of security at the hotel; she had never seen anything like it. The first checkpoint was at the very edge of the hotel complex, still by the main road, which was manned by around half a dozen men; a few were heavily armed police officers and the remainder were security guards. The taxi stopped, and the driver was questioned by an armed policeman; the back of the car and the boot were searched thoroughly, and once the officers were satisfied that all was well, the car was allowed entry. Further down the lane, there was a similar checkpoint. As the car drove on, Farah noticed that there were armed men on the roof of the hotel building, a sight which quite took her by surprise. And the final security check came just inside the hotel entrance by way of a bag check and metal detector machine. Farah couldn't help but feel a little alarmed as they went through each checkpoint, and she considered what a faff it was going to be every time she left and returned to the hotel, although she comforted herself with the thought that given Pakistan's recent terrorism troubles, it was probably better this way, even if this was a side to Pakistan that was going to require some major getting used to.

Farah walked over to the reception desk; it was a large, square structure which sat in the middle of the huge, marble-floored foyer. There were red velvet chairs and sofas, and large, bright fresh flower arrangements on gold-rimmed glass tables.

Farah informed the receptionist of her booking, which he checked, and then confirmed.

'There is a message for you here, Miss Jilani,' he told her. The receptionist was a taller than average man, dark skinned, with striking black hair, and a neatly trimmed thin black moustache and beard. He handed her the room key and the envelope containing the message, and clicked to attract the attention of the concierge to take Farah's bag to her room.

Farah's room was more than comfortable, having all the trappings and amenities you would expect in an international five-star hotel. The room was a combination of solid, dark wooden furniture, pale walls and neutral-toned soft furnishings. It looked and felt comforting, and familiar; if she tried really hard, she could almost imagine she was back home.

She threw herself on the large, plump bed, and opened the envelope she had been handed at reception. The note read:

I have arranged for a lawyer to see you in connection with Razia's incarceration.
His name is Imran Shah – contact him on 516298541.
Mention my name when you call.
All the Best, Yours, Mr Amin

Farah sank further into the softness of the bed, closed her eyes, breathed out slowly and felt an instant sense of relief. She had hastily flown to Pakistan on the crest of a wave of anger, but hadn't really thought with any seriousness about what she would do when she got here; she was clueless about how the system worked over here, about who she would see, or where to even start. At least this Imran Shah should know where to begin.

She took a quick shower and phoned her mum to announce her safe arrival. As she had expected, she was subjected to a further list of dos and don'ts now she was in Pakistan.

Then she gave the lawyer a call. After the introductions, they went on to discuss the case. Farah didn't hold back with the details, and her suspicions of Zaheer.

'So, what do you think can be done at this stage for Razia? How do we get her out of prison?'

'Miss Jilani, may I be frank with you?'

'Please do.'

'I think you must face the fact that there is not much hope of Razia being freed.'

'Excuse me?' Farah responded with clear horror in her voice to this sweeping statement.

'The facts speak for themselves. She was caught red-handed with drugs in her bag. She can offer no explanation as to how the drugs got there if she didn't put them in herself. And this suggestion that if was Zaheer Mansur . . .'

'What about it?'

'I would urge you to be cautious, Miss. Perhaps you are not familiar with the way things work here, but making such serious allegations against such an important man, such an important family in fact, is a dangerous thing to do, and I am not entirely comfortable with this line of attack.'

Farah was dumbfounded and didn't hesitate in making her next move.

'In that case, I am afraid it will be impossible for us to work together.'

'What? Are you sacking me?' he asked, surprised.

'That's exactly what I'm doing; good day to you,' replied Farah, and ended the call.

It was a bit harsh perhaps, Farah thought to herself, but she knew she couldn't work with a lawyer who clearly didn't have his client's best interests at heart; a lawyer who was more concerned about the upset he might cause the Mansur clan than about working hard to get his client out of prison and seeking justice for her. She would have to think of a plan B, but presently she had no idea what that was going to be.

25

The next morning, while Farah was having breakfast, the receptionist came and found her at her table, where she was enjoying an *aloo paratha* with spicy scrambled eggs, and a cup of *desi* cardamom tea, whilst at the same time mulling over what to do next. She thought that telephoning her contact at the British High Commission would be a good place to start; perhaps she would be able to recommend a suitable lawyer. Farah pulled up her details on WhatsApp and was about to message her when a cursory glance at the profile revealed she was 'unavailable', with a message underneath that read 'enjoying the sun in Barbados'.

Farah let out a sigh; things were not panning out as she had hoped. She felt agitated at having reached yet another stumbling block so soon after her arrival.

The receptionist interrupted her breakfast to inform her that there was a lawyer called Mr Ali Omar on the telephone for her.

'Really? I don't know of anyone by that name,' replied Farah.

'I know Mr Omar; he is a regular here. He is a top lawyer; one of the best in fact. You can take the call in reception if you wish.'

Farah hadn't been impressed by her dealings with Pakistani lawyers thus far but thought it wouldn't do any harm to speak to him.

'Hello,' said Farah after she had taken the receiver.

'This is Ali Omar,' came the voice on the other end of the telephone. The voice was husky as opposed to deep, laced heavily with an American accent. 'Hello, Miss Jilani, is it?'

'Yes, this is Farah Jilani.'

'I am contacting you about the young woman found with drugs at the airport.'

Wow, news certainly travelled fast around this place, thought Farah. She was curious.

'How do you know about that?'

'I am a local lawyer here, and it's not long before word spreads; it's a small world around these parts when it comes to these things. If I'm not mistaken, you are looking for someone to represent the young woman.'

'Yes, I am as a matter of fact.'

'I am willing to take the case on, if you wish.'

He sounded very sure of himself, thought Farah. She hadn't actually asked for his help yet.

'You are? Why?'

'Because it is exactly the sort of challenging case that I

relish. Call me a champion of the underdog, or whatever else you wish, but that is who I am.'

Farah wasn't sure what to make of this lawyer who was so keen to take on such a problematic case.

'I see. Well, perhaps we could sit down and talk about it and see where we go from there.'

'Excellent. Let's meet and discuss the case properly before we plan a course of action, lawyer-to-lawyer, so to speak.'

'Yes, let's do that,' Farah agreed.

'You are staying at the Marriott, that's one of my favourite haunts anyway. I have a couple of appointments this morning, so I can come over at, say, around one-thirty, if you could come and meet me down by reception. Will that be OK?'

'Perfect,' replied Farah. She put the phone down, but as she walked away, she wasn't entirely sure if she had just done the right thing. He sounded very assertive, but Farah was prepared to stand her ground should he not be the right lawyer for the job.

When Farah approached the reception desk, she couldn't see anyone who looked like a lawyer. There were a few men standing in one corner. They were all suited and booted, and very official-looking. They were engrossed in conversation, and from what little Farah could gather from the chatter, they appeared to be politicians, or something of that ilk.

She walked up to the tall, dark-haired receptionist and asked if anyone by the name of Ali Omar had called for her.

'Mr Omar is standing just there, Ma'am, right behind you.'

Farah turned around, expecting to see someone in a smart tailored suit, a crisp pale shirt and a silk tie, clutching a briefcase or perhaps some files in his hand. Ali Omar was of medium height, with long, wavy shoulder-length black hair, parted off centre. He had brownish green eyes, a scruffy moustache and a beard. The look was completed with a black T-shirt and dark brown leather jacket, frayed sky-blue denim jeans and a muddy-looking pair of grey trainers. To Farah's eyes, he looked like a wannabe rock star. Oh God, she thought to herself, the last one was all official sounding but had no backbone at all, and this one looks like he must surely spend more time washing his hair than looking through his files.

He was just finishing a call.

The man put his mobile phone in the back pocket of his jeans and stepped forward.

'Miss Jilani?'

'Yes.'

'I'm Ali Omar, pleased to meet you.'

The American accent seemed even stronger in person, perhaps because of the way that Ali looked. Was it real, or a bit manufactured?

On Ali's suggestion, they went and sat in the terrace café outside. Ali took his jacket off and hung it on the back of the chair, and seemed quite at ease with the temperature. Farah thought it was much too warm and sticky, but the terrace area itself was a delight to sit in. The sofas were comfortably arranged with scatter cushions, and the large beige parasol provided plenty of shade from the scorching sun.

'Do you like the hotel?' he asked her.

'Yes, very much so.'

'It's a great establishment, although it has had its fair share of tragedy.'

'Really?' asked Farah, waiting for him to tell the story.

'Well, it was rebuilt after the bomb attacks during the terror-ridden post-9/11 period, as you may remember. There were countless attacks which caused countless tragic and needless deaths, not to mention the long-term damage.'

'And now?' asked Farah, with a little concern.

'Don't worry. The security situation around the country is much better now, although we Pakistanis know better than to rest on our laurels. There are still sporadic bursts of bombings and attacks, but, generally speaking, at lower levels and on a smaller scale than was the case a few years ago.'

Ali then turned his attention towards the food, and proceeded to order what seemed like half the menu for what was supposed to be a light lunch. Farah began the task of going through the case from beginning to end, with as many details as she could cram in. Ali scribbled away on his notepad, in between mouthfuls of Mughlai lamb *seekh* kebabs with tandoori *naan* and mint chutney, and he said nothing whilst Farah presented her case.

When Ali had finished jotting everything down, with meticulous precision, albeit in a handwriting style that most would struggle to read, he sat back. He twisted his pen around in his hand gently, and Farah could see that he was turning it all around in his mind; he did so for a little while. Probably a bit longer than he needed, Farah thought to herself, but nevertheless she waited patiently.

'OK,' he said, 'so the first thing I must do is speak to the prosecution and the court, and see exactly what is going on with regards to the charges and potential hearing dates; see how far the case has actually progressed. In the meantime, I will arrange for us to visit her in the prison as soon as possible.'

This all made logical sense, but it made Farah feel a little out of control. He wasn't asking her; he was telling her what was going to happen. However, on the flip side, she had to acknowledge that she was out on a limb here, out of her own territory and comfort zone, and she had to allow him to get things sorted, because helping Razia was most important.

'Yes, that is imperative. She will be feeling alone and frightened, so we need to see her as soon as we can,' said Farah, and she then poured herself another glass of iced lemon water.

'We will go first thing in the morning,' Ali continued. 'I will come and collect you from outside the hotel at eight a.m, unless you hear otherwise from me. In any event, here is my card with my mobile number.'

'What about your fees?' she asked him.

'Don't worry about that,' replied Ali dismissively, with a shake of the head.

'But you have to get paid; you can't live off fresh air,' Farah protested. However, as she looked at the state of him, Farah felt that he looked as though that was exactly what he must have been doing.

'Seriously. Don't worry about my fees.'

Farah thought this was most odd. A lawyer not worried about his fees? Should she be worried? she asked herself. Who was this guy? She knew nothing about him; she only had the word of the receptionist as to what a great guy slash lawyer he was. How did she know she could trust him?

Ali was beginning to sense her hesitation and unease, thought Farah, for he jumped in straight away before she could ponder for too long.

'I think the High Commission feel partly responsible for not keeping a closer eye on Zaheer Mansur,' Ali added. 'I think you will find they will help out on the quiet, if they can. Let's not worry about money at this stage. Let us just concentrate on getting an innocent young girl out of prison.'

Farah hoped his words would ring true, but she had to wait and see. She recalled the words of the taxi guy at the airport: 'This is Pakistan, and anything goes.' She couldn't just assume that everything was as it seemed, especially after what had happened to Razia. She knew she had to proceed with caution.

26

Exactly as he had promised, Ali was waiting in the car outside the hotel entrance promptly at eight o'clock. The long white saloon car, a Toyota of some description, had a driver in the front; Ali was sat in the back, busy shuffling through some papers.

When Farah stepped out of the air-conditioned building into the already intense morning heat, the blast of hot air almost took her breath away. She hadn't expected this kind of all-consuming heat so early in the day in April. She was thankful that the car had been parked right outside, just steps away from the hotel.

Soon they were on their way.

'What's the prison called? And where is it?' asked Farah.

'It's called Central Jail, in Rawalpindi, locally known as Adiala Jail, as it's off Adiala Road, which is just a few miles away from Adiala village. The prison has a very interesting history,' said Ali.

'Really?'

'Oh yes. It was built in the seventies and eighties, during a particularly problematic period, although it would be fair to say that there's rarely been a time in its history when Pakistan has not endured problems. Have you heard of General Zia-ul-Haq?'

'I've heard his name, but I must confess, I don't know much about him,' was Farah's honest answer.

'He presided as the self-declared leader of the country after his audacious *coup d'état*. This prison replaced the old District Jail, and there was a very particular reason as to why General Zia had decided that the old prison must go: it was the jail in which the previous leader of Pakistan, Zulfiqar Ali Bhutto, had infamously been executed. General Zia ordered that the District Jail be demolished and turned into a recreational park. He most likely feared that the old prison building would have become a shrine to the former leader, to which people no doubt would have flocked in their droves – something he wanted to avoid at all costs.'

'Wow; shrines are a big deal here, right?'

'Oh yes, shrines are commonplace. The biggest one is Data Darbar in Lahore; the devotees attend in huge numbers, day and night. And there's Khari Sharif, which is not far from here. The shrines of people regarded as saints, you could say. And that description can extend to politicians too. People still flock to Mazar-e-Quaid, the mausoleum of Mohammed Ali Jinnah, in Karachi. You have to watch the pickpockets, mind you.'

'I see.'

The journey to the jail took over an hour, during which time Ali explained to Farah as best he could the intricacies of the Pakistani criminal justice and court system. His talk of procedural delays, embedded corruption, administrative oversights and the like didn't fill Farah with much hope, and in fact it irked her a little.

'You paint a very gloomy picture; what happened to your plan to get an innocent girl out of prison?' she asked Ali, as she pushed her sunglasses off her face, and perched them on her head. She wondered if this level of doom and gloom was really necessary or appropriate; it appeared as though he was hinting at failure before they had even got started.

'I know it all sounds very pessimistic. But you must realise that things here don't work like they do in the UK. Believe me, I had the shock of my life trying to adjust to the legal system here after working in the States. In Pakistan there are two different systems that operate side by side – one for the rich, and another for the poor. If you're wealthy, the chances are you can get away with pretty much anything, even murder, for if you have the money, then all doors are open to you. You just have to speak to the right people, hire the best lawyer, identify the correct loophole, throw the right people the adequate amount of cash, and there you go. Job done. If you're poor, on the other hand, as our client is, then it's a totally different story. Without power, money or influence, you will be stuck in the system for years – a system that comprises delays, ineptitude, inequity and, quite frankly, a total disregard for the underprivileged in this society. If you happen to be female, then your fate will be even worse. Women are, to put it bluntly, often simply left to rot.'

Farah didn't know what to say to that, at least not to Ali. She felt perturbed by what he had just said. This was all so alien to her. She began to think about all the times in the past when she had complained about the British judicial system, moaned about court delays, or the attitudes of certain judges, or the never-ending rises in court fees. However, having heard Ali's take on the legal system in Pakistan, she swore to herself not to take the legal system for granted when she got back to the UK, and to actively appreciate all those aspects of her life which were so privileged when compared to Razia's. But the thing that really niggled her was her realisation that things were far worse for Razia than she had thought, merely because of her gender. She felt responsible for having placed Razia in a precarious position in the first place, and now she felt compelled to get her out of it. Whatever it took.

She felt a little overwhelmed by her private thoughts of Razia, so she pushed her large sunglasses back down over her eyes, and looked out of the window. The landscape was very dry in parts, and yet quite lush in others. They drove past tiny villages and farms. She could see women walking along the edges of their villages, going about their daily routines, dressed in traditional *salwar kameez* with *dupattas* swathed around them. She could see some with *gharas* expertly perched on their heads; each one of the round clay pots in which they fetched water from the wells would be very heavy, yet some carried two or three. The car passed alongside men toiling away in the fields with their bare hands, digging the soil with the most basic of tools or tending to their crops that were now beginning to take shape. Other men were stood on the roadside by their carts, selling traditional fast food; there were freshly fried spicy samosas and pakoras, *chana chaat,* and there were stands selling *kulfi*, a cardamom-infused milky ice cream. Other men were sat next to their carts with their donkeys parked up a little way behind them. The carts were weighed down with various fresh fruits and vegetables, including tiny spotty bananas, slender pale red onions and bright plum tomatoes. There wasn't a burger joint or a pizza shop in sight.

Farah thought about these men and women fetching water, or digging fields, or selling their goods at the roadside, all in the baking heat of the unforgiving sun. She had found taking just the few steps from the hotel door to the car door difficult this morning, and the heat wasn't even at its peak yet. These men and women would work in these fields and stand on the side of roads like this up and down the country, for hours, just so they could earn enough to feed their family *dhal* and *roti*. She felt a sudden pang of sadness, a strong feeling of grief, such as she had never experienced before; a fierce and unexpected sense of attachment to these people, and their struggles, even though they were all perfect strangers to her.

Then her mind turned sharply towards Razia. Razia was not a stranger. Razia was someone she had opened her home to, someone to whom she had made a promise to keep safe.

'I guess what I need to know is, what are you thinking in terms of how you are going to get Razia out of there?' Farah asked Ali. 'She hasn't done anything wrong, and I think you are already convinced of her innocence.'

'I hear what you say, and I have no reason to doubt you,' said Ali, allowing a smile to escape as he did so. 'But I still need to speak to her. I have to make sure I hear as much as possible from her, first hand. Once I've heard what she has to say about it all, then I will be able to give you a better idea of what we should do.'

Farah was beginning to relax now; despite finding him a little irksome initially, she had to acknowledge that he was in fact not a severe, draconian Pakistani man, which was the preconceived image that had been fixed in her head. She was starting to warm to him.

'How come the American accent, and not a Pakistani one?' she asked.

'That's because I went to high school and university in the US.'

'Really?'

Farah was surprised; it was rare for men, or women, to return to Pakistan once they had gone overseas. The country suffered massively from the 'brain drain'.

'Yes, really. My uncle lives there with his family. I went over to live with them as a teenager. After school and college, I studied international law at New York University, and after that I started work at one of the top attorney's offices in the city. I was doing well. My family used to come out and visit me every year. I was there about fifteen years in all. I only came back to Pakistan five years ago.'

'Why?'

'Why what?'

'Why did you come back?'

'Well, my parents and sister still remained in Pakistan.'

'Yes, but you say you had a really good job. And your family visited you.'

'Yep.'

'So, why *did* you return?' Farah probed.

Ali looked away for a moment and started to fiddle with his hair.

'It's kinda complicated,' he replied. His face clouded over and Farah could see that she had hit a raw nerve, although she hadn't meant to. Nevertheless, she was intrigued. The generally composed Ali had exhibited a tiny chink in his armour. She wondered why.

Farah could now see the prison in the distance; it was a large fortress in the middle of nowhere. There was nothing surrounding it for miles. There was vast open rural land in every direction as far as the eye could see; patches and swathes of dry, barren territory that was mainly flat, although some hills could be seen further in the distance.

'OK, we're almost there,' Ali said.

Now Farah could clearly see the intimidating prison building looming. And as the commanding jail came into focus, so did Farah's fears about the task ahead.

27

The front entrance to the prison was very distinctive; it had an extravagantly designed arch built around the prison door, reminiscent of Mughal-type architecture, which she had seen in television documentaries back home. If you were ignorant of what the door opened up to, you could be forgiven for thinking that it might lead you to somewhere far nicer than a prison, but once inside, the grandeur of the exterior soon slipped out of your mind.

Farah and Ali were shown to a small, grey-looking meeting room. It was windowless, dimly lit, and completely bare, save for a small table and four chairs. It had a very particular stench. Sweat, urine and tears came to Farah's mind, as she struggled to breathe. She felt sick, and she swallowed hard to fight the feeling.

Razia was brought in by a female guard. Ali and Farah had already seated themselves on one side of the table; Razia came in quietly and sat opposite them. She folded her arms under her *chaddar* and didn't speak. The guard left and locked the door behind her. The sound of being locked in startled Farah; she felt the room close in on her.

Razia's eyes were sunken, and she had her *chaddar* wrapped tight around her head and most of her face, right up to her nose, so that it was only her sunken eyes that were visible.

'*As-salamu alaykum,* Razia,' said Farah.

'*Wa alaykumu as-salam, Bibi ji.* Sorry, I mean Farah *ji.*'

'You know you can just call me Farah. This is Ali Omar; he is a lawyer, and he is going to help you.'

Razia's eyes shifted wearily towards Ali. She suddenly sat up straight, and her eyes opened wider. She looked at him for a few seconds, but she didn't say anything.

Ali gave a small nod of the head, and a faint smile.

Razia stared at him with an increased intensity for a few moments and then she looked down.

'That's right, Razia, I'm going to help you, but I need you to tell me everything you can.'

'Everything?' she asked.

'Yes, anything and everything that helps me to understand why you have been put in jail. Please, don't be afraid. Talk openly and freely and try and tell me everything that you can remember; every detail, however insignificant you may think that detail may be,' said Ali.

Most of Razia's face was still hidden under her *chaddar*, but her eyes welled up, and then she started to shake a little. This reminded Farah of the very first time she had seen Razia, cowering in the corner of the kitchen in London, cornered and scared. This wasn't what she had expected today. She knew Razia would be upset, but she had expected her to look more hopeful once she realised Farah and Ali were here to help her.

'Please, don't be worried,' said Ali.

'*Ji*, Ali *Sahib*.'

'And there's no need to call me *Sahib*. Ali is just fine.'

Farah shot a glance at Ali. The look was enough for Ali to soften his tone a little.

'You can call me Ali *bhai* if you like; would that be better?' Ali said to Razia gently, obviously trying his best to sound as reassuring as he possibly could. It was the first time Farah had heard this soft tone in Ali's voice.

Razia's face was still tense, as though she was there in body, but her mind was somewhere far away, thinking about her mother, perhaps, whom she still hadn't seen. Razia nodded her head, but she didn't seem to be present.

'I understand your family work at the brick kiln for Mr Mansur's older brother? Is that right?'

'Yes,' replied Razia. Her voice was low, and she trembled a little as she spoke.

'For what reason were you sent to England, if you normally worked at the brick kiln alongside your family?'

'My family, mainly my brother, wanted to get me away from someone. A young man from a neighbouring village, who also works at the brick kiln with his family. His name is Ahmed. We want to marry each other. Ahmed and I love each other.'

This was the first time Farah had heard about Ahmed; she thought about Razia's tender age, and yet how certain she was that she wanted to spend the rest of her life with this man. Farah was now thirty, and was nowhere near this point. She wondered if it was naivety or true love on Razia's part.

'OK, so what actually happened?' Ali asked.

Razia's *chaddar* had now slipped below her chin, but it still covered all of her head. She continued to sit with her arms crossed under the *chaddar*, and went on.

'Ahmed and I love each other and want to get married. Ahmed was going to speak to his family about asking for my hand in marriage. He was going to break off his betrothal to his cousin, and marry me instead. But before he could do that, my brother saw us together. He was absolutely furious. After he beat me, he locked me up, and it was he who decided that I should come away with Mr and Mrs Mansur, because I might bring shame to the family honour if word of my relationship with Ahmed got out. I know that in the eyes of my family I behaved dishonourably, but that was not my intention, nor Ahmed's. We just want to be together, as husband and wife.'

Farah felt a bit numb. She had known nothing about the reasons why Razia had been sent to London. If she was honest with herself, she hadn't really bothered to find out. She had no idea about how much this girl had really suffered at the hands of not just Zaheer, but her brother also. And yet, all she had wanted was to marry her love. Farah had the freedom to

186

marry and couldn't find her way there; Razia knew who she wanted to marry and was denied the freedom to see it through.

'I have been through the details about the abuse you suffered at the hands of the Mansurs with Farah, and she told me how she came to your rescue. But I would like you to tell me everything in your own words,' said Ali.

Razia recalled all the gruesome details of London once again. Ali scribbled the information down on his notepad as fast as it emerged from Razia's mouth; he showed no emotion as he did so and barely looked up throughout the whole of Razia's narration. Although what she was saying was very familiar to Farah, it wasn't any easier for her to listen to it all over again.

Ali then shifted his attention to what had happened after Razia left London.

'Now we need to focus on what happened during your journey back to Pakistan,' said Ali. 'You must tell me every little detail, however trivial it may seem to you.'

'Yes, Ali *bhai*, I will try my best. When I came off the plane at Islamabad, I only had a small suitcase and a handbag with me, both of which Farah *ji* kindly gifted to me. As I entered the airport building, two ladies in uniform came up to me and asked me my name. I told them my name, and they said that they were going to take care of me, and take me to a place to rest between the flights. They said they had been instructed to look after me until I boarded the next flight, and that I was not to worry about a thing. One of them took my suitcase and said she would look after it for me, and the other lady took my arm and showed me the way to another part of the airport.'

'Just as I thought,' muttered Farah. Razia and Ali both looked at her. 'Sorry,' she added calmly, but inside, she was raging at the thought that Razia's innocence had been exploited to this extent, by people who were supposed to look after her.

'Where was that, where did they take you?' asked Farah quickly. Ali shot a stern look at her, and she in turn glanced towards Razia and waited for her to answer.

'I don't know the name, but they took me to a very nice place, with beautiful soft brown and cream coloured armchairs, and shiny square and round glass tables, and big televisions, and a nice, clean washroom. And they gave me lots of tea, and pastries and biscuits.'

Poor Razia, thought Farah. She would have had no idea at all; she must have been so mesmerised by the shiny surroundings and personal service, and understandably so. She had probably never even dreamed of such luxury, let alone seen it.

'OK. It sounds like they took you to the Rawal Lounge. How long were you there?' asked Ali, whilst looking down, as he continued to make notes.

Farah observed that he didn't look up much; perhaps Ali was trying to hide some emotion, even anger, that he might be feeling, she pondered to herself.

'I was there for about an hour, I think,' Razia replied.

'What happened after that?' intervened Farah, as Ali continued to scribble his notes.

'Nothing, really. The lady who had taken my small suitcase came back with it. I was told to go to the security desk by the exit doors, to get in line to board the flight to Lahore. There was a policeman there with a small dog. The dog kept sniffing my suitcase, and barking. They opened and checked the contents of my suitcase. The clothes were all there just as we had packed them, but they found something wrapped inside one of the items of clothing. They said they found drugs. I was so shocked. I have never even seen drugs. I don't know how they got there.'

There was now a nervous edge to Razia's voice. Farah could sense that she was reliving the moment and feeling the pain of it all. Farah felt for her desperately, but knew she must remain collected.

'Did you get the names of the women in uniform who accompanied you?' asked Ali, now looking intently at Razia.

'No. They didn't say who they were. They were wearing some badges that had some writing on them, but I didn't really look at them.'

There was a brief pause. Damn, thought Farah. The names would really have helped. Yet Farah had to acknowledge that she really couldn't blame Razia for not noticing them; she had put her complete trust in the women.

'OK, please continue, Razia, you're doing really well,' remarked Farah, who was listening intently, and at the same time trying keep her frustrations in check.

'The police took me to a police station for a short while and then brought me to this prison, and that is all I can tell you.'

Razia's face suddenly darkened. Her eyes began darting from side to side. Farah could see the panic rising.

'How long am I going to be in here?' Razia placed her hands on the table in a prayer pose, and began to sob. Farah reached her hands out across the table towards Razia.

'Are they mistreating you in here?' Farah asked.

'My room is overcrowded and it is always noisy; there are so many women in there, some with lots of children, and they cry day and night – the mothers and the children – they all cry and wail, and I don't get any sleep. There is so much misery. None of us have done anything wrong. There is one woman who has been here for seven years and she is still awaiting her trial. What if that happens to me? I don't want to stay here for seven years. I cannot be here for seven years. Or maybe it will be more than seven years? Then what? I want to start my life with Ahmed. I want to see my mother. Please, I'm so scared. I . . .'

Razia's voice trailed off. Farah quickly got up and walked round to her, and tried her best to console her. She placed her arms around her and held on tight.

'Hey, listen. I have come all this way, and I have brought the best lawyer with me, and all of this is with the sole aim of getting you out of here. Please, you need to be strong. It's going to take a bit of time, but we will get there. We will get you out of here.'

She noticed Ali looking at them both. He was quietly watching Farah cradling Razia. Perhaps it was not something he would usually do for a client, she thought, but there didn't seem to be any sense of disapproval on his part as far as she could make out. He just observed silently.

'But I don't know if I can do it any more. I can't take this place. You *have* to help me, Farah *ji*, you simply have to. I am losing the will to live!'

'Don't talk like that. You will get through it. We are here for you. Ali and I will fight to get you out of here. And I'm sure Ahmed will be waiting for you when you get out.'

Farah didn't want to make promises she couldn't keep, but she also didn't want to leave Razia feeling worse than she had found her today. As they took Razia away, still sobbing and pleading for help, Farah knew in her heart that the few morsels of assurance that she had thrown Razia's way were just empty words, for she couldn't in all honesty make any guarantees. She could hope, and she could pray. She wasn't certain of anything beyond that. Ali claimed to be the best lawyer around; clearly he knew the system well, and he made all the right noises about trying his best for Razia. But Farah had to ask herself two questions. Firstly, how well did she actually know him? The answer to that was simple: she didn't know him at all. And secondly, why had Razia look so freaked out upon seeing him? This latter question she could not answer, but was determined to investigate.

28

That evening Ali had offered to take Farah out for a dining experience which, according to him, she would never forget. Although she wasn't entirely sure about spending the whole evening with Ali, she nevertheless accepted the invitation gratefully, as being away from home, she didn't know where was safe to eat, and where was not. She felt like a bird whose wings had been clipped; technically she could do whatever she wanted, but she knew that as a foreign woman alone in this country her choices were severely limited. Practically speaking, she couldn't really do anything much alone. She was in a place which, despite being the land of her roots, was to all intents and purposes foreign to her, although her parents would be aghast if they heard her say such a thing. Also, she didn't mind spending additional time with Ali because it would allow them to continue discussing Razia's case.

Ali drove them himself, and the twenty-minute trip turned into a twenty-minute mini-conference about Razia. Farah expressed her wish that she had checked properly about the flight change, or, better still, accompanied Razia.

'There was no way you could have known what was in store for her,' said Ali. 'I honestly think that they would have got her with or without you.'

'They?' asked Farah.

'By "they" I mean the Mansur family, but, yes, Zaheer more specifically in this case. They are a brutally powerful family, and they are used to getting whatever they want, by any method they choose, so I really don't think you should feel guilty.'

Farah was grateful to Ali for his attempts to ease her conscience, but, however kindly they were meant, Farah knew they could not lessen the guilt that ate away at her.

Ali pulled up by a bustling street-food market. Farah knew that Lahore was recognised by all of Pakistan as food central; a culinary heaven, with a proud history behind its array of Lahori specialities, they included chicken *haleem*, lamb *nihari*, mutton *paya* and the famous *halwa chana puri* breakfast. However, from the appearance of the market it seemed to Farah that Islamabad was now beginning to catch up.

When Farah stepped out of the car, the thing that first struck her was the sticky warm evening air. After a few seconds she noticed that the atmosphere was tinged with an off-putting roadside smell, a putrid aroma. It made her feel quite queasy. However, as soon as they crossed the road, this was quickly replaced by the very different aromas of the foods that were being cooked nearby and which carried through the air; spicy, sweet, fragrant and pungent.

The open-air food bazaar was teeming with people. It seemed that the somewhat sleepy daytime Islamabad only came to life in the evening, or at least it did so here. There was a certain amount of theatre that accompanied the scene, as chefs created their dishes with much drama: the sizzle of the food hitting the oil, the spices and herbs being thrown into the pans from a height, the tossing and the turning of the ingredients, all accompanied by copious amounts of noise. She had never seen such an alluring sight before, and very much enjoyed getting a glimpse into this part of her cultural heritage.

Farah observed the people around her, just as she liked to do in England. There were groups of friends wandering about, whole extended families sitting and enjoying their meals, and couples walking around slowly, chatting away. They were all out savouring not only the food, but also the more subdued evening air, which, although still warm, was far cooler than the unbearable daytime heat. The people here tonight were different to those she often observed back home; the groups were bigger, there were more generations in each group than she would see back in England, and they were a much livelier bunch.

Ali led the way to a stall that, according to him, made the best tandoori chicken and *naans* in the world.

There were three men working away behind the stall. They all looked hot and sweaty. The man at the front took the orders and served the food, and the two behind him were busy sticking their hands in and out of the blazing hot tandoors, as they produced brightly coloured seared, tender chicken pieces on the bone, which were placed on top of hot *naans* that were as fluffy as white clouds speckled with the chars of the fire in the tandoor. The *naans* were first generously spread with *desi ghee*, and then the succulent chicken was placed on top. Alongside this was a generous helping of a lemon-juice-drenched red onion and tomato salad, fresh lemon wedges and a zingy green chilli mint and coriander chutney.

Farah and Ali took their plates and *nimbu pani* drinks, and strolled over to a table and sat down opposite each other. They started eating the food in the only way that Punjabi food should be eaten: with their hands. Hands were the best tools for tearing strips of sunset-red coloured chicken from the bone, which was then tucked inside a ripped piece of *naan* along with the salad and chutney, and then every mouthful was savoured fully. It was very simple food but it tasted spectacular; the sharpness of the lemon, the spice of the marinade on the chicken, the crunch of the onions and the contrast of the mellowness of the *naan* with the heat of the chutney all produced a popping taste sensation, like a multitude of firecrackers going off in your mouth. Farah had eaten food of this type in restaurants back in England, but the authenticity of this food and the purity of the ingredients left her feeling defrauded, as though she had been eating a fake version back home this whole time. This was the real deal.

They were both so hungry that they ate without much conversation initially. Once their hunger subsided a little, the talking started.

'This is an amazing place,' said Farah. 'It's so lively, and atmospheric. And this food is awesome. My parents would love it.'

'Then you will have to bring them here,' Ali said.

'Hmmm,' said Farah absent-mindedly, as she continued to take in the sights and sounds that surrounded her. Even though it was dark, she noticed that everything around her was bright and colourful, from the food to the lights around the stalls, to the clothing and jewellery worn by the women who looked so pretty and relaxed. Added to this was the traditional music that played in the background. She liked it here. She liked it very much. And now she was beginning to understand why her parents always saw themselves as Pakistani first, for she realised in an instant that they would fit in with this crowd beautifully.

Their seating area was now crowded, and an elderly couple approached their table, as two of the seats were empty. They asked if the seats were free and Ali told them to go ahead.

The lady was short and cute and very Pakistani looking, and on close inspection she didn't look as old as she probably was. She was still svelte, and very stylish. She had a pretty sky-blue flower-print scarf wrapped around her neck. Her red nails were beautifully polished. She smiled at Farah, who smiled back. The old man was grumpy, and had his head down as he tucked into a plate of chicken *pilau* rice, so much so that all that everyone else at the table could see was the round shiny bald patch at the top of his head.

'It is a lovely evening, isn't it, my dear,' said the lady to Farah.

'Yes, it is,' Farah replied.

'Seeing youngsters like you two takes me back,' continued the old lady. 'It was our forty-fifth wedding anniversary last week. It only seems like yesterday that we got married. How long have you two been married?' asked the lady, looking at Farah initially, and then towards Ali.

Farah's face and mind went blank, as she tried to work out if she had heard correctly. The lady had assumed they were married, and Farah wondered if this public, family-style arena was not the sort of place where unmarried couples would usually hang out, hence the question.

'Do you have any children?' continued the woman.

'Oh, erm,' muttered Farah, 'actually we're—'

'A year!' Ali declared. 'We've been married just over a year. How time flies, doesn't it, darling? A year has passed so quickly. But it's too soon for children yet, wouldn't you agree, dear?' he said, smiling at Farah.

Farah threw a cold glance at Ali, although she felt she couldn't now contradict him without the lady asking ten further questions.

'Oh my goodness, you are still practically honeymooners!' said the old lady, as her eyes lit up and she raised both hands excitedly. 'How lovely.'

'Yes, lovely,' said Farah, 'anyway, we must be off.' She glared at Ali.

'What? Already, darling?' Ali teased.

The old lady continued to look at them with a dreamy smile.

'Yes, already,' said Farah, and got up from the table.

'*Khuda hafiz*,' they said to the couple. The old lady waved goodbye. The old man continued to eat his food.

When they were far enough away, Farah couldn't contain her annoyance any longer.

'What did you do that for?' Farah asked him; she was infuriated at the way he had just laid claim to her as his wife. She didn't feel there was any need for the tall tale.

'Oh, come on. It was just a bit of fun. She had already assumed we were a couple; imagine how disappointed she would have been if I had told her otherwise. Anyway, on a serious note, if I had said we were unmarried, she would have assumed we were dating, and then she would have asked fifty questions, believe me.'

'Maybe,' Farah said. 'But one thing is for sure.'

'What's that?' Ali asked.

'I'm going to have to watch you. You are far too convincing a liar for my liking.'

Ali let out a brazen laugh. But Farah wasn't joking; she would have to watch him. The evening had been lovely in some ways, but it also made her question how honest Ali really was. If he could lie so easily to an old woman, it begged the question: could she really trust him?

29

Zaheer Mansur sat in the reception area of the government building in Islamabad. He anxiously fidgeted with his mobile phone, checking for messages that weren't there, flicking from screen to screen, from email to browser. He had been waiting for over half an hour, having arrived punctually, after being summoned by the minister's top aide. He had only just set foot back in Pakistan when he received the phone call informing him where and when he must attend, and who he would be seeing. This man was today going to tell him his fate. Without realising it, Zaheer let out a quiet grunt as he thought about the power that this man had, or thought he had, to decide his destiny.

The room in which he sat restlessly was very plain, and lacked any noticeable charm or character. Zaheer was sat on a dark wooden chair. The dull yellow walls were bare, aside from a round digital clock, which was hung slightly lopsided. There was a large brown plant pot in one corner, with a sorry-looking plastic display that did nothing to make the room look any cheerier.

A young woman entered the room. She had a high ponytail which swung from side to side as she walked. She wore red high-heeled sandals, and was dressed in a dark grey *salwar kameez*. She told Zaheer that he could now go into the office which was down the hallway and second on the right. He acknowledged her half-heartedly, with a dismissive nod.

Zaheer walked up to the room; he quickly went through the key issues in his mind, and feeling prepared, he knocked on the door. He heard the muffled sound of the word 'enter', and went in. He was greeted, somewhat coldly, by the man who was sat on the other side of the desk, a Mr Hamid. He had never met him before, but then he never usually had cause to meet civil servants of inferior rank in this way.

Mr Hamid was a grave-looking man, perhaps in his early sixties. He was dark in complexion, clean shaven, and wore thick black-rimmed glasses. He looked as though he was wearing a toupee. He asked Zaheer to come in and close the door and sit down in the chair opposite him.

Mr Hamid carefully pushed a pile of papers to one side and placed his hands on the desk space that he had cleared. He rested one palm on top of the other. Mr Hamid looked Zaheer up and down in a disapproving manner, with a sour expression on his face, a little like a headmaster would look towards the boy at school who had done something very naughty and had brought the whole school into disrepute. This wasn't a situation that Zaheer was used to or comfortable with.

'You must be in no doubt as to why you are here,' Mr Hamid said. He spoke unusually slowly, dragging and teasing each word out. Zaheer wanted to give this man a piece of his mind; how dare he speak to him like this? This whole charade was ridiculous, Zaheer thought to himself. He recoiled at the sense of power this man seemed to think he had over him.

Instead of rising to the bait, Zaheer answered calmly, 'Yes, Sir.'

'You have placed us in some difficulty, Mr Mansur. From my understanding, you are accused of mistreating your maid, a Miss Razia. Said maid, on her way back to Pakistan, was found to be in possession of drugs in her suitcase, and it appears that, at least unofficially, she is alleging that you framed her. Apparently you are the only person she can think of who, shall we say, had an axe to grind.'

Zaheer wondered what specifically Razia might have said, what details she had given to the police.

'Has she given an official statement to this effect?' Zaheer enquired.

'No. We have managed to delay this for now. We wanted to speak to you, and try and ascertain exactly what we are dealing with. However, this British lawyer who brought up the whole issue back in London, a Miss Jilani, has teamed up with Ali Omar. You must know, or at least you ought to be made aware, that Omar is the best lawyer around for these types of cases, and we won't be able to delay matters indefinitely. So, I wanted to ask you straight, and I expect a straight answer from you; did you have anything to do with those drugs in Razia's bag?'

Zaheer looked Mr Hamid straight in the eye and answered firmly, 'No.'

Mr Hamid let out a noisy sigh.

'In that case, do you have any ideas as to why and how she might have ended up with drugs in her suitcase?' Mr Hamid asked.

Zaheer kept his calm countenance and cleared his throat before he replied.

'No, Sir, I cannot. I have no idea what happened. She left my house with Farah and Mr Amin, and I believe she went to stay with Farah whilst her flight was being sorted. After she left my house that night, I did not hear from her or see her again.' Zaheer shifted around in his chair a little, but he resolutely maintained eye contact with Mr Hamid at all times. He knew he couldn't be seen to waver in any way. His every move was being watched and his every word was being noted.

Mr Hamid placed one hand under his chin and shook his head slightly. Zaheer wondered what was going on in that little brain of his; it was hard to make out anything from his gormless face.

'I hope for your sake you are being honest with me,' Mr Hamid warned Zaheer. 'When Ali Omar gets after something, he is like a dog with a bone. Whatever has or hasn't happened, he will get to the bottom of it sooner or later. In the meantime, whilst I appreciate what you have said, having looked at the circumstances, I have no option but to suspend you, pending the outcome of Razia's court case.'

'Yes, Sir. OK then, I will wait to hear from you.'

'You do that,' Mr Hamid said. 'Goodbye. And please close the door behind you.'

Zaheer stepped out of the room, and shut the door gently. He closed his eyes for a moment, inhaled a deep, long breath, and clenched his fists by his side. As he did so, he felt a renewed surge of energy enter his body. He opened his eyes and walked swiftly towards the exit.

30

Farah put the telephone down, having spent the last ten minutes speaking to Razia's parents. Farah had insisted on talking to Nusrat, so she could personally reassure her about her daughter. At least she was able to tell her that she had seen Razia, and that she was 'OK'. She didn't say much more than that. She didn't tell her about how difficult Razia was finding things. She also didn't tell her how tough she herself had found it to see Razia in such a state. She didn't tell her that her daughter had looked gaunt and seemed to have lost weight, although she had been thin enough anyway and had precious little to lose. Farah had instead done her best to keep the conversation as upbeat and as positive as she possibly could in the circumstances.

No sooner had the call ended than the hotel phone rang; it was a lady from reception informing her that Ali was waiting for her downstairs. Oh, yes, Ali, she thought to herself. The man she had now become dependent upon to try and secure Razia's freedom, even though she barely knew him. She thought about the contrast with London, where she was in charge of her clients and their files, where she called the shots, where she decided how the case proceeded. Here, she felt more like a helpless bystander, and it was something she was not used to.

Farah grabbed her scarf and bag and left her room to make her way down.

When Farah got downstairs, she saw that Ali was chatting to the male receptionist with the large moustache. They were both laughing. For a split second, she felt out of place, and far away from home, and from everything that was familiar to her.

When Ali noticed Farah, he waved at her.

'I wasn't expecting you for another half an hour,' said Farah, as she approached him.

'I know, I'm sorry, I came early without any warning, but there has been a development,' Ali replied, and mid-speech, he started to make a dash for the exit. Farah followed right behind, half frustrated but also half excited about what this development could be.

'Really? What is it? Do tell,' Farah urged, as she followed him through the exit doors.

'I'm pretty sure I've managed to track down the women who took care of Razia when she arrived at Islamabad Airport. And they should be on duty now, so we need to rush to try and catch them.'

'OK, great. Let's go,' said Farah, who, whilst she had her misgivings, was nevertheless relieved that Ali had managed to make some sort of a breakthrough in Razia's case. Right now, she knew that her own feelings didn't come into it; securing the best outcome for Razia was of paramount importance.

The driver dropped them as close as possible to the airport building, and they made their way towards the main entrance. As they approached the steps, Farah noticed the little boy selling the *thasbees*; the same boy she had seen on the day she had arrived.

'Wait one moment,' she shouted to Ali, who was a few steps ahead of her. Ali stopped in his tracks just before the entrance doors to the airport. He spun around to see what was going on.

Farah walked over to the little boy. He was in the same shabby clothes that she had seen him in on the day that she had landed, only they were even filthier than they had been then. There were other noticeable differences in his appearance; he had a gash just above his right eyebrow, which had scabbed over, and, on this occasion, he was barefoot. His feet were so dusty you couldn't see the actual colour of his skin. She didn't know what it was about this little child, but she felt for him. She knelt down to talk to him.

'Are you OK? *Thum teek ho?*'

He nodded his head, but didn't speak.

He held out a *thasbee* for her. It was strung with striking turquoise beads, like the colour of an unspoiled ocean.

This time Farah gently took the prayer beads from his hand. The boy's face beamed with a wide, partly toothless, radiant smile, and also revealed two cute little dimples which appeared on either side. Farah grabbed some rupees from her bag and handed them to the boy.

'*Shukriya*, Ma'am,' he said.

'Farah, come on,' shouted Ali. His shout made the boy jump, and he quickly ran off. How strange, thought Farah, that the severity of Ali's voice should frighten the boy in this way.

'I'm coming,' replied Farah.

'It's sweet of you to care about people such as that little boy,' said Ali, 'but if you're not careful, then you'll—'

'Have a line of beggars as far as the eye can see. I know, I know,' Farah interrupted.

They were shown into to a quiet corner of Rawal Lounge. The area they sat in was furnished with smart black leather-effect sofas and a low, square, pale wooden coffee table, which was topped with a few lifestyle magazines, and a couple of the morning's newspapers. The television closest to them was running the day's main story on the national news channel, about a train derailment in rural Sindh, where there were dozens of suspected casualties and injuries.

A small male employee approached them with two cups of tea along with a plate of biscuits and pastries, which he placed on the table. Farah thought about the fact that this was the same place that Razia had been brought to on that fateful day.

She had been so enthralled by the comfortable seating on which they now sat, so taken with the delicious refreshments which they were now enjoying and so awestruck by the big television which they now glanced at intermittently.

After about ten minutes a young woman appeared. She was dressed in the official airport uniform, and introduced herself as Najma. She was tall and slim, with a large, prominent gold and ruby nose stud which dominated her facial features. She wore a maroon-coloured lipstick, and her dark hair was scraped back into a high bun. She sat down. Ali introduced them both, and then asked her about exactly what happened on the day of Razia's flight.

'I remember being told by my senior that this girl Razia was to be looked after during the period between the two flights. The job was given to me and my colleague, Sadia. We were told to collect her when she came off the Heathrow flight, explain to her what was going on, which we did, and then take her to Rawal Lounge, and there she would stay until it was time for her onward flight to Lahore.'

'Did you stay with her the whole time?' Ali asked, whilst writing away on his notepad, not looking up when he asked the question.

Farah looked intently at her, and she noticed that Najma thought about the question carefully for quite a few seconds.

'No. We simply escorted her from one place to another. Once we had ensured she had reached Rawal Lounge, we left her there.'

'And did you see her again? asked Ali.

'No,' replied Najma, most definitely, 'I didn't see her again.'

'And what about Sadia?'

'I can't speak for her, because after we left this girl in Rawal Lounge, we went our separate ways to see to our own duties.'

Farah wasn't at all convinced by this Najma character.

'Well, we will discuss that with Sadia when she comes in,' Farah commented.

'You can't do that,' Najma said quickly.

'What do you mean we can't do that?' asked Farah.

'Sadia isn't here any more. She left her job a few days ago.'

'Really? Where has she gone?' Ali asked her, sounding concerned that the other girl had gone before he'd had a chance to question her.

'I don't know. I never really knew her all that well. She had only been working here a few months, and now she's gone off somewhere else. She is from somewhere down Karachi way, and that is probably where she has gone. But I don't have an address. My seniors have already tried to phone her, in readiness for your visit, but it's a dead line. And they only had a temporary hotel address for Islamabad on their file. I don't think anyone really knew very much about her at all in fact. She kept herself to herself.'

Farah felt a surge of exasperation. It was just as she had expected: the drugs had been planted, and then the suspect had disappeared off the face of the earth. The job had been done well, she thought to herself.

'One final question: do you remember Sadia taking Razia's little suitcase from her as she walked away?' asked Ali.

Najma thought for a few moments, to Farah's ever-increasing frustration. The woman was still unconvincing in her eyes.

'Perhaps she did. I really can't tell you for certain. I wasn't paying all that much attention. My job was simply to deliver her to Rawal Lounge, which I did. I don't recall any more than that.'

There was a small, stretched-out pause. All three of them sat there, none of them quite knowing what should be said next. Farah had a mind to call her out, as an out-and-out liar, or at least someone who was holding back from telling the full story. Perhaps Ali noticed Farah's dissatisfaction; he directed a quick glance at her, accompanied by a brief shake of the head.

Najma broke the awkward silence.

'Look, I've answered all your questions. I've told you everything I know, so can I go now? I have a lot of work to do. We have an important foreign dignitary flying in today, so we are very busy with all the extra security,' she said.

'OK,' Ali replied, but Farah observed that he now also wore a look of dissatisfaction on his face.

'Thank you for your time and your help,' added Farah. The woman gave Farah a slight smile, and left.

'What now, Ali?' asked Farah.

'Back to the drawing board. Looks like your Mr Mansur did a proper stitch-up job. The only question is: why?'

'Why?' asked Farah, looking perplexed. What a daft question to ask, she thought to herself, and coming from a supposedly accomplished lawyer like Ali. 'Isn't it obvious?'

'No, not really,' replied Ali, as he shook his head. 'Perhaps you can explain what is so obvious to you?' he asked. Farah wasn't expecting the question to be bounced back at her in this way and felt she shouldn't have to spell it out.

'He was exposed as a man who beat a girl, who he kept as a modern-day slave, and now he has lost his cushy post in the UK as a result. So, I guess revenge would be the obvious answer to your question.'

'No.' Ali shook his head vehemently. 'I don't buy it.'

'You don't? I don't understand.' What on earth was Ali trying to say? Farah asked herself. The facts spoke for themselves.

'It doesn't add up. Sure, what happened was embarrassing for him, but he comes from a family that makes money off slave labour at the brick kiln. This is not a big deal for him. Also, he's been suspended on full pay and privileges pending the outcome of Razia's case. It's in his interest not to bring attention to himself.'

'What exactly are you saying, Ali?'

'I'm saying, why would he be so angry that he would resort to this? And why are his lawyers, and the police, delaying a formal interview with our client? Razia must know more than she has said. There is something else here. We need to speak to her again. Right, back to the car; I will make some calls on the way and make sure we see her today.'

'OK, let's go,' said Farah. She grabbed her bag and followed him out of the room, although she was unsure what to make of Ali's mini rant. Farah felt a little out of the loop sometimes, both culturally and in terms of the legal technicalities, and she didn't think Ali really appreciated this. However, she was happy to park this to one side as it was becoming increasingly evident to her that Ali was going to do everything he could to free Razia. And she couldn't ask more than that.

She was, however, dreading going back to the prison, and having to face Razia once again in that hellhole of a place.

31

For the second time that day, Ali and Farah were asked to sit and wait, but the room at the prison was far less inviting than the lounge at the airport; there were no decent furniture, no glossy magazines, no tea and no biscuits. This room at the prison, Farah thought, smelled even worse than the last one, if that was possible. The reek of what seemed like blood and sweat was overbearing. They sat patiently for almost thirty minutes, waiting for Razia to be escorted in. Time seemed to pass even slower in Farah's mind as she chewed over, once again, the events that had led to Razia's incarceration, and her own role.

'I wonder what's taking them so long?' asked Farah, looking to Ali for some sort of a response.

'Me too; they are taking ages.'

'You do think everything is OK, don't you?' asked Farah. She didn't get much from Ali, only a slight nod of the head.

A few minutes later, the door opened.

'Aha!' Farah said. 'Here she comes.'

But to her surprise, a man walked in, and announced himself as the jail's superintendent. Ali seemed well aware of who he was, but still looked surprised to see him walk in. What did this mean? Farah asked herself.

The superintendent was dressed in his full uniform. He slowly walked over and sat down on a chair on the opposite side of the table.

'I understand that you are both here to see one of our inmates, a Miss Razia Begum.'

'That's right; I called earlier and was told to be here for three p.m. Where is she? What's taking so long?' Ali asked.

The superintendent hesitated. He cleared his throat abruptly before he spoke again.

Farah started to feel tense; there was a grave look on the superintendent's face. She could feel a sticky heat creeping up her neck and into her cheeks. She swallowed hard, and waited with her hands clasped together in her lap; waited for him to speak.

'Erm, I'm afraid I have some bad news,' announced the superintendent. His eyes were set on the table that separated them; his face remained grave.

'What's the matter? Is Razia ill?' asked Farah, beginning to feel the sense of alarm that had been creeping across her neck and cheeks now start to spread throughout her body. She started to chew her bottom lip.

'No. It's not that. She's not ill.'

Farah let out a sigh. Ali softly tapped his fingers on the table. More excruciating seconds passed, and finally the other man spoke.

'I'm afraid that Miss Razia has committed suicide.'

'Good God! No!' Farah gasped.

'*Inna lillahi wa inna ilayhi raji'un,*' Ali said quietly.

'To Allah We Belong and to Him We Shall Return,' Farah whispered to herself. She looked ahead at the blank wall in front of her, into nothing.

'What happened?' Ali asked the superintendent.

Farah couldn't speak. She turned her face to one side, and let her tears flow.

'Just that. She killed herself.'

'How? When? Where?' Ali shouted, and banged his right fist down hard on the grotty table with each word. 'I want details!'

Ali's violent outburst momentarily snapped Farah out of her trance-like state.

The superintendent let out a long, uneven sigh. He shrugged his shoulders and shook his head.

'She used her own *dupatta* to hang herself. It happened just over an hour ago, in her room; the other women and children who she shared the cell with had all gone into the courtyard to eat their lunch. She had refused to go out and insisted that she wasn't hungry. When they got back they found her hanging, and they raised the alarm.'

Farah sat in a hopeless silence; Ali was now also quiet. The room felt icy cold, and a deathly hush occupied the air. Farah could see a scarf in her mind. It was white; she imagined Razia might have used a white one. She didn't know why.

'I really am very sorry; we are constantly making efforts to try and reduce prisoner suicides, but we can't watch them all the time. It seems that she just couldn't carry on. Evidently, prison proved to be too much for her.'

'She told us as much the other day,' Farah said, turning towards Ali, finally finding her voice. 'She said she was losing the will to live. She should never have been in prison in the first place! But of course, if it hadn't been for me . . .'

'You mustn't say that,' said Ali, jumping in. 'She was the prison's responsibility.'

'I cannot comment on any of this,' said the superintendent. 'As I said before, I really am very sorry. We are making the necessary arrangements. Her body will be transferred early tomorrow, to reach her family home around midday, where-upon I assume that they will perform the *jannazah* and bury her as soon as is practical, should you wish to make your own preparations to go and pay your respects.'

'Thank you for letting us know,' said Farah.

Ali said nothing. Farah could hear him breathing heavily. He was still angry.

How was she ever going to face Razia's mother? What on earth was she going to say to her? These thoughts buried themselves deep inside Farah's mind as they left the prison.

32

LAHORE

As Ali and Farah queued at the airport, waited at the departure lounge, and then boarded their plane, they did so largely in silence, aside from any comment or remark that was unavoidable. Farah was still trying to make some sense, any sense at all, of what had happened to Razia, and she felt Ali was struggling to do the same.

During the flight between Islamabad and Lahore, which lasted just under an hour, Farah and Ali remained quiet and thoughtful. Farah considered how Ali had only met Razia once, yet he still looked like he was grieving. His reaction was not born of a personal attachment to his client, rather she sensed that it was centred more around the fact that this had happened on his watch. Farah appreciated that he gave her the space and time to grieve. She sat still in her seat, in a stunned stupor. She was grateful for the lack of any small talk, and that he didn't offer any empty tokens of condolence and nor did he mumble any clichéd phrases that were supposed to show sympathy or empathy. She was just allowed to be. And although she was surprised at this silent patience on his part, she was very thankful.

While Ali had not known Razia well, or for long, Farah felt that in the short time since he had met Farah and heard Razia's story, he had resolutely made up his mind to seek justice for her. She recollected their many discussions over the past days about how the woeful tale of this girl called Razia was the woeful tale of thousands and millions of girls and women all over Pakistan. Women were not seen as equals in this patriarchal society. They were disadvantaged from the moment that they entered the world – because they were female. But the misfortune of being born into poverty, it seemed to Farah, meant that the existence of these girls would always be all the more difficult. Farah had sensed this to some extent before, but since she had come to Pakistan and dealt with this case, she now knew that girls and women like Razia were always some man's belonging or commodity; they were always expected to be someone's dutiful daughter, or obedient sister, or virtuous wife, or devoted mother, or indeed a submissive slave to their master, as in Razia's case. If they stayed in line, and within the boundaries of what was perceived to be an honourable existence, and if they never strayed from these norms, then perhaps, just perhaps, they would be all right in life. But if they deviated in any way from the accepted rules and customs of the family and the society in which they existed, they would be punished by that same family and society. This would be so even if they were not guilty of any wrongdoing, even if it wasn't their fault. She could see how Ali had developed a burning passion as a lawyer to help such victims. She could see that he wanted to be a bearer of some light in what was an increasingly dreadful, dark world for such women. But in this case, it had not been possible, and Farah wondered if his silence was indicative of his reflecting on his own sense of failure, just as she sat and reflected on how she had failed Razia in so many ways.

Farah sensed his anguish, and she broke the silence on the flight.

'What are you thinking?' she asked him.

'I'm thinking, I should have picked up on the signs earlier.'

'What signs?'

'There was more to this case than met the eye,' replied Ali.

'You did everything you could,' Farah reassured him.

'No, I could and should have done more. I should have gone back sooner to speak to Razia. I should have pushed for a formal interview with the investigating officers, instead of allowing the continuation of the systematic delaying tactics that I knew were being employed. I didn't move fast enough.'

Ali shook his head despondently.

'You mustn't be so hard on yourself.'

'Mustn't I? The regret will always remain. The loss of an innocent life that I might have been able to prevent will always stay on my conscience.'

Farah gave him a small, warm smile, and then looked out of the window. Ali was hard on himself, she thought, and that was never going to change.

After their brief conversation, Farah sank back into her own quagmire of reflection and tribulation. Logic told her that she wasn't to blame, just as she had told Ali that he wasn't, but deep down in her heart, and in the pit of her conscience, she felt morally responsible for this young woman's death. There were so many ifs and buts circling around in her head. The thoughts and regrets picked away at her conscience bit by bit.

Perhaps, Farah thought to herself, if she hadn't intervened in the first place; perhaps if she had kept her nose out like Paul had suggested, then Razia would still be alive today. Yes, she might have continued to receive physical and mental abuse, and no doubt she would have continued to suffer as a result, but at least she would still have been alive, and her family would have seen her again, eventually.

Farah's mind then turned to Razia's trip back to Pakistan. She beat herself up again about the fact that she had allowed Razia to travel on her own. How could she have been so naive as to send her off by herself all the way back to Pakistan, especially after the threats that Zaheer had made? She cringed at her own idiotic sense of superiority when she had thought that she had 'sorted' it all; she thought she had 'dealt' with Zaheer. Nothing could have been further from the truth; her sense of triumph had skewed her perception so much that she couldn't see the danger that lay ahead.

And then her thoughts turned to the most difficult issue of all: how was she now going to face Razia's mother? How was she going to explain that despite her promise to look after Razia, her daughter was now being returned to her in a coffin? She turned and looked at Ali, who had put his seat back and closed his eyes; she was comforted by the fact that he was accompanying her, and she would not have to face the family alone.

The silver saloon hire car and its driver were waiting for them when they emerged from Lahore International Airport. This was the airport that Razia should have arrived at, but she'd never made it. Farah thought about Razia's family, waiting for hours, worried sick when she didn't show. And then her thoughts turned to her own parents, and her father in particular. Lahore Airport was also known as Allama Iqbal Airport. Seeing the name of the late poet in large letters reminded her how last year she had accompanied her father – who was a huge fan – to a celebration of the work of Allama Iqbal and William Shakespeare at Shakespeare's house in Stratford-upon-Avon. There was a rapturous commemoration of both poets. The evening had featured important artists from both cultures, and there seemed to be an overwhelming agreement that both these poets had shared a similar vision, though they were centuries apart; their works related strongly to human emotions that went beyond cultures, place and time. As she squinted to block out the sun from her eyes, she remembered one of her father's favourite poems by Allama

Iqbal: 'The Message of Dawn'. He would often recite it to her when she was younger, usually when he would enter her bedroom first thing in the morning and open the curtains, and the sunlight would stream in. She never could remember it all, except the last two lines:

> Remain lying in comfort still, come again shall I
> Make the whole world sleep, wake you up shall I.

Hearing these words had always been a source of comfort to her as a child; they had given her a sense that her father would always be there for her, every morning, every day, no matter what. She suddenly missed her parents. More so today than ever before. She wanted to hear their reassuring words, to feel their warm embrace, to know that they would hold her and tell her that everything would be all right. And then she felt a pang of guilt; how could she feel sorry for herself in this way when she considered the enormity of the situation faced by Razia's family?

The drive from the airport on the hottest day of the year so far proceeded in the same manner as most of the journey from Islamabad: wordlessly. When their car reached the edge of the village, she got out slowly, as did Ali. She looked at him, as the tormenting sound of weeping echoed from somewhere in the village. She knew they wouldn't really need to be led or directed as to where they should go; they could simply follow the agonising noise of the wailing. Farah pulled her scarf over her head, and they made their way along the rickety, uneven path.

As they advanced into the heart of the village, Farah could see the small, simple dwelling from where the sounds of the women crying were emanating. It looked more like a mud house than it did any kind of a home Farah was used to, but this had been Razia's home, the home she never made it back to, until now, in a coffin.

A small, elderly lady came quickly towards Farah, and took her by the arm to lead her to where the women were assembled; she stopped for a second or two to inform Ali that he should to go to the house next door, as this was where the menfolk were gathered. Farah looked at Ali, and in that instant, she felt something. It was the feeling of not wanting to be separated from him. Perhaps he sensed this, she thought, for he gave Farah a reassuring nod, as if to say, 'you will be OK'.

The old lady continued to lead the way, and Farah followed anxiously behind; her arm was still being held by the woman.

There were many women gathered outside the house, standing around, crying into their scarves and *chaddars*. Farah entered the house and saw that the courtyard was not very big at all, and it was heaving with mourners all crammed into the tiny space. The sudden increase in the intensity of the noise of the weeping women penetrated right through Farah's head. She was guided by the old lady through the rows of women, until Farah reached the middle of the yard. Then the sight before her took her breath away, and for a few seconds Farah felt as though her breath would not return.

For there she was. There was Razia, lying in peace. She was a picture of serenity. She was draped in soft, pure white sheets, much like a newborn who is wrapped in white blankets when it enters the world. Only her face was visible. Just as she would have been enrobed when she had entered the world, so she was now covered on her departure. Razia's face was tranquil, her skin smooth and flawless, without a mark or a blemish, aside from her scar. Her eyes were peacefully closed to the world, closed to all of its noise and pain, oblivious to all of its sorrow and trouble. Sat next to Razia, on a chair, as she could no longer stand, Farah could see a lady who she knew must be Razia's mother. She was bent over with a hunched back, and cried without tears for she had cried herself dry. She repeated Razia's name, as she stroked her daughter's forehead, and wept emptily. Farah thought back to her promises to this woman that she would help her daughter, that she would free her from prison and bring her back home.

Farah swallowed hard and went over. She was going to introduce herself when Nusrat turned to notice her; Farah could see that her eyes were sore, and the look of anguish on her face revealed the relentless agony she must have endured since receiving the news of her daughter's death.

'Farah?' asked Nusrat.

'*Ji. Bahut afsos*—'

Nusrat cut her short, and suddenly embraced her, and

sobbed. She must have stayed there, holding Farah tightly, for a good few minutes. Then she pulled away, and looked carefully at Farah, who saw that her eyes were struggling to open fully; they were painfully swollen from crying.

'I'm so sorry,' said Farah softly.

'Why are you sorry?' asked Nusrat, turning her gaze back to her dead daughter's face. 'You must not apologise. This is Allah's will. She belongs to Allah, and to Him she will now return. We all will.' Farah did not always practice her religion as well as she perhaps felt she ought to, but she did have a spiritual connection with the basic tenets of her Islamic faith, and hearing Nusrat say this touched her, and made her think about how, at times like this, their shared faith was a source of comfort in the face of such adversity. 'None of us will take any of this world or any of our possessions with us. We will go as we came. We came into this world empty-handed, and we will leave empty-handed,' added Nusrat. She then fixed her eyes back on Farah. 'I know you were very kind to my daughter, and you tried to help her. But it wasn't meant to be. Nothing can happen without Allah's permission. He plans and we plan, and He is the best of all planners. This is what was written for her.'

The words, though spoken kindly, only heightened Farah's already frayed emotions. She could not believe the sheer courage of this woman. This was a poor, uneducated lady, a slave labourer, from one of the most disadvantaged sections of Pakistani society. Yet here she was, grief-stricken beyond belief, behaving in a more dignified manner than anyone else that Farah had ever come across in her life. Whilst a part of Farah, her spiritual part, believed that there was an element of preordainment and destiny to life, she could not accept it in this context; this was not God's will, this was down to the evil actions of one man.

'I'm so very sorry. I had no idea anything like this would happen. That she would end up in prison and . . .'

Nusrat held Farah's hand tightly, and spoke to her in a soft, maternal tone.

'You acted only with kindness; I know that. And my daughter was not guilty of anything other than being poor. If you are poor, and on top of that if you are a woman, then you have the lowest position of all. Who can help you other than Allah? Do not reproach yourself. I do not blame you. This was her kismet. And now she has left me with a lifetime of grief. But it is Allah's will. We cannot fight the will of the Almighty.'

Nusrat turned and looked at Razia again, and gently stroked her forehead.

'Look at my daughter; she is at peace now. She looks the same to me as she ever did; her face so beautifully round, and perfect like a painting, aside from a scar that was not there when she left me.'

Zaheer, thought Farah. Every other sentence reminded her of the wickedness of that man.

Nusrat looked at her daughter almost as though she were meditating.

'I could search the whole world over, and you could offer me all the world's riches, but never would I find, and never could anything replace, that most precious of all things, which was my daughter Razia,' said Nusrat.

'Say your goodbyes, Sister, the men are coming to take her for the *jannazah*,' said the old woman who had brought Farah in to the house.

'*Alvida, meri ladli*,' said Nusrat, and then bent down and kissed her daughter's forehead. 'Goodbye, my precious daughter. I will see you very soon in His Kingdom.'

Farah could hold her grief in no longer. She brought up to her face one end of the scarf that was wrapped around her head, and sobbed, unable to say anything further, and unable to watch any more.

Some of the men entered the yard, and four of them, two of whom were Razia's father and brother, lifted the *manji* on which Razia lay. Her father was teary, but her brother's face was without feeling or emotion; he was dim and silent. He didn't even twitch. Farah felt a sense of anger, of resentment, that this man had the honour of carrying Razia to her grave, when he had been instrumental in paving her path to it in the first place.

The women moved to leave a path, and the men quietly carried Razia away, out of the yard, along the narrow alleyways and towards the graveyard which lay just outside the southerly border of the village.

*

Ali went with the men, towards the field where all the village funerals took place. Ali felt no strangeness or awkwardness at participating, though he had not known Razia or her family. He had partaken in many funerals during his life, and there was a general sense of familiarity; rich or poor, it didn't matter, the prayers and purpose were the same.

Razia was placed at the front of the field, in the correct position so that her head was in the direction of Mecca. The imam took his place, also at the front, to the side of Razia, and the congregation of men began to file into neat rows, ready for the imam to begin the funeral prayers. Ali was asked to stand in the front row by Razia's father. He obliged, for he knew that this was a mark of respect that had been afforded to him by the family, in recognition of his position as a guest who had travelled from afar to share in the family's grief and be a part of the funeral prayers.

The entire congregation faced in the direction of Mecca. There was silence; once the imam was satisfied that the men were ready, he approached Razia's father and asked for his permission to commence the *jannazah*, which her father gave. The imam announced the details of the funeral; the deceased's name, her family's particulars, and then he began the recitation of the prayer in Arabic. The imam's voice was truly melodic, almost hauntingly so, and as it flowed into Ali's ears, it made him think deeply about the prayer and its purpose. He was not an overly religious man, but he was inherently spiritual, and the occasion stirred Ali into reflection; as he uttered the words in Arabic, he focused intently on the meaning of this ritual, and with closed eyes and a heavy heart, he found himself praying intensely for peace for the soul of this young girl.

As the men stood in congregation and prayed, the women back at Razia's house tended to their tasks. Those women closest to the family helped to prepare a simple meal for the mourners. The remaining women and girls sat and recited the Quran and said special prayers for the departed.

After the funeral, Ali met Farah back at the family house, just outside the front gate, and they both expressed a wish to leave immediately; however, Razia's parents were most insistent that they stay and have something to eat.

Farah and Ali knew that it was good manners to stay for food if the grieving family insisted in this way. They stepped to one side for a quick chat.

'What do you think? Are you OK to stay for a bit longer?' asked Ali. 'If it's too much for you, I can press the matter and we can just hang around in the departure lounge at the airport.'

Farah opened the gate slightly and popped her head in to see Nusrat, who despite having just sent her daughter's coffin on its way, was busily preparing the food for her and Ali to eat. She owed her this much at least, thought Farah. She turned back to Ali.

'No, Ali. It's OK. Let's stay.'

Ali gave her a subdued but warm smile.

They accepted the invitation and joined the others to eat a

simple meal. Ali went to the neighbours' house to sit with the men, and Farah entered Razia's house. The men and women ate in different houses, just as they had sat in segregation to grieve.

Everyone was sat on the floor on old sheets and blankets in well-ordered rows. Even though Nusrat had tried her best to convince Farah not to sit on the floor, she had insisted on doing so, and insisted on eating the same food in the same manner as everyone else.

The meal consisted of tandoori *rotis* and *dhal*; both were homemade, and whilst the food was simplicity itself, it was delicious. The yellow-orange *masoor dhal* had been tempered with freshly fried chopped red onions, ginger, garlic and green chillies. The *rotis*, having been made in the tandoor, had the aromatic, smoky taste Farah associated with barbequed food. Eating this meal took Farah back to London, and the taste of Razia's beautiful cooking on that fateful evening at Hans Place. She remembered how extravagant the menu had been that night, compared with the modest meal she was fed today. She recollected the food that evening tasting divine. And she also recalled how Aneela had floated around all evening taking the credit for everything that Razia had slaved over in the kitchen. The terrible memories of that dinner party would forever be stuck in her mind.

'Is the food all right?' asked Nusrat, prompting Farah to come back to the present.

Nusrat sat next to Farah and fussed over her, making sure

she had enough to eat, and that her *rotis* were fresh so that they were soft and easy to eat; but no matter how fresh and soft they were, Farah couldn't muster up an appetite. They had also gone to the trouble of buying cold bottled water for Farah and Ali. Nusrat said she didn't want them to drink the water from the well in case it upset their stomachs.

'Our debt has been paid,' remarked Nusrat whilst she placed a fresh chapatti in the *roti* basket in front of Farah. Farah remembered that Mr Amin from the High Commission had assured her that this would be done. It was good to hear that he was a man who stuck to his promises.

'That's good,' said Farah. She took a few long sips of the cold water. The heat was suffocating, and she had no idea how she had survived the day.

'New housing has also been arranged for us in Lahore, close to some distant relatives on my husband's side. We hope to move as soon as the mourning period is over. Things will never be the same again, but at least it will be a fresh start.'

What sort of a fresh start could it really be for this poor woman, now that her daughter was dead? Farah asked herself. She found each mouthful hard to swallow; Farah could not get the image of Razia's corpse out of her mind, and as she looked on helplessly at the sorrow that she saw in Nusrat's face, Farah could not console herself in any way, let alone console Nusrat.

The mourners had eaten quickly and drifted out of the houses in a hurry. Farah had been to many *poorhis*, the gatherings where mourners sat and comforted the deceased's family, and usually people sat for hours, right up until the evening. Farah was puzzled.

'Why has everyone left so suddenly?' asked Farah. Nusrat sighed heavily, and then went on to explain.

'They all have to get back to their work at the brick kiln. Making one thousand bricks a day is not an easy task, my dear child, even if you work for eighteen hours a day.'

Farah asked Nusrat if she and Ali could be escorted to the brick kiln to see it for themselves, and Nusrat went off to have a word with her husband.

She came back having quickly arranged the visit; she said Karim was happy to accompany them.

When Farah met Ali and Karim outside the front gate, Ali drew her to one side.

'I'm not sure this is a good idea, Farah,' he said.

'Why not?' replied Farah, who was curious, and quite determined. 'Now that we are here, I really want to at least pay a brief visit to the place where Razia spent so many years of her young life toiling away. I want to see for myself the sort of work that she had to do. It can't do any harm, can it?'

'I don't know. I guess we could go for a short while, if it will be of any comfort to you,' said Ali, before he added, 'but we need to be quick, I don't want us to be seen hanging around for too long.'

They followed Karim down the lane.

33

Karim marched ahead, and Farah and Ali followed him closely. They walked down the winding paths of the village and beyond, as the kiln lay about a five-minute walk from the edge of the village.

It was now mid-afternoon, and the sun was still beating down like a scorching flame that showed no signs of burning out. As Farah and Ali approached the kiln, they could see the workers in the distance, most of them squatting, or hunched over.

As they got closer, Farah noticed that they were working in the most primitive of conditions. In fact, she thought, it was like stepping back in time some 200 years or more.

There were men, women and children, all with their heads down, working quickly. Except for the very young children; they amused themselves whilst their parents and older siblings carried out their tasks. The toddlers played in the dirt, and the babies clung to their mothers' backs in homemade slings, or lay on a blanket to one side, entertained by the toddlers. The older children were busy at work. What surprised Farah the most was that none of the children were crying or playing up. Farah felt a tremendous flow of sorrow rush through her, as if this day hadn't been sad enough already, as she considered how for such children, life was so different compared to those back home. No schooling, no playtime, no leisure, just working hard to help their family reach the target number of bricks; day in, day out. Nothing else existed. The workers made their bricks, they were paid a pittance and they barely survived.

Farah and Ali approached the nearest family; a man, and presumably his wife, and their two young children, a boy and a girl, aged perhaps three and four, who sat close by. Karim introduced them, and then enquired after the man's father.

'Where is *lala* today?' he asked.

'He couldn't come today, Uncle. His health is very bad. I have had to take out another loan to buy his medicines. What can I tell you about our woes, Uncle? With Mother gone, and Father too ill to work, and my children too young to help, it is down to the two of us to make the bricks. We never seem to get enough done, no matter how many hours we put in.'

The man was relatively young, as was evident from the fact that he addressed Karim as 'uncle', but he looked much older. The gruelling work in the blazing heat had taken its toll, and the premature lines on this man's face bore witness to this. The man told Farah and Ali that he had worked here since he was five or six years old; he had never been to school and was totally illiterate. This was all that he had known for the past twenty-odd years of his existence. Farah wanted to cry. On a human level, she felt desperately sad for him; she wanted to help these people, and felt there must be a way to do that.

'Doesn't the landlord provide you with any help with the healthcare or medicines at all?' Farah asked, although when Ali looked at her strangely, she felt she may have asked a silly question.

'No, Madam. Nothing. We have nothing, and we receive nothing, except a lifetime of debt that we can never even dream of paying off, and which these children of ours will most definitely inherit.'

Farah had already known about the problem in broad terms but seeing it for herself really brought home to her the magnitude of it. This was the same fate that Razia's family had been facing until the events that unfolded led to a change in their circumstances. Razia's family were going to escape all of this, but at what cost?

Farah turned to look at the kids. Poor, dirty, malnourished kids. Kids that knew no other existence. They continued to play in the dirt, in between uncertain looks at the visitors; they seemed confused to see them, and Farah could see why. She doubted very much that these children saw smartly dressed strangers like Ali and herself at the brick kiln very often, if ever.

The wife had not stopped to talk, but rather she had continued working. She kept her head down and toiled like a human machine. As she worked, Farah wondered she how managed to keep her *chaddar* on her head the whole time; it never slipped off once. She was hideously thin, and her slender hands were covered in the sloppy mixture which she quickly prepared and shaped into the mould, and then slapped out onto the ground. Farah had never seen anything like it. It was like turning a jelly out of its mould or patting a just-cooled cake out of its tin, and yet those comparisons could not do justice to the sheer hardship that they suffered in order to carry out this work. There were rows and rows and rows of such bricks lying out to dry in the sun. Thousands of them.

Whilst Ali continued to talk to the male worker, Farah wandered off to one side. He noticed her absence after a few minutes.

'Is everything OK?' Ali shouted out to her.

'Oh, yes; I just needed to check my mobile. I will be with you shortly,' she called back. She walked a little further away in some haste, abruptly pushed her hair away from her face and tried to focus on the screen of her phone, as she typed fiercely.

Ali nodded and continued talking to Karim and the worker.

Ten minutes later, they headed back to Razia's house, and as they stood by the gate outside, Karim insisted that they come in and have some cold drinks. Nusrat came out and repeated her husband's request.

'You still have a few hours until your plane is due to take off;

please come in and have some soft drinks. I have already sent someone to the village shop to fetch some cold bottles.'

As most of the mourners were now at the brick kiln, aside from a few ladies who had stayed behind to comfort Nusrat and help with the chores, Farah and Ali both went into Razia's house, and sat on the *manji*. The drinks were served to them as soon as a young boy dropped them off. Farah and Ali spent another half an hour with Razia's parents, who seemed, Farah thought, to be comforted by their presence. Perhaps because they had been the last ones, aside from those inside the prison, to see her alive.

As they were talking, there was a knock at the gate, and a man entered.

'*As-salamu alaykum*, Munshi *ji*,' said Karim. 'This is Munshi *ji*, he works for Mansur *Sahib*,' he introduced Farah and Ali to Munshi.

Munshi was the only chubby person Farah had seen since she got to the village. He liked to eat, that was obvious from his large, flabby frame. He was on the short side and wore a smart beige *salwar kameez*. He had a receding hairline, although his hair was still black, it was obviously dyed, and he wore silver-rimmed round glasses. He carried a clipboard and a pen with him. Like 99 per cent of the male population in Pakistan, he had a thick black moustache.

'The master would like to see you,' Munshi said.

'The *master*?' Ali responded.

'Yes, erm, Mr Mansur. Senior.'

'Why?' Farah asked.

'As a gesture of friendship, that is all. Perhaps you would be kind enough to partake in some afternoon tea?'

Farah looked at the man with some uncertainty. What was going on? Why in the world did Zaheer's brother want to have afternoon tea with them?

Ali and Farah proceeded behind Munshi towards a monstrously large 4x4 Toyota Land Cruiser. Munshi got into the front, Farah and Ali jumped into the back, and the driver started the short journey towards the Mansur ancestral home. Once they were away from the kiln, there was an increasing amount of greenery to be seen; they passed a pretty wooded area, and a stream trickled by. It was perfectly picturesque, especially when compared to the arid landscape of the dirty brick kiln they had visited just a short while ago. Farah turned to look at Ali; he looked serious, almost moody, and she really didn't know what to make of it.

Farah did expect the family home to be grand, but she was quite unprepared for the dramatic appearance of the *haveli*. The mansion was an architectural delight, dating back over 120 years, or so Munshi told them. It was a very wide building; the lower floor was much larger than the upper. It was washed in a creamy colour, a muted tone that was very soothing to the eye. The building was enhanced with numerous archways, beautifully designed pillars and expertly crafted columns. It was appealingly symmetrical. The path that led to the front was dotted on either side with neat rows of orange and lemon trees planted alternately in the parched soil. In fact, everything around them looked dry and thirsty, standing forlorn due to the unrelenting heat which took over everything in its path.

Just as they were entering the hallway, a boy, aged about twelve or thirteen, came out from one of the doors to the side of the hallway. He stopped briefly to check his mobile phone, then looked up and met Farah's gaze. For a split second she felt unnerved, inexplicably so, but then the boy rushed past them and darted up the grand staircase. He was followed by a middle-aged woman, presumably his mother, who carried a rucksack in her hands. She stopped in her tracks, and gave a brief nod to Farah and Ali, which was accompanied by a hushed *salaam*, which they both returned. She then followed the boy up the stairs.

They were both shown into probably the largest sitting room that Farah ever entered. There was enough space for perhaps two tennis courts. At least this room was not hot; far from it, for as soon as they stepped inside, the air conditioning made her feel as though she had walked from the unbearable heat of a baking desert in midsummer to the coolness of a dew-covered mountain top in winter. The freshness suddenly and quite unexpectedly brought to Farah's mind several verses from the Quran, which she didn't read as much as she felt she ought, but did usually make an effort to try to read every Ramadan. She recalled the verses where paradise is described as a place where there will be a constant cool breeze and no heat or fatigue will touch those fortunate enough to dwell there, although she thought neither of the Mansur brothers were ever likely to enter the gates of paradise.

The coolness was where the similarity with paradise stopped. The room was decorated with large, showy, obtrusive portraits of various family members, past and present. This included one of Zaheer, which caught Farah's eye as soon as she entered the room. It was a hand-painted portrait hung on the wall above a fancy glass-fronted display unit. Zaheer was wearing traditional clothes: a white *salwar kameez* and a black waistcoat. His face bore a faint smile, and it was as if his countenance was saying he was untouchable, invincible even. Farah looked away, uncomfortable with his image watching her from the wall.

They were shown to the seating area with three large, soft burgundy sofas, each resting on a decorative walnut frame. The wood extended to display fancily carved armrests. The large rectangular wooden coffee table in the middle was topped with an abundant arrangement of fresh flowers, a shiny gold cigarette box and an Urdu newspaper.

'Please, make yourselves comfortable; I will arrange for some cold drinks and snacks, and inform Mr Mansur that you are here,' said Munshi, and then he walked off.

They both sat on the same sofa. It was so large that at least six people might have fit.

Farah looked towards Ali, but he said nothing. Right now,

there was something about his silence that unnerved her. She looked hesitantly around the room, which was imposing in both its proportions and its appearance. It was awash with gleaming marble floors, complicatedly woven rugs, modern and antique furniture and delicate ornaments that adorned every corner, table and dresser.

Farah didn't speak, and Ali maintained his silence. She didn't quite understand why Ali was so hesitant to speak; was he annoyed about having been roped into coming to this place, or was it perhaps the fear of being overheard?

Mr Mansur walked into the room with a sense of presence that was hard to ignore; he had an authoritative manner, dripping with self-importance and grandeur. He was dressed in a finely made and neatly pressed pale blue *salwar kameez*, and over it he wore a dark blue traditional waistcoat with bright gold buttons. He was taller and larger than Zaheer, but he definitely bore a resemblance to his younger brother, particularly around the face.

'*As-salamu alaykum*,' Mr Mansur said, although he only looked at Ali; he did not meet Farah's gaze.

'*Wa alaykumu as-salam*,' they both replied.

He shook hands with Ali, and then proceeded to sit on the sofa directly opposite them.

There were a few moments of silence; Ali and Farah looked at him, and yet he still did not acknowledge Farah in any way.

'I don't wish to be rude, but we have a flight to catch back to

242

Islamabad in a couple of hours. Why exactly did you invite us here?' Ali said.

Mr Mansur raised one eyebrow.

'You are not going to engage in even a few pleasantries?' he asked, still looking only at Ali.

Farah also looked at Ali, who did not respond, and sat with his arms folded.

'Very well then. Seeing as you have got to the point, so will I. Word did reach me that you were trespassing on my brick kiln and speaking to my workers.'

Farah sat up, shocked by this accusation, but upon reflection she wasn't surprised that he should say such a thing, if his brother was anything to go by. He was most likely a bully, just like Zaheer. Well, she had stood up to Zaheer, she thought to herself, so no reason why she couldn't stand up to his brother.

'Firstly, we weren't aware that we were doing anything illegal,' she said, 'and secondly—'

Mr Mansur raised his hand, palm facing towards Farah, and she was suddenly unable to finish her sentence. Farah didn't know what had happened to her; this brute of a man, who still hadn't looked her in the eye, perhaps because he saw her as being beneath him because she was a woman, raised his hand and she just stopped talking. She didn't mean to, she wanted to carry on, but it was a knee-jerk reaction on her part. It was as though he had physically shoved his hand in her face, invaded her personal space.

There was a pause before Mr Mansur Senior continued.

'I don't know all that much about you two, about your *zaat paath*, but let's get one thing straight right now; we are *khandaani* people.'

Farah couldn't believe the sheer conceitedness of this man, the way he talked about his caste and bloodline. How could he claim they were of an honourable background and lineage when they behaved like criminals?

'We have centuries of noble traditions and customs,' he continued. 'One of those attributes is that we as a family do not involve ourselves in matters that are beneath us. We have a certain standing in society, and it would not be becoming for us to engage in petty, small issues – unless, of course, we are left with no choice.'

The atmosphere in the gigantic air-conditioned room grew even cooler as he continued.

'Miss . . . er . . .'

'Jilani,' interjected Ali. Farah thought he must have sensed her hesitation, which was rapidly growing into a sense of agitation, and she was grateful to him for the intervention.

For the first time Mr Mansur turned and looked at Farah.

'Miss Jilani. Yes. I believe my brother warned you not to interfere in his private matters. And yet you proceeded to do so. Now look at the end result. Perhaps you would have been well advised to heed the warning, no?'

She was still unable to speak; this supercilious man, and his menacing words, were making her feel uneasy. He was managing somehow to completely overpower and intimidate her, and despite having Ali by her side, she felt nervous.

'Do you understand what I'm saying?' Mr Mansur asked, still looking at Farah.

'Are you threatening us?' Ali asked.

Mr Mansur smiled slowly. His eyes crinkled, and he let out a small laugh.

'Why, there is no need to jump to such a baseless conclusion. I am doing no such thing. I am merely pointing out a few essential facts which you would both do well to keep in your minds.'

Farah noticed that Ali had clenched his fists. She knew him well enough now to realise he would be feeling very angry, but she admired the fact that he kept his steadily brewing rage inside and maintained a calm outward façade.

'I think we can judge the facts for ourselves, and make up our own minds, without any pointers from you. Now if you don't mind, we have a flight to catch, and must be on our way,' said Ali, with a sense of finality.

'Yes, but before you go. There is one more thing.'

Farah noticed he turned his gaze towards her; it unnerved her, and for a split second he reminded her of Zaheer, which added to her unease.

'Miss Jilani, I have to say, you are playing a very dangerous game with your latest antic.'

'What antic?' asked Ali.

Farah began to shift around in her seat, but didn't say anything. Ali looked at her, probably, she thought, for a hint as to what Mr Mansur might be talking about. Farah looked away.

'Oh, hasn't she told you? Miss Farah here has started an online petition. She wants not only, as she sees it, justice for Razia by implicating my brother, but she wants a thorough investigation by the authorities of the conditions at the brick kilns, and consequently, she wants the family to be investigated.'

Farah now turned to look at Ali, and she noticed his face begin to constrict; he squinted his eyes, as if he were trying to understand what he had just heard. Farah could see that Mr Mansur Senior had also registered the complete bewilderment on Ali's face; he displayed a wry smile, and seemed to be enjoying the moment.

'Oh, wait now; it gets better. She is also petitioning for an investigation into the local police, who she claims are on the Mansur payroll, and, not content with stopping there, she even wants the local judiciary to be investigated.'

'Why shouldn't you all be investigated?' said Farah, as she sat up tall to retaliate. 'I know how badly you treat your workers, and how they can never escape the debt. And I know that you pay the police off, even the judiciary, so that they will turn a blind eye to all the offences you commit.'

Farah then turned her attention towards Ali, who sat open mouthed.

Mr Mansur Senior leaned over and shot a stern look at Farah.

'You know no such thing. And nor do you know the consequences of what you are doing.'

'Has the petition been up long?' Ali asked Farah, but the response came from Mr Mansur.

'I believe it was put up today.'

'When you wandered off with your phone?' Ali asked Farah.

'Yes,' she replied. 'But—'

'She will take the petition down as soon as we land back in Islamabad, if not before; it's not been up long, so there's no harm done,' said Ali.

Farah glanced at him with an injured look, but she didn't contradict him.

Mr Mansur Senior raised his right eyebrow high like the wing of a bird of prey. The men locked eyes.

'You have my word,' added Ali.

'Ali, you know why I—'

'Not another word,' Ali said to Farah through gritted teeth.

34

The pair left the house in silence. Ali marched on ahead, and Farah quickened her pace to try and keep up with him.

Their driver was already waiting in their car; Farah had barely even closed her door when Ali instructed him.

'*Gari challao, jaldi*; straight to the airport, as quick as you can.'

Once they were on their way, Ali finally spoke to her and did not hold back.

'What the hell did you think you were doing! Why didn't you run this stupid petition idea past me first?'

Farah was stunned at Ali's audacity. While she understood that, clearly, he thought she had done something wrong, she didn't care for his self-important tone.

'Why? You think that I need your help or guidance? Or worse still, your consent? Your typical Pakistani male narrow-minded attitude is finally coming out I see!'

'Nonsense! Utter nonsense!' Ali shouted.

He clenched his fists and Farah edged away a bit. Her actions had clearly unnerved him for some reason, although she couldn't fathom why; on the face of it, he was overreacting spectacularly, and she didn't get it.

Ali shifted in his seat to look directly at Farah.

'You will delete that petition, and promise me that you will never pull a stunt like this again.'

'But—'

'But nothing! You have no idea what you are playing with. Promise me!'

'I don't see why I should!'

'Farah, stop being so belligerent! You're not in England any more. And you clearly have no inkling of what sort of people you are messing about with; what people like the Mansurs are capable of. No amount of protesting on your part is going to make a jot of difference to me, nor will I change my mind as a result. I mean it. You will get online right now and scrap that petition, before anyone notices it. I'm not asking you. Do you understand? I'm *telling* you.'

They stared silently at each other for a few seconds.

'OK, OK,' said Farah, finally relenting. She had put the petition up in the heat of the moment, after she had seen the state of the brick kiln, especially having witnessed young children working alongside their parents in the baking heat. She hadn't really thought about the consequences; evidently Ali knew that side of affairs much better than she ever could.

'My battery has died. But I promise, I will do it when we get to the departure lounge just as soon as I have charged my phone,' she added.

Ali nodded his head, and his mood softened. He offered Farah a slow, reassuring smile, his anger now having subsided. Her promise to remove the petition was all it had taken to ease the tension on his part.

'Look, I know it's probably hard for you to understand where I'm coming from. But you have to believe that it is a genuine concern on my part. Some actions, which may seem benign, or fair and just, can have devastating consequences,' said Ali.

Farah didn't respond.

'Can we just forget about all this?' Ali asked. 'The hardest part is over now. We got through the funeral, difficult though it was. Razia died, in the most dubious of circumstances to my mind, but regardless, her death was a tragedy for everyone concerned. No amount of hastily-put-together online petitions, or feelings of guilt about her death, are going to bring Razia back, are they? I have regrets too; there are things I should have done differently, but none of these thoughts will bring her back.'

Farah shut her eyes, and quietly thought about what a tough day it had been.

'Look at me,' Ali said.

She stayed as she was.

'Look at me,' Ali repeated, this time softly.

Farah opened her eyes and looked into his; his gaze was soft, and tender.

'You will get through this. *We* will get through this.'

She responded without any words, but instead with a slight smile; he responded with a generous smile back. She took a soothing breath in and started to relax.

As they sat in the departure lounge, Farah stayed true to her word and charged her phone and then set about the task of removing the petition.

A man came out from the nearby café and walked around among the waiting passengers, shouting in a high-pitched voice with a strong Pakistani accent, 'Sandwich, pizza, burger. Sandwich, pizza, burger.'

The man's voice trailed off as he headed towards the other side of the lounge, still shouting 'sandwich, pizza, burger.'

'Are you hungry?' Ali asked Farah.

'Err, no, thanks,' she replied, momentarily looking up from her phone.

'Are you sure you don't want any "sandwich, pizza, burger"?' asked Ali, mimicking the man's strong accent.

'No, I'm fine,' said Farah, smiling in spite of herself.

She put her phone away in her bag.

'It's done. The petition's gone,' she told Ali, who mimed a 'thank you'.

When the announcement to board the flight to Islamabad

came, Farah let out a huge sigh of relief. It had been a very difficult day, and she was ready to get on that plane.

When they reached their seats, Ali sat back and tried to get comfortable.

'So, what are your plans now?' he asked.

Farah sighed as she looked out of the window. She felt tired, and a bit numb, after the turbulent day.

'To go back to London, I guess. I will phone first thing tomorrow morning about getting a flight out as soon as I can.'

Ali leaned over and peered out of the window as the plane taxied across the tarmac and headed towards the runway. Farah could hear him breathe, and his proximity made her feel strange.

Ali slowly sank back into his own seat, breaking the short interlude of intimacy, and he buckled his seat belt.

'Why are you in such a hurry to leave?' Ali asked. Farah could tell that he was trying to sound blasé, but he didn't quite manage it. He repeatedly picked away at a loose thread on his jeans as he spoke.

'I'm not particularly in a hurry, as such, but there isn't really much purpose in my staying here now. I need to get back to my work; to some sense of normality.'

'So, there's nothing, or rather no one, that you're in a rush to get back to?' Ali asked, to Farah's surprise. She turned away from the window and looked at him.

'No. There is no one. Other than my family, of course. Why?'

'I'm just curious. I mean, I thought you'd be attached or something.'

Was he actually interested in her? Farah asked herself. No, she concluded quickly. He was probably just being inquisitive, and even if he *was* interested, she knew better than to go there again, to have any personal involvement with someone who was a professional contact only.

'You mean at my age! You sound like one of those aunties who come around to our house, or the ones you meet at weddings; the first thing they ask is "When are you getting married"?' Farah said, in a mocking Pakistani accent.

They both smiled. He seemed to understand where she was coming from.

'There was someone,' said Farah, 'but it didn't work out. We never got to the marriage stage; we almost did, but not quite, and it's over. My mum is now fretting because she has a daughter aged thirty who is not yet married – forget married, not yet even engaged!'

'It's not so different for us guys, you know. My mum asks me the same thing pretty much every day, and whenever I see them, so do the aunties, and uncles, and my cousins; the list goes on. Although, I must confess that my mother is laying off me a bit at the moment because my sister is getting married soon, and so she is busy with all that.'

'When is your sister getting married?' asked Farah. Perhaps she had revealed too much about herself already, she thought, and she welcomed the opportunity to change the subject.

'In just over a week's time. My kid sister is tying the knot before her rapidly aging older bachelor brother.'

Although on the surface it looked like Ali was making a joke of it, Farah sensed that perhaps there was more to this subject than he was letting on.

'So, you have a sister? How old is she? What does she do?' Farah asked.

'She's a doctor, she's twenty-eight now, and she's made my parents extremely happy by agreeing to marry one of the doctors she met at her hospital. He is from a family of top medics, which has pleased my father no end.'

'That's lovely. Congratulations to you all.'

The sister had made the seemingly perfect match; maybe Ali was feeling the pressure, thought Farah.

'It's the *mehndi* on Friday evening, and the wedding is the week after. Why don't you hang around until then, and come along?'

Farah didn't say anything immediately. She took a few moments to think about the impromptu invitation. She didn't really fancy going. She wouldn't know anyone at the *mehndi*; she would look and feel out of place. But Ali had been so kind to her since she arrived in Pakistan, and he had gone above and beyond with Razia's case.

'You would be one of my VIP guests. What do you say?'

'VIP guest, you say?' Farah chuckled.

'Definitely.'

'How VIP?'

254

'The most VIP-est of all the guests. Extra food, extra *mitai*, front row seat, all that kind of stuff,' Ali said, his palms wide open.

Farah thought about it for a few seconds. Did he actually mean all of this, or was he just teasing her?

'Extra *mitai*, you say?'

'Of course!'

'And does the definition of "extra *mitai*" include *khoya barfi*?'

'Naturally!'

'And *gulab jamuns*?'

'That goes without saying!'

'OK. You're on!'

'Brilliant! But there's something that I think you need to do before then,' Ali declared.

'Oh yeah? What's that then?'

'I think you need a dose of sightseeing. And I will take it upon myself to be your personal tour guide.'

'That sounds like an offer that I simply cannot refuse.' Farah half smiled and locked her hands together in her lap. She was beginning to look forward to it already, although she also felt guilty at the prospect of having fun when she thought of Razia and all that had happened.

35

ISLAMABAD

Farah caught a glimpse of herself in the large mirror in the corridor outside her hotel room. Today she wanted to look less the lawyer and more the casual tourist, so she had donned a long, *kurtha*-style pink and grey *kameez*, with black leggings. She had left her hair down, and it fell below her shoulders in layers, like shiny black silky thread.

It was now half past three in the afternoon; Farah made her way down to reception and caught a glimpse of Ali waiting for her. She remembered the very first time she had seen him, in almost exactly the same spot. She remembered thinking how scruffy he was. He didn't look all that much different now, but she no longer saw him as that unkempt strange man any more.

She was just a few feet away from Ali when her mobile phone rang.

'Excuse me one minute, Ali,' she said, looking down at it. 'I have to take this – it's my mum.'

Ali nodded, and then he walked to one side to give her some space.

'Hi, Mummy. How are you?' Farah asked.

'I'm fine, darling, but more to the point, how are you? And when are you coming back home? You were very upset about Razia when I last spoke to you. Understandably so. But still, I have been really worried about you. What can I do? I'm a mother after all. I can't help but fret about you, especially as you are so far away.'

'I'm feeling a bit better now, Mum. It was just such a massive shock at the time. I hadn't expected it at all. Anyway, you can stop worrying, as I will be coming home soon; I will let you know just as soon as I've sorted out my return flight. I'm just about to go out now to do a bit of sightseeing, but I will call you later, or first thing in the morning. Give my love to Dad.'

'OK, *beti*. We are looking forward to seeing you. You go off and enjoy yourself, but please, be very careful, there are pickpockets galore in the touristy areas.'

'Yes, Mum,' replied Farah.

'Before you go, there is just one thing I wanted to ask you. I'm pretty sure I know what the answer is going to be, but there is no harm in asking, is there? Just in case!'

As she spoke, the pitch of her voice grew in intensity.

'What is it, Mum? Go ahead, ask me.'

'You haven't, whilst you have been out there, by any chance, met a nice Pakistani man who is also an eligible bachelor?'

Farah could hear the tongue-in-cheek attitude in her mother's voice.

Usually, Farah would have half-heartedly scolded her mum for asking such a predictably annoying question, and then she would have laughed, because in the end she would have found it funny. They both would have giggled. But today, as soon as her mum said what she said, Farah looked straight at Ali. She was staring at him, and she couldn't help herself. She had to stop this, she told herself, for so many reasons. He was a colleague, and there was the first red flag. He treated her like a child sometimes, which irritated her enormously. They lived thousands of miles apart; her life was in England, and she would be leaving soon. They were too different; she was far too British, and he was way too Pakistani.

She ended the call quickly.

'Is everything OK?' Ali asked, as she approached him.

'Yes, fine, thank you,' Farah replied quickly. 'Shall we go?'

Ali told her he was taking her to Daman-e-Koh. He was driving the car himself today.

'Tell me about this place that we are going to, and why you've decided to take me there,' Farah demanded, as soon as they were on their way, driving through the capital's traffic.

Ali gave Farah a sideways look and smiled. In contrast to his sometimes erratic behaviour, he seemed happy today, and if he was trying not to give away just quite how happy he was, he was not doing a very good job.

'The name Daman-e-Koh literally means foothills; in this case, the foothills of the Himalayas. We are going to a viewpoint which is about halfway up Margalla Hills and provides the most spectacular sight of the capital. By going at this time, as well as seeing its beauty in the daylight, we will also get the evening view in a short while; you'll like it, I promise.'

The drive up the hills was simply staggering. The car zig-zagged and wound its way through a sea of green, and Farah leaned out of the window and took in the view of the peepal and eucalyptus trees, which stretched as far as the eye could see. There was a heady, warm breeze that fluttered through her long hair, and she gently breathed in the musky, woody scent. She couldn't explain it, but she felt a connection with this land, with all of this space before her; she felt free, and a sense of joy soaked through her, but once again, her euphoria turned to sadness as her mind soon floated towards Razia.

Ali parked up the car when they reached their destination, and they walked the short distance to the vantage point. There were only a few people around, and even they looked like they were making tracks. A family of four were walking back towards the car park, chatting away. There was a couple still hanging around, gazing at the views. The two of them looked like newlyweds. The young woman wore a red *salwar kameez*, which was embroidered around the neckline with shiny beads and sequins, and she had her red chiffon scarf wrapped loosely around her neck. She had chunky, traditional jewellery in the form of gold *jhumka*-style earrings which had a pearl set in the centre of the flower-shaped section that sat on the earlobe. She wore a matching necklace, and clattering red and gold bangles which sang a playful tune every time she moved her hands, or swept her hair back. Farah looked at the earrings as they swayed gently with each movement of the young woman's head, she suddenly decided that she really liked them, and wondered why on earth she had never worn *jhumkas* before. They brought to her mind an old Bollywood song that her father often listened to: 'Jhumka Gira Re', sung by Asha Bhosle. She remembered the scene from the film in her mind's eye; the actress was dressed very traditionally in an Indian pink *choli* and blue *lengha* with pink trim, and she twirled around and swung from side to side as she sang, and there was a crowd gathered around watching her dance.

Farah then noticed the telltale sign on the young woman of the recent nuptials; the still bright red-orange henna patterns drawn on the backs of her hands. Her young husband gazed into her eyes, and smiled dreamily at every word she uttered. They looked and behaved like a couple very much in love. She couldn't help but feel a twinge of jealousy. Would she ever know this feeling? she asked herself. Would she ever be this sort of a blissful newlywed?

Ali led Farah up to the middle of the curved railing, from where a panoramic view of the city was visible. Beyond the gently curving hillsides of Margalla Hills lay the city of Islamabad in all its splendour. Farah noticed that despite the number of buildings that flanked the neat roads and avenues, the city was astoundingly green. Although there was so much to see, one building sat boldly right in the middle of this vast view: the majestic Shah Faisal Mosque. Her eyes could not help but be drawn to the iconic white building shaped like a Bedouin tent, with its four minarets standing proudly around its inner section. It looked so serene, so peacefully situated; she wondered how uplifting it might be to pray in there.

Ali and Farah sat next to each other on a bench, and they slowly took in the sight. It was still daylight, and the air was warm and soothing.

'This is so beautiful; I mean, just jaw-droppingly amazing. I've never seen anything like it,' said Farah.

'I knew you would like it.' Ali said. 'By the way, how was your mum? She phoned earlier, right?'

'Oh, my mum. My mum is fine. She's as mad as a box of frogs most of the time, but she's fine. She wanted to check I was OK, and also, she wanted to know when I'm going to be back.'

'I see. Does she have a *rishta* lined up for you?'

Was he serious, wondered Farah, or was he just joking when he asked if her mother had a prospective suitor and betrothal in mind?

'Probably, knowing my mother.'

'So, what happened with the marriage that didn't happen?' Ali asked.

Farah thought about the question for a few moments, not sure what to say or where to begin. She started to fiddle with the hem of her dress; the *kameez* was edged with a pretty, pale pink lace, which matched the pink flowers in the print of the material.

'I'm sorry, I didn't mean to pry,' said Ali.

'No,' Farah responded. 'It's OK. To be honest, it might do me good to talk about it, because I haven't really spoken about it much to anyone. There was someone at work – he still works there. Tahir, his name is. We were attracted to each other pretty much from the day we first met. I hadn't felt like that about anyone before. He felt the same way; we fell for each other, and neither of us felt that we could stop it.'

Farah paused for a few moments, as she remembered the pain she had gone through. She hadn't realised but it still felt a little raw. Ali waited quietly, and she continued.

'But there was a problem. A big problem.'

'What was that?' Ali asked.

'He was already married,' Farah replied.

'Oh,' was Ali's short, sharp response. She wondered what he must now think of her.

'Well, he was separated, to be precise. He had been coaxed into a marriage quite a few years ago that had been arranged by the elders. He hadn't had any say in it. By the time we met, she had been back at her parents' house for a while. He said he was planning to divorce her, but then for one reason or another it didn't happen. On top of that he was twelve years my senior, so there were multiple issues that my parents were going to have a problem with. The age gap wasn't a deal breaker, but obviously his marital status was. Eventually he got around to talking to his family about giving her a *talaq*, but his next idea took me by complete surprise.'

Farah hesitated.

'Go on,' Ali urged her.

'He suggested that instead of divorcing her . . . I become his second wife.'

Ali sat up straight upon hearing this.

'Wow,' he said in response.

'Wow, indeed! I could hardly believe my ears. But he meant it, and that signalled the end for me. We split up. He all but begged me to give it another go, but I couldn't go back. I felt as though he had deceived me. Maybe he hadn't; looking back, I don't think he intended to, and he was certainly put under a lot of pressure by the elders to preserve the family *izzat*. But that's how I felt – betrayed. I had wasted my best years on him. When the feeling's gone, it's gone. I wanted to put it behind me and move on. And that's it really.'

Ali didn't say anything. She wondered what he was thinking. Did he think badly of her? Not that it should matter. She would soon be on her way back home and they would probably never see each other again.

'Are you disappointed in me?' Farah asked. He looked straight ahead at the vast city that lay before them.

'No, I'm not,' he said finally.

There was a long pause. Farah felt as though she was holding her breath without even meaning to. Ali turned his gaze away from the view and looked at her. His face was serious.

'What an idiot. I wouldn't have done that to you. I would have realised what a good thing I had and never let you go!' Ali said, still gazing straight at her.

Farah was taken aback. What he thought of her mattered; it mattered to her. She didn't know why his having a good opinion of her was so important to her, or when this had become a reality. But it was.

'What about you then?' Farah asked.

He looked away pensively into the distance, and as he did so, it was as though he had drifted somewhere far, far away. There was a long silence, and then he began to speak.

36

The summer heat was now just on the right side of bearable, and today in particular, the weather was very conducive to an afternoon walk through Central Park. They had just finished an Italian lunch. A walk helped to reduce, at least for Ali, the sleepy effects of the carb-heavy, cheesy meal in which he had overindulged. Sofia, on the other hand, had barely picked at her seafood dish.

Central Park was teeming today with walkers, joggers, sport enthusiasts, tourists and entertainers. Ali and Sofia headed out of the park through the gate by the Met museum.

Above the short back and sides, Ali's hair was brushed back neatly off his face and fixed into place with expensive clay that ensured it didn't budge all day; he wore dark blue jeans today, and a red polo shirt added a splash of colour.

They walked by the roadside to try and avoid the further throngs of tourists that were gathered nearby, mainly on the wide steps leading up to the iconic museum building. Many of the tourists were posing for photographs on the famous stone steps, wherever they could find a small space. The girls posed, as still as mannequins, leaning one way or the other after each shot, pouting ferociously, as their other halves did their best, before someone walked into view, to snap an amazing photograph that would be worthy of being uploaded on to Instagram. New York was as noisy as ever; a symphony of voices and car horns glided through the air as though the wind itself carried it all right past your ears in a continuous flow.

Ali reflected on how it was an ever prevalent hum that, once you got used to it, you barely noticed, for it was as much a part of the fabric of the city as the imposing skyscrapers and the dazzling lights. And it was like this no matter where in New York you happened to be, whether in the financial district in the morning rush hour, or outside Bloomingdale's around lunchtime, or in Times Square at night. After so many years, Ali had got used to it, but there were times when he desperately craved silence.

'Why do you have to go to Pakistan now? It's not exactly great timing with our engagement only two weeks away,' said Sofia in her polished American accent, as she walked along with Ali. She had her arm tightly locked inside his.

'You know why,' said Ali. 'Amir is my oldest friend; we went to school together. I have known him since the age of five. He is opening his own law firm, and it's a big deal for him. I feel I should be there to support him. I will be back in a week, along with my parents; my mum is going on about bringing presents for you and your family and wants me to help her choose.'

Sofia let out a wispy sigh.

'Well, I suppose it will have to be OK; if you promised him then I guess you must go. Just as long as you don't forget about the engagement ring!' she said, wagging a finger at him.

'As if you, or my mum, would allow me to forget about that! I've heard of nothing else these past God-knows-how-many weeks, months even. No, my life wouldn't be worth living if I did that. Rest assured, the ring will be ready for collection from Tiffany's just as soon as I get back.'

Ali was now keen to get on with things; the engagement was just around the corner, and he would be relieved once it was out of the way so they could finalise things for the wedding.

'I meant to ask, have you read my latest blog?' Sofia enquired, as she flicked her dead straight, streaked brown hair off her face. It didn't really need flicking. It was just a habit of hers. She always flicked strands of her hair at timely intervals, without thinking. She did have beautiful hair, thought Ali. In fact, she was beautiful full stop, even if he didn't tell her that as often as he ought to.

'No, honey. Things have been absolutely mad at work. Sorry. What's it about?'

'Botox.'

'Botox?' asked Ali. He stopped in his tracks. He didn't know whether to laugh or feel exasperated that she spent so much time on such shallow stuff.

'Yeah, silly, you know what Botox is,' said Sofia. She placed her well-manicured hands on her hips, and thereby accentuated her thin waist. Ali noticed her bright red gel nails, which glistened. He saw that her short, fitted red top matched almost exactly the colour of her long nails. The top, coupled with her skinny designer jeans, showed off her slim figure. Sofia always had time to strike a dramatic pose, he thought, no matter where she was and what she might be doing. At times Ali found it amusing, and at other times it was plain irritating.

'Of course I know what Botox is! Why are you writing about it?'

Sofia rolled her eyes.

'Because that's what beauty vloggers do! And don't you dare say it's not real work. Botox is so important nowadays. It's pretty much the same as having your hair done or having a pedicure. It's as normal as applying make-up.'

Ali shivered at the thought. Why women felt the need to stick needles in their faces to achieve some phoney kind of beauty was beyond him.

'Actually, I was thinking of it for myself,' she added.

'Why would you want Botox? You don't have any wrinkles.'

'No, I was thinking of it more for plumping up my lips. The fullness of your lips does diminish as you get older,' she said, and then promptly pouted her lips.

'You're pretty enough as you are,' he said.

268

'Yes, I know. And you enjoy my full lips right now, don't you? But what about when we've been married a few years, and I'm getting on a bit, huh?'

'You don't need Botox now and you won't need it then either!'

'Honestly, you're so old-school,' Sofia teased.

'And you're so am-dram!'

Ali hailed a taxi. The cab driver pulled over, and they jumped in.

'Let's not fight,' said Sofia. She snuggled up tight next to Ali in the back of the cab. She placed her head on his shoulder. He gently placed one arm around her; he enjoyed these quiet, thoughtful moments. Ali's life hadn't always turned out as he had planned, from moving to the States as a teenager, through to the choice of his life partner, but he was a realistic optimist, and always tried to embrace the good in whatever situation he happened to find himself.

'I can't wait for our engagement party,' said Sofia. 'The venue is amazing, my dress is gorgeous, the food is going to be fine dining at its very best; it's all just as I wanted it. It's going to be perfect. Just perfect.'

'Nothing in life is perfect,' said Ali, looking straight ahead at the busy traffic along Fifth Avenue.

'Less of the negativity, please. I only want happy, positive vibes!' said Sofia, before she landed an affectionate kiss on his cheek.

She was right, thought Ali, life was for living, and perhaps he ought to lighten up a bit.

Ali's mobile phone rang. He whipped it out of his pocket and saw that it was his mother phoning from Pakistan. He answered the call immediately. He loved to hear her soft voice; it instantly made him feel at home.

'Hi, Mum. Yes, I'm well. So is Sofia, and her parents. I'm flying from JFK tomorrow evening. I will message the flight details to you in a bit, and give you a call later on.'

'Give my *salam*,' Sofia instructed Ali.

'Sofia is here with me. She sends you her *salam*. OK, Mum. I've got to go now. Love you too. Bye.'

Sofia abruptly took her head off Ali's shoulder.

'I swear you tell your mum you love her more than you do me,' she said.

37

ISLAMABAD

When Ali got to his family home in Islamabad, he was immediately accosted by his sister, who crept up from behind him. He wrapped an arm around her and patted her head with his free hand.

'Welcome back to Pakistan, *bhai*!'

'It's good to be home, Sis.'

Whilst Ali spent most of his life in the US now, this was still home for him. The aroma of the traditional food being cooked in the kitchen wafted his way; another reminder that he was back home. His apartment in New York lacked any such comforting homely touches.

The driver walked in behind him and took Ali's bags up to his room. Ali's mother rushed from the kitchen into the large, marble-floored hallway, and went over and kissed Ali softly on his forehead. He immediately noticed that her face bore a wide, twinkly smile, and her eyes danced joyfully. It had been some time since she had last seen him.

'It's so good to have you home, son. It's been far too long. You always rely on us to visit you, but you need to come over more,' said his mum.

'Well, that will be even more difficult for him now he is marrying Sofia, as he will be laying roots in New York,' said Ali's father, who had wandered into the hallway and stood right behind his wife.

'*As-salamu alaykum, Aba Jan*,' said Ali.

'*Wa alaykumu as-salam*,' replied his father. He was taller than Ali, and had an overbearing presence. His hair was now receding, and he had rather large, bulging eyes. Ali's father did not move from the spot on which he was stood. Ali did not attempt to move towards him either. There was no embrace, not even a handshake.

They all proceeded into the dining room, where the maids had laid breakfast. The food looked even more enticing than it had smelled. There were freshly made *aloo parathas*, and plain ghee ones, aromatic cardamom and cinnamon *desi* tea, fried eggs sunny side up, spicy scrambled eggs, *keema handi* and hot buttered toast. They all sat together, and started to tuck in. Ali's mum couldn't help fussing over her son, just as Ali had expected, and she started piling his plate high with the food.

'Slow down, Mum, or you will fatten me up so much with all this *desi* food that I won't fit into my clothes when I get back to New York!'

'You never fuss this much over me, *Amee!*' complained Ali's sister, in response to which she was shot a stern look by her mother.

'Of course I do! But because you are here all the time, and it is a regular occurrence for you, you neither notice nor appreciate it! *Kapathi!*'

'Yes, you pest! You just don't appreciate it!' added Ali.

Ali's sister let out a giggle; her mother joined in, reluctantly at first, but soon the laughter of the two women filled the room. Ali smiled at them, and then he started to eat his food. He realised in that instant how much he missed them both; missed their homely touches, their comforting words and their jovial nature.

His father let out a short but loud, and probably unnecessary cough, which resulted in them all turning to look at him where he sat at the head of the table. Once he had the attention of all three of them, he placed his floral china teacup down on the saucer, raised his head slightly and began to speak.

'Son, I am proud of you,' said Ali's father. Ali could pretty much guess what was coming next. 'By agreeing to marry Sofia, you have done a very good thing. And that good thing is that you are going to unite two strong families that will become all the stronger for the union. Her father's business is very much thriving; he now has thirteen grand malls all over Pakistan, not to mention his numerous luxury hotels. And as for our side, our factories are going from strength to strength.'

Ali took in a deep breath and braced himself for what was coming next.

'You know, it was always my ardent wish that you would one day join, and eventually take over, the family empire; I cannot deny, as you well know, that I was sorely disappointed when you opted to become a lawyer instead. I was not only disappointed. Truth be told, I was angry. However, that said, this decision of yours to agree to marry Sofia does go quite some way to make up for your past mistakes.'

Finally, Ali's dad was a tad proud of him – although only he could convey a compliment in such a critical way; Ali felt it was like a dagger in the guise of a flower.

For his entire life, right from his decision as a child to take up swimming instead of cricket, or his choice as a teenager to learn to play an electric guitar instead of taking classical music lessons, or his decision to become a lawyer instead of the big boss factory owner, Ali had always felt that he could do nothing right. And whatever his accomplishments, whether it was his academic success, or coping with living in the States as a teenager without his immediate family around, or securing a job with a top law firm in New York – his father had never congratulated him.

Unlike the two women of the house, who shared many similarities with each other, Ali knew that he and his father were as diametrically opposite as it was possible to be. His father's cold nature, condescending tone of voice and mean choice of words were, Ali hoped, in huge contrast to his own character. Ali had been more influenced by his mother's warm, engaging personality, which was free of any of those traits that signified a sense of self-importance or grandeur. Ali desired to be nothing like his father. He wasn't driven by money; perhaps because he had never been without it, or maybe because he found his father's constant pursuit of it so off-putting. The truth was that his father had never really understood him, or even tried to do so with any sincerity. And Ali had certainly never understood his father's desire for more, more, more, even though he had enough worldly riches to last him a hundred lifetimes.

Amir's office was located on the second floor in a dated, old-fashioned office building in central Islamabad, a stone's throw away from the law courts. There was a good turnout. Ali knew that Amir was well connected in the legal fraternity, and well respected for his professional, and honest, approach to his work. Amir made no bones about the fact that he was a lawyer for one reason and one reason only – to help those in society who needed his help the most. Ali saw him as a sort of champion for the underdog, a dedicated human rights activist, a prolific women's rights campaigner and a strong advocate for reform. Consequently, Amir had friends in high places, but Ali also got the feeling that he had a fair few enemies in those upper echelons too.

Amir had managed to make a name for himself as soon as he had started working, when he was fresh out of law school, after he took on a notorious case of a family seeking justice for the rape and murder of their daughter at the house where she had worked as a maid. The brutal sexual assault had been followed by the strangulation and then dumping of the body in a squalid side street in the centre of Rawalpindi. Rapes were committed daily, and most never gained any attention, but this case was different. The victim's family alleged that the young woman had been raped and murdered by none other than the son-in-law of the chief minister of the province. The money, power and influence of the family had caused every attorney to give the case a wide berth, every attorney except for Amir. After much persuasion, the senior lawyer at his firm gave him permission to pursue the case, which he did with rare vigour, and with a depth of analytical thought seldom seen in most lawyers, let alone in a lawyer as young as he was. Amir's meticulous attention to detail, his hounding of the police to ensure they were accountable for every piece of evidence, however miniscule, and his dogged resistance to all the bribes, inducements and threats that were flung his way, added to the fact that the trial had been presided over by one of the few judges who did not fear the rank or influence of the defendant's side, meant that against all the odds and predictions, he won the case and ensured justice for a victim and her family who had felt they were voiceless and invisible.

After that, Amir went from strength to strength, and he was soon recognised as the unofficial people's champion, a lawyer who cared deeply for the most deprived and defenceless in society. Ali worked hard in New York, but he didn't think he could ever compare himself to Amir, who worked on the ground with some of the most disadvantaged in society. As Amir worked the room now, Ali could see the magic he possessed; he had a deeply caring and yet charismatic quality about him which was rare, and it wasn't hard to see why he was adored by those around him.

The launch party was simple but very well attended; it was in stark contrast to the lavish parties Ali was used to attending back in New York where the champagne flowed freely, although he himself was teetotal, and blini canapés topped with smoked salmon and caviar were handed out like candy by the pretty, and often scantily dressed, waitresses. Ali tucked into a large samosa which he first dipped into a zingy tamarind sauce.

'Man, these samosas are amazing. Fluffy yet crispy pastry, and the spicy *keema* filling is just on the right side of hot; not bland, and not so fiery as to take my head off! And the *imli* chutney is perfect. Some things just aren't the same abroad.'

'No, I guess they're not, *yaar!*' Amir responded, as he smiled and patted his friend on the back. 'That was quite a description! I'm not sure now whether you came back for me, or for the food! But it is good of you to come, I really do appreciate it. So, what are you going to be doing whilst you're here?'

'Nothing much. I was hoping to hang out with you for a bit, if you can have a few days off work,' said Ali.

'Sorry, old friend, I just don't have the time. It's taken me a while to finally get here, to fly solo, and now I must crack on.

I'm as busy as busy can be. But you can join me on the job if you want; that's if your prim and proper Western sensitivities will allow you to slum it with us plain and simple sorts!'

Ali knew Amir was joking, but he had to think twice about Amir's last comment. Had he really lost touch to that extent? he asked himself. He thought about his corporate law team back in New York; the building he worked in was in a prime location within the heart of the financial district, and he carried out his legal work in plush offices that overlooked the New York Stock Exchange. The meetings took place in state-of-the-art conference rooms, or over fine dining in one of the many high-class restaurants nearby.

'Hey!' Ali protested. 'I may live in the Western world, but I haven't forgotten where I'm from.'

'But are you aware of how bad things really are over here?' Amir asked.

Ali had left for the US as a teenage schoolkid, and only came back occasionally. Even then, whenever he did return to Pakistan for his brief visits, he stayed within the confines of luxury: an air-conditioned mansion, several air-conditioned cars to choose from, modern marble-floored shopping malls, and the best restaurants in town.

'Yes,' replied Ali.

Amir looked at him a little sceptically.

'It's pretty full on, a lot of dashing here and there, court to court, jail to jail, sitting in smelly rooms with smelly clients. It can be a bit ugly to tell the truth. You sure you want to?'

'Of course, man.'

Ali nodded his head eagerly, but he did wonder; was it really going to be all that bad?

'OK, in that case, be here first thing,' said Amir, with a wide smile on his face.

That first visit to the prison was something that Ali would never ever forget. He had never before strayed from within the circles of privilege to see the 'real' Pakistan, the places where you would find the most disadvantaged in society, be it in a government hospital where patients shared beds, or a prison that had dozens of inmates crammed into one cell, or a slum-like village with open sewers where children played in filthy water.

On this first trip to a Pakistani jail, it was a hot, dry day, and the journey was full of anticipation on Ali's part. As he sat in the car, he tried to picture the prison based on what he had seen in the movies or little glimpses of images online; prisoners lining up eagerly for their food or squabbling over cigarettes smuggled into the jail was what Ali pictured in his head. He couldn't quite manage to form any coherent image in his mind as to what the inside of the jail would be like.

The first thing that hit Ali when he walked into the room was indeed the smell. An awful, unforgettable, rank smell that was so overpowering it was almost suffocating. He felt as though he was going to pass out. The prison meeting was in a tiny, filthy room, with terrible lighting. It wasn't possible to discern what colour the walls must have originally been painted, for they were now a cauldron of shades; dirty grey and murky brown, speckled with large splatters of black in big patches and small specks. Ali was a million miles away from his corporate boardroom.

The prisoner sat before them and cried, having been framed by his landlord for a murder that had been committed by his landlord's son. The prisoner was hideously thin, very dark, and had bloodshot eyes. He rested his skeletal hands on the table as he spoke.

Amir asked insightful questions, and took down every detail the prisoner uttered, rarely looking up from the notebook in which he scribbled so fast.

'I believe you said one of the villagers saw you walking past his house at the time that the murder supposedly took place?' asked Amir.

'Yes, and he is my only alibi,' replied the prisoner, 'but he is refusing to give a statement.'

'Why is that?' asked Amir.

'I can't say for sure, but I think my landlord had paid him money to keep quiet. The man has a poorly child; his son has kidney problems, and I think he has been promised money for the treatment if he keeps quiet.'

Amir sighed as he wrote.

As they left the jail, Amir explained to Ali that it was far too easy for the rich and powerful to do this in a society where money talked. Bribery and corruption were rife; the rich could pay off just about anyone, and consequently stay out of prison, just as long as someone else would take the rap. Ali had always had an inkling about the injustice that existed here, but seeing it with his own eyes was a different thing altogether. Something that the accused had said in that room that day had always stuck in Ali's mind: 'Jail is full of people who haven't killed anyone, and outside is full of murderers who roam free.'

It was not just the visit to prison that Ali would forever remember; the whole week in Pakistan with Amir had been an unforgettable experience for him. Whatever he did back in New York, however hard he worked, it was always done in ultimate comfort, and he always dealt with the privileged. He never had to consider the woman who was locked up just because she wanted to marry the man she loved, or the manservant who was incarcerated on trumped-up charges so the master could get away scot-free, or the children who were born into and spent their formative years in prison with their mothers because there was nothing else that could be done for them. Their childhood was robbed from them, they were locked away in the grimmest of conditions, when they should have been out playing. It was all so wrong, so unfair, thought Ali; there were so many grave problems here, and to some extent, Ali was relieved that he would soon be leaving them behind.

38

NEW YORK

Ali arrived back in New York with his parents two days before the engagement was due to take place, with just about enough time to sort out the last-minute details, including picking up the diamond ring. He found it difficult to take his mind away from Pakistan though; thoughts of some of the people he had seen whilst shadowing Amir occupied his mind. He realised just how fortunate he and Sofia were, but that didn't detract from the sadness he felt about what he had witnessed.

He had a rough idea of what the engagement function would be like. Although Sofia had tried to run all the details past him, much of it had bounced straight off him, without penetrating his mind or memory. It was going to be very much her day, as she had been given free rein to plan the party exactly as she wished.

The exclusive fifteenth-storey rooftop function room at the hotel was the venue for a seated dinner for forty. Ali knew it was a special place indeed; it afforded unobstructed, enviable views of the star-studded Manhattan skyline. The view of the city was so clear, so vivid in its colours and textures, that it was almost as though one was looking into a painting, rather than seeing the city itself. The image, though alluring, seemed to Ali like a glittery façade: pretty, but ultimately phoney and insincere.

The food was 'fine' dining in the best and most Western sense of the word. There was not a traditional curry or biryani in sight. This decision had been made to please Sofia, rather than to cater for the food tastes of the majority of the guests, Ali included, but that didn't detract from the fact that the dishes were exquisitely prepared and served. Ali wasn't surprised by Sofia's menu choices; she was not one for cultural attachment when it came to such decisions.

The guests sat at the immaculately arranged tables; the tall candles and luxurious fresh flower centrepieces were neatly placed, as were the polished cutlery and crystalware. The generous number of uniformed waiting staff began to arrive with the drinks and appetisers. For the first time, Ali thought about how much money had been spent on this event; an eye-watering amount. He reflected on the poverty and in-justice he had seen in Pakistan, and just couldn't marry the two in his head.

Ali and Sofia did their rounds, meeting and greeting the guests, who were mainly from the upper echelons of Pakistanis settled in and around New York and New Jersey; some had come from further afield in the States, and a few of their parents' very good friends and closest relatives had even flown in from Pakistan. Ali entertained talk about their Pak-American businesses, their children's Harvard graduations, their latest multimillion-dollar contracts, their involvement in high-level politics, and yet he found it difficult to focus on the detail of anything that was being said. He mainly listened, nodded and added a few words here and there; the troubles of Pakistan which he had witnessed were still uppermost in his mind.

After the main course, the families decided that they should carry out the engagement ceremony, before they all moved on to dessert.

Ali and Sofia sat in the middle of the head table, with their parents on either side of them.

Ali's father stood, with his usual air of self-importance, and the guests all looked in anticipation towards him, as he proceeded to make the announcement. Ali took in a deep breath for the moment had now arrived.

'*Bismilla ar-rahma niraheem. Alhamdolillah*, we are all gathered here today, on this auspicious occasion, to witness the *mangni* of Ali and Sofia. I am so very proud to be stood here in front of you, as this union is one that fills my heart with joy.' He looked towards Sofia's parents, who smiled, and looked equally pleased. Ali's mum gently stroked her son's arm. 'So, without further ado, I think we should proceed with the formalities of the engagement ceremony, an act that will bring the two families one step closer to being bound in an everlasting alliance. Over to you both.'

Ali and Sofia stood and faced each other. The moment had come for the official presentation of the ring. Soft traditional music played in the background, the strokes of a melodious sitar danced playfully with the gentle, bouncing beats of the tabla. Sofia smiled at Ali; she looked the part beautifully, thought Ali, as he really focused on her properly for the first time this evening.

Ali carefully took out of his pocket the distinctive blue Tiffany box, which had been so precisely tied with a crisp white ribbon. Sofia's smiled widened as Ali started to open the box. He opened it slowly, and savoured the moment; all eyes were on her, eagerly awaiting her reaction. However, her beaming smile suddenly faded when she saw the ring. He wasn't sure why her smile vanished, but he continued nevertheless; he took the solitaire diamond ring set in platinum out of the box and placed it on her finger, to the cheers and applause of the guests. The two sets of parents hugged and embraced each other, and there were shouts of 'mubarak' from them and the guests.

However, Sofia's face continued to look childish and sullen, which Ali couldn't fathom; he had never seen such an unattractive expression on her face before.

'What's the matter?' Ali whispered in her ear, whilst the merriment around them continued, and they took their seats again.

'It's nothing,' Sofia replied.

'Are you sure? If it's nothing, then why the glum face?' Ali asked.

'Well, it's just that . . .'

'What is it?' Ali asked again, smiling at everyone, but waiting for an answer.

'Is this a two carat diamond?' Sofia asked.

'Yes, just as you wanted,' Ali replied.

'No, I asked for two and a half.'

Something inside him snapped, like a rubber band that had been stretched just that little bit too far. He suddenly saw the dark dingy room in the jail, where he had listened to prisoner after prisoner recount misery after misery. He looked around him and saw the extravagant room that he was sat in right now, and then he saw Sofia's dismal face and the diamond ring.

'Are you serious?' Ali raised his voice.

'Be quiet,' she whispered in his ear, 'everyone is looking.'

'No! I won't be quiet! This is a complete joke!' Ali said, standing back up. 'I just put a frickin' two carat diamond ring on your finger, as my commitment to you for our forthcoming marriage, as my pledge to be your husband and to agree to spend the rest of my life with you, and all you can say is that you wanted two and a half carats? No thanks, no kind words or loving gestures?'

Sofia looked at Ali in total shock.

'There are people out there, all around the world, who are fleeing wars, and starving to death, and being tortured, and there are men and women and kids and babies who are homeless and have nothing to eat. What the hell, why look so far away? There are people sleeping rough just around the corner from this place, right in this city, and all you can think of is the size of the shitty stone?'

'Ali! What are you doing? Sit back down,' his father ordered sternly.

Ali looked around the posh room, and out towards New York City in the night sky. He looked at everyone around him. It was as though they were all holding their breath. They all waited; waited for him. No one moved. No one uttered a sound. Ali turned and looked down towards Sofia; she was without remorse, and he felt sickened.

Ali's father broke the silence.

'Ali. Whatever has happened, or has been said, by either of you, put it behind you. It doesn't matter.'

'No. Sorry,' said Ali, as he shook his head firmly. 'This *does* matter. It may not matter to anyone else, but it matters to *me*. I'm sorry, but I can't do this. This is a complete sham. I only agreed to this stupid match to please *you*. Out of respect for you, as my father. I agreed to it because it is what *you* wanted. You never bothered to ask me what I wanted. But I'm telling you this right here, right now; I can't spend the rest of my life with a woman who measures happiness and success with such shallow concerns like the size of her diamond ring, or the latest hideous designer trends, or the need for Botox.'

Ali slowly looked around the room as all the eyes continued to observe him. He felt as though he was in a room full of complete strangers; he couldn't relate to anyone. None of these people meant anything to him right now.

'Sorry to ruin your evening, folks, but this party is over.'

And he walked out of the room.

39

ISLAMABAD

It had just gone 7 o'clock. The night had descended as a shroud over the day; the view was now akin to a sea of stars, as the lights shone away in the distance. The Shah Faisal Mosque continued to glow in its own commanding space, as its illuminated boundaries and minarets blushed brightly.

Farah thought for a few moments about everything Ali had said. She wondered at the amount of courage it must have taken for him to go against his family, and particularly his father, in this way; she had once hoped for a similar display of courage from Tahir, but it had never materialised.

'Wow! That's quite a story,' she said.

'Isn't it just,' Ali said slowly.

'But you didn't say how you ended up back in Pakistan. Did you literally run away from it all?'

A tinge of sadness glazed over Ali's face.

'Just a few weeks after Diamondgate, something tragic happened, that brought me back here.'

Farah didn't say anything. She allowed him to take his time. She could see that whatever it was, it had affected him deeply.

'Amir was killed. Here, in Islamabad.' Ali almost choked the words out.

'Oh no. I'm so sorry to hear that. What happened?' asked Farah.

'What always seems to bloody happen to good people in Pakistan!'

Ali let out a stifled sigh. He continued to look into the distance.

'He was on a demo against police and judicial corruption, along with other lawyers, and members of the public. It was a very large gathering, and it was getting tonnes of media attention. The camera crews and news reporters were all there. He was one of the organisers of the demonstration. But he was "run over", Ali said, quoting and unquoting with his index and middle fingers on both hands.

Farah could see the pain in his eyes. And she could hear that same pain in his voice, as he struggled to speak.

'You don't think it was an accident?' asked Farah.

'It's hard to know with any certainty exactly what happened, but the witness statements seemed to suggest that somebody had called him on his mobile phone. As a result of this call, he left the large gathering and started to walk away from everyone, I assume he was walking to wherever it was that the caller had asked him to go, for whatever reason, Lord knows. As he crossed the road, a car came out of nowhere at high speed, and crushed him into a pulp.'

Farah tried to imagine Amir being called to his death in this way.

'The driver escaped from the scene and was never found; neither was the car. No one caught it on camera because Amir had walked away from the cameras, which were glued on the opposition party leader, who had suddenly turned up to support the rally and was making an impassioned speech. It was deemed to have been an unfortunate accident; just a hit and run.'

'Obviously whoever carried this out did a thorough job in making it look like an accident; we both know accidents always leave traces,' said Farah.

'I agree. It was an execution that had been planned to precision. From what I'd heard, Amir had taken on a few too many influential people, and someone decided they would shut him up for good. So, you see my concern about your trying to take on these sorts of people with online petitions and the like.'

Farah looked away for a second, unable to meet his gaze. She fidgeted with the hem of her dress. She felt guilty about having had such a go at him about that petition, for thinking that he was being controlling and patronising; she now understood that he was only trying to protect her.

'Did you ever find out why?' she asked him.

Ali took in a deep breath, which he held on to for a few seconds before he exhaled.

'You don't have to go on if it's too painful.'

'No. It's OK,' Ali assured her. 'Amir had decided to represent a young Christian man who had been accused of blasphemy. You must know what it's like in this country if you even mention the word "blasphemy", let alone stand accused of it. This young guy worked at a factory. There was some sort of a dispute between him and some of the other workers, they colluded to accuse him of making derogatory remarks about the Prophet Mohammed. If you're found guilty of that here, it's punishable by death, unless the madmen kill you first.'

Farah continued to listen intently.

'The workers went to the factory boss, who in turn went to the police. The factory owner was a very powerful and exceedingly corrupt guy; he had friends in high places. This young Christian man never really stood a chance. As soon as the accusations were uttered, he was arrested and dumped in prison, and no one was prepared to represent him. No one, except for Amir, of course.'

'Actually, I think I read about this case,' interrupted Farah. 'I remember the reports of how this man had supposedly committed blasphemy, and the ensuing political and public pressure that had been put on the courts to sentence him to death.'

'Probably, the world's media were all over it. In the end, it became very personal, especially for the factory owner, who began putting himself out as some upholder of Islam, a modern-day warrior fighting against blaspheming scoundrels. He in fact had political ambitions and seized upon this opportunity to kick-start his political career. He knew that it was imperative that he was seen to win this case; he is indeed now in a position of power within the government. Anyway, Amir rattled people. He was adamant that he would bring out the truth, adamant that the case should be a turning point to dissuade people from using the blasphemy laws as a means of religious persecution or as an easy way to wage personal wars or vendettas. But he never got to finish it.'

'That's terrible,' said Farah. She felt an acute sense of sadness at the loss of this beautiful life of a talented young man who represented all that was good. And then her thoughts turned to Razia, another loss of a good and innocent life. In Razia's case, she still felt guilt as well as sorrow.

'What's even worse is the fact that he wasn't the only one killed. The young Christian guy was executed.'

'Good God!'

'I know. It sends a shiver up your spine, doesn't it? But that is Pakistan. A tale of two halves. The good and the bad. The breathtakingly beautiful and the downright ugly.'

Farah looked straight ahead at the striking night view. It gave her goosebumps; this was Pakistan, she thought to herself. A melting pot in which there was so much to love but also much to loathe.

'So you came back to continue Amir's work?'

'Initially, it was just meant to be a short visit. When I came over for his funeral, I was told by Amir's father that, in his will, Amir had left the law firm to me. He had said that he understood that because I lived in New York I wouldn't be able to see to the day-to-day running of the firm, but he wanted all major decisions to be made by me. I couldn't believe he had entrusted it to me. I knew how much having his own firm had meant to him. He had worked tirelessly. As soon as his father told me that, I suddenly had this urge to carry on his legacy. It didn't fade when I got back to the States. I felt miserable over there. I felt lonely, and stranded; someone without purpose. I was working all the hours God sent, but for what? I couldn't honestly say what it was for. Yes, the money was brilliant, but what else? Money was not enough.'

Farah hadn't seen him in this light before; she tried to imagine the unhappiness he must have felt at being part of a rat race that gave him no personal satisfaction.

'So I quit my job. I quit New York. I moved back and took over the law firm. I came back home.'

'Wow. How did that go down with your family?'

'My mum was overjoyed to have me back. So was my sister. Above all, they both just wanted me to be happy. But things were awkward with my father, and to be frank, they still are. He can't forgive me for backing out of marrying Sofia. We barely speak. But the one advantage of being a rich kid is that your father has such a large mansion that you can go days without having to set eyes on him!'

They both let out a laugh, and then stared into the distant canvas of bright flickering lights in the dark, still night.

Farah took the pause as an opportunity to reflect on the time she had spent with Ali today; she had seen a totally new side to him, which had taken her by surprise, but in a good way. She felt they had connected on a deeper, more personal level, and she was comfortable with that. She was comfortable with him, and even felt comfortable with Pakistan, despite everything she had learned there.

The ringing of Ali's mobile phone startled them both, and broke the tranquillity of the moment.

'*Salams*, how are you? Yes, I can see you tomorrow . . . my office . . . no problem . . . yes . . . but what . . . oh . . . yes, I will. See you tomorrow.'

Ali ended the call. He looked puzzled.

'Is everything OK?' Farah asked.

'I'm not sure. That was a lawyer friend of mine. She's coming to my office first thing tomorrow morning to see me. She says it's urgent.'

'See you about what?'

'She wouldn't say over the phone. She said she has to tell me in person. But she specifically asked that you are also present.'

'Me? Why would she want me there? I don't even know her.'

'My thoughts exactly.'

Farah had an uneasy feeling; she couldn't help but worry that Zaheer, or perhaps his brother, was up to something, but the question was: what?

40

Farah sipped slowly from her cup of masala tea.

Sat opposite her, behind his desk, Ali was busy on a telephone call, so she placed her cup on the desk, and wandered about the office. It was a good-sized room. In fact, it was spacious compared to most offices in London. There were files and documents everywhere. The clutter led to Farah feeling a solidarity with Ali, for she believed that lawyers were of a particular ilk, the same the world over – be it London, New York or Islamabad. If you didn't trip over a file at least once a day, then you were in an extraordinarily tidy office, which was a rarity.

There was one framed photo on the wall: Ali with Amir. The two were stood smiling, in a garden or park somewhere. Amir was a tiny bit shorter than Ali, and a tad darker. He had a neat moustache and wore smart black-framed glasses. She noticed the photo had captured the closeness of the two; the manly embrace, the beaming smiles, the jovial expressions on their faces. Farah thought about the immensity of the loss for Ali.

There was a silver-edged, rectangular clock on the wall which had clearly not had its batteries replaced for some time, for the face was displaying the time as 2 p.m. as opposed to 9 a.m., and the date was some six months past.

There was a bookshelf in one corner. It was quite dusty; evidently Ali wasn't one for the furniture polish. It held a good selection of law books, but also some non-legal books too: poems of Rumi, a book on Baba Bulleh Shah and a biography of the late great Abdul Sattar Edhi.

As Ali came off the phone, there was a knock on the door and a middle-aged lady walked in.

Ali walked over and greeted her, and then made the introduction.

'This is Jabeen *Baji*, and Jabeen *Baji*, this is Farah.'

After the exchanges of the *salams* and how are yous, they all sat down.

Jabeen was in her early- to mid-fifties perhaps. She had short, frizzy black hair that had a thick cluster of grey strands. Over her dark blue dress, she wore an oversized black blazer.

'Would you like some tea, *Baji*?' asked Ali.

'No, thank you, I would if I had the time, but alas, I cannot stay long,' she replied.

Farah waited anxiously. Why would Jabeen want her to be present?

'I guess you must be wondering what I am doing here, and why all the secrecy. It's a sensitive matter. I had to see you face to face, both of you.' Jabeen spoke quickly, clearly and to the point.

'I was at the Adiala Jail yesterday, in the women's section,' she continued.

Farah sat up straight when she heard the name of the prison where Razia had been.

'I had gone to see a client of mine. She put a request in saying it was urgent. I didn't think there could have been much development in her case, but you know my nature, I have to check things out, so I went along to see her.'

'OK,' said Ali, 'so, what happened?'

'I was right in one respect; there was no progress with her case. However, she didn't want to see me about herself, but she wanted to talk to me about one of your clients. I believe this client is now deceased – someone by the name of Razia?'

'Really?' Farah asked. She was listening intently; hearing Jabeen now mention Razia's name confirmed her suspicions.

'Yes. My client told me that she and Razia had become quite good friends and that Razia had entrusted her with a very important letter. She told my client that she must not under any circumstances open it, but that if anything should happen to Razia herself, then my client was to make sure that Miss Farah received this letter.'

Farah and Ali said nothing. Farah was taken aback. She

couldn't believe it, but then, Razia had always trusted her; deep down, she knew that.

Jabeen delved into her handbag and whipped out the letter. She placed it on the desk. It wasn't in an envelope. There was just a piece of lined paper folded around it.

'My client was true to her word and she has not opened it; in any event, she can't read. But she honoured her promise to Razia and she kept it safe.'

Farah looked at the folded piece of paper that sat on the desk; the last piece of communication from Razia.

'Well then, I'm going to be on my way, I have to be in court by ten o'clock.'

'Thank you for coming,' said Ali.

'Yes, thank you so much for this,' Farah added.

The door closed and they both sat back down and continued to look at the letter. 'It was meant for you, Farah. You open it,' said Ali.

Farah slowly picked it up and took away the outer lined paper. She carefully unfolded the letter, and saw that it had been written in Urdu. Razia's first language, but not hers.

'I can only read Urdu a little; I can understand it, but I can't read it very well,' said Farah, suddenly feeling embarrassed that she couldn't read Razia's last message, even though it was addressed to her. She was embarrassed as a lawyer who was used to reading documents for herself, but also as a woman of Pakistani heritage. How little she had bothered over the years with her own culture, she thought.

'Will you read it?' she asked Ali.

He took it off her and had an initial cursory look.

'It seems to have been written in very simple Urdu, but of course if you want me to read it, I will.'

Farah nodded. He cleared his throat a little and began.

My dear Miss Farah *ji*

I hope you are well.

Firstly, forgive the writing; my Urdu is very poor, and there may be many spelling mistakes. I never attended school, but I was lucky enough in my childhood to have received lessons from a neighbour who taught me up to a very basic level.

The fact that you are reading this letter means that I am no longer in this world. I have written this letter and told my friend in my cell that if anything happens to me then she must get this letter to you. And so, as you have this letter, that day has come.

I want to thank you for everything you have done for me. I am very grateful and please know that I do not blame you for my being in prison or anything else that happens.

I have had time in prison to think about everything, and I believe that I now know the reason, at least partly, as to why Mr Zaheer wants to harm me. Because he does want to harm me.

If I am suddenly found dead then please know that I

did not harm myself, but I was killed. This is because I am to be interviewed soon, and Mr Zaheer does not want me to speak and tell anyone what he thinks I may know; because of this, I fear I may come to some harm.

When I first arrived in prison, I was visited by a man and a woman who pretended to the prison officers that they were my relatives. But, in fact, they were sent by Mr Zaheer with a warning that if I said anything about him, or against him, then they would harm my mother, or me, or both.

I wanted to tell you when I saw you yesterday, but you had a man with you and I could not be sure that he was not also sent by Mr Zaheer, that he had not tricked you and made you believe he was here to help, when really, he could have been in cahoots with Mr Zaheer.

Ali paused.

'Wow, I had no idea. Poor girl, imagine how I must have made her feel,' said Ali, his voice laced with regret.

'You weren't to know; neither of us knew the level of control and pressure Zaheer was imposing upon Razia,' said Farah.

'You can be excused; I should have known better. I should have thought of letting you see her alone first. Why didn't I think of that?'

'Don't do this to yourself. Like you said to me, regret won't bring her back. In any event, I think she must have trusted you on some level; she must have known Jabeen would need to contact you to reach me.'

Ali sighed, and continued reading.

If I am fortunate enough to see you again, I will tell you in person, and I know you will make sure that my mother is not harmed.

But in case I do not see you again, I must tell you by way of this letter. Once you have read this, please do not do anything until you can be sure of my family's safety, especially the safety of my mother.

When I was in London, I accidently overheard a conversation between Mr Zaheer and another man. I do not know who this other man was. They were in the lounge, and Mrs Aneela was out of the house. Before leaving, she had left me the strict instruction to polish the floor in the hallway. I was getting on with this when I overheard some of the conversation, because the door was slightly open. When the two men came out and saw me there, they were startled. After the guest left, Mr Zaheer quizzed me for some time; he asked me how long I had been there and what I had heard. I panicked, and I lied; I said that I had only been there for a minute, even though I had been in the hallway for a lot longer than that. I don't think he ever believed me. And it seems that he may not be prepared to take any chances.

I did hear some of the conversation. The man who had been with him had said something like 'when the deal is signed, the million dollars will be in your account'. I heard them say that no one must know, even by accident, about the arrangement. They talked about emails and documents, and Mr Zaheer said, 'don't worry, I have a friend who takes care of this for me. It's all stored away safely.'

The truth is, I do not know what any of this means, but I am sure that it must be important. That is why I am letting you know. I am sorry I cannot tell you anything else.

Thank you once again. You were very kind to me. I don't think anyone could have been nicer than you were to me. I feel sad that I will not see my mother again, or Ahmed, who will always be the love of my life.

Yours gratefully.

Razia

Ali and Farah initially sat in stunned silence, and the only noise was the buzz of the traffic coming from the busy street outside the office.

Farah felt a multitude of emotions, but it was her anger which spilled over first.

'The vicious brute; how could he murder such an innocent, beautiful young woman? This was nothing short of a cold-blooded execution, and yet it looks like he will get away with it.'

'Not necessarily. Let's look at the evidence. What do you think all this means?' Ali asked her.

Farah shook her head.

'I haven't got a clue,' she replied. 'Zaheer referred a lot of work to the law firm, in return for cash payments, and perhaps they weren't declaring the fee arrangement to the Law Society. But – a million dollars. That's on another level.'

'Yes, I agree. This is something on a higher scale, international maybe.'

'Can't we take the letter to the police and have them investigate?' she asked.

'Not unless you want the mother's death on your conscience.'

Farah dropped her head in her hands momentarily.

'That said, if we can get hold of any evidence somehow, relating to what is in this letter, then depending on what we find, we can go to the police and get protection for the family pending their investigations. If we have evidence, then they will have to investigate. They won't do it on the strength of this letter though.'

Farah could sense that Ali was concerned; bearing in mind the impulsiveness with which she had launched the online petition, she could perhaps understand why.

He leaned over the table towards her.

'You do understand where I'm coming from, Farah? Lives are at stake here.'

'Yes. Of course, you're absolutely right.'

Farah sighed. She knew she would not be able to rest until she had done something to bring about some justice for Razia. But what?

41

Farah was ready to attend Ali's sister's henna function. She took a good look in the mirror in her hotel room before going down. She had really made an effort this evening to blend in with the crowd and play her role in the evening's festivities; her two-tone emerald and pale green *anarkali kameez* was dotted with sparkly gemstone work around the neckline and waist. She had done the whole traditional *mehndi* event look; *desi*-style jewellery, kajal eyes, red lips. She had even gone and bought some *jhumka* earrings. She knew she looked very different, and she was amazed at how her usual resistance to traditional dress seemed to have melted away of late. She was very happy with what she saw in the mirror.

This didn't go unnoticed by Ali, who came to pick her up.

'You look amazing,' he said as soon as he set eyes on her. Farah was initially flattered by the compliment, but this soon turned to a feeling of embarrassment. She surprised herself. She liked the fact that he had noticed and liked the way she looked, but she told herself not to make too much of it; she would be going back home soon and that would be that.

'Thanks,' she replied, and looked away, aware that she was blushing.

'I was thinking about the letter,' said Ali. 'It's been on my mind.'

'I've been thinking about it too. But it's your sister's *mehndi* today; maybe we should put the discussions about Razia on hold for tonight?'

'I guess so,' he replied.

'Anyway, I'm sure Razia would have wanted you to enjoy your sister's henna night,' said Farah.

Ali gave her a reassuring smile, and they set off.

It was a short drive to his home, which was situated on an exclusive road in Islamabad. The house, like so many others Farah had seen in the capital, was large, and grand, and sprawled over a very wide plot. Farah thought back to the very first day she had seen Ali; he came across as so scruffy looking, almost impoverished, that she would never have guessed that he came from such a wealthy background or lived in such a huge mansion. Nothing about him ever gave that away. He was always humble.

The exterior was currently decorated from top to bottom with bright lights, hanging down from the roof to the ground like glittery flower garlands, a sure sign of wedding celebrations. Farah thought of how she had once dreamed of a colourful, traditional *mehndi* and a perfect wedding day, but now these dreams seemed more and more unattainable to her as time went on.

When they arrived, the evening's celebratory activities were just getting underway, and Ali got a bit of a telling off for being late from several people as soon as he walked through the front door. After he had introduced Farah to his mother and some of the other relatives gathered in the large hallway, he ran upstairs, and within two minutes he was back down, dressed in a white *salwar* suit with a bright green scarf, as per the colour code – green for the girl's side, red for the boy's side.

Those gathered in the hallway were close family – aunts, uncles, grandparents, cousins – and they all had a role to play in the evening's proceedings. They were ready and poised in their colourful outfits, not too formal, but decorative and vibrant, as was usually the case with *mehndi* parties. When they were all satisfied that they had everything they needed with them – *mitai*, *mehndi thaals*, garlands, rose petals, gifts – they started to make their way towards the back of the house.

The function was taking place in the back garden, in an enormous creamy coloured marquee, complete with flashing and static lights, chandeliers, fresh flower decorations and enough seating for at least 200 people. There was a large stage, decorated with red and yellow flowers and plenty of green foliage, and a good-sized dance floor right in front of the stage.

309

Ali escorted Farah towards the marquee. It was a perfectly warm evening. There was a slight breeze that exuded a heady scent of the fresh flowers, particularly roses and jasmine, which were abundant, whether growing in the gardens, freshly picked and used as decorations for the archways and tables, or secured with pins in the women's hair. There was also the distinctly woody scent of the actual henna, as groups of girls sat around the marquee having their henna designs applied onto their hands and arms. Traditional *mehndi* music and songs played loudly, and people sat and stood happily milling around, chatting and laughing. Farah didn't know whether she should feel like an impostor, or really honoured that Ali wanted her to be part of such an intimate family gathering.

As soon as Farah and Ali walked into the marquee, he was accosted by several of his male friends.

'Hey, *yaar*. Haven't seen you in ages,' moaned one of them, as they shook hands in the manliest of manners. His friends then looked at Farah.

'This is my friend, Farah,' Ali said, ignoring his mate's complaint.

They exchanged *salams*; Farah could sense that Ali's friends were curious about her. In fact, she had been receiving quite a few looks, and she could have sworn she heard a few guarded whispers as they had both walked past people. It made her feel a little on edge. On the contrary, Ali was very relaxed; he was enjoying the evening. She had never seen him quite so relaxed before; he was all smiles, and perfectly at ease.

The female relatives decided that it was time to start the *dholki*, so they gathered at the front of the marquee, to the side of the stage where they had laid a soft covering on the floor, and scattered the area with plenty of cushions of all different colours, shapes and sizes; some were sequined, some satiny and sparkly, others were soft and velvety, but they were all bright and eye-catching.

The ladies belted out their traditional folk songs to the beat of the *dholki*. All those who were not part of the singing party gathered round and clapped and cheered, especially at the funny lyrics in some of the songs.

Oh Mother-in-Law, five sons you have
Two of them are bad, and two of them are drunkards
But the fifth, my beloved, is like a blossoming red rose.

Farah had heard many of these songs sung at *mehndi* functions back home in England, and listening to the women filled her with a feeling of nostalgia. She remembered in years gone by sitting next to her mum as she had played the *dholki*; often Farah used to bang a spoon on the wooden part on top of the drum, as she had tried, although not always succeeded, to keep in rhythm with the beat of the drum. The ladies now sang an old folk song which was her favourite:

Henna, oh henna
We sisters have all gathered to adorn you
With the henna
Sitting all around you
With tearful eyes, and happy faces.

Upon hearing the melodies and words of these familiar songs, Farah found that whilst she didn't know anyone here apart from Ali, and even Ali she only really knew on a professional level, she was starting to relax, and even beginning to enjoy the evening. She stood amongst a group that comprised Ali, his friends and his cousins, male and female. They were all of a similar sort of age and chatted away. As Farah looked at him, she felt as though she had known Ali for a lot longer than their short acquaintance. It was like they were old school friends, where the familiarity was embedded, and so they found each other's company easy, and the conversation came naturally. They kept catching each other's eye; perhaps it was just one of those things, or perhaps it wasn't. She tried not to look too deeply into it, for she felt happy to be right here, right now, with him, to take pleasure in the moment.

Ali's mother got up and left the singing to the other women and came over to speak to her son.

'Come on, *beta*, it is time for you and your cousins to bring your sister in. Sorry, Farah, I am going to have to take him away from you for a little while,' she said, with a soft smile on her face.

'That's fine, of course,' Farah replied.

'OK, see you in a bit,' said Ali, and wandered off out of the marquee. The others in the group also drifted off in different directions, the time having come for them to fulfil their own roles and attend to the duties they had been assigned.

Just as Farah and Ali's mother were about to start chatting, his father came along. Farah immediately noticed that he was a tall, proud-looking man; he held his head unnaturally high. He didn't look very happy considering the occasion; his face almost bore a grimace.

'I must introduce you. This is my husband,' Ali's mum said. 'And this is Farah, Ali's friend.'

'*As-salamu alaykum*,' said Farah.

'*Wa alaykumu as-salam*,' he replied.

'I'm sorry, I need to go check on things,' said Ali's mum.

'Don't worry,' said her husband, 'I will keep Farah company.'

Ali's mum disappeared off towards the exit from the marquee. Ali's dad stood next to her in silence for a little while. Farah started to feel quite uneasy.

'So, you are from the UK?' Ali's father asked eventually.

'Yes, that's right.'

'What does your father do?'

Farah was taken aback by the abruptness of the question.

'He's a driving instructor,' Farah replied.

'And what about your relatives in Pakistan. What do they do?'

Farah was even more surprised at this question but replied out of politeness.

'I'm not entirely sure, Sir, but I think they are farmers.'

'Farmers?' Ali's father repeated, raising his right eyebrow as he did so.

'Yes, they do *kethi badi*, that's what my father always told me.'

Ali's father went quiet again for a little while.

'What is your intention now?' he asked her.

'Sorry? My . . . my intention?' Farah asked, perplexed.

'Yes, your intention?' he said coldly.

'I don't know what you mean, Sir.'

'Are you trying to say that you are not understanding me?'

He leaned over slightly, to look directly at Farah. She could see from the determination in those eyes that he was going to make sure she heard every word he said.

'OK, let me make myself clear, so there can be no misunderstandings further down the line. I hear that you have been hovering around my son rather a lot recently. I understand there was some case you needed his help on. I am also led to believe that case is now over.'

'Yes, it is, not to anyone's satisfaction, but there isn't much more that can be done,' said Farah.

'Well, in that case you will be returning to the UK shortly?'

'Yes. Imminently.'

'Good. Keep it that way, because if you have any designs on my son, then you can forget it. I don't wish to appear unkind, but obviously, we are not of the same social status. Many a girl has tried to snare my son with a view to climbing the social ladder, but you see, he can only marry a girl who is our equal, and I'm afraid that excludes somebody like you.'

Farah was astounded. No one had ever addressed her in this way. She didn't allow herself any time to process the shock though; she reacted instantly.

'With all due respect, Sir, firstly, I don't think you have any right to comment on my private life or jump to any conclusions about the relationship between myself and Ali. And secondly, I think it is *you* who is so very keen to climb the social ladder – otherwise why would you have been so upset when Ali broke off his engagement to Sofia?'

Ali's dad looked enraged; his face started to turn red, and he seemed stuck as to what to say next. Farah saved him the bother, for she carried on, and didn't hold back. She was going to return home soon, and most likely she would never see this irritating man again, but moreover, she could not just allow him to get away with saying all this nonsense about her or Ali.

'My father may be a driving instructor, Sir, and he may come from a farming family, but quite frankly, he's worth ten of you. And another thing; thank God your son is nothing like you. You don't even know me as a person, but you think so highly of yourself that you feel it's all right to approach me and insult me without a second's thought. Your son, on the other hand, is a decent, polite and kind-hearted man. Unlike you, he is a true gentleman.'

His mouth dropped open. Farah was certain that Ali's father would now think she was a thoroughly insolent young woman and wonder how she had the nerve to talk to someone as important as him in this way.

'Enjoy the rest of your evening,' Farah added, and walked off with her head held high.

Inside, her blood was boiling. Then the procession started, and Farah caught a glimpse of Ali walking his sister into the marquee down the aisle. She tried to push the unpleasant exchange out of her mind and began to relax. Seeing the siblings together, witnessing their affectionate bond, made her realise even more just how different they were from their father.

Ali's sister wore a traditional green and yellow *lengha*, and her hair was braided with yellow and white flowers which hung down to one side. Her scarf was pinned beautifully at the crown of her head and around her shoulders, so that it dropped down elegantly. Floating above her was the red *dupatta* that was traditionally held over the top of the bride-to-be as she came in on her henna night. The four corners of the large, heavily embroidered red and gold scarf were held by four members of the family: Ali was at the front to her right, and three male cousins held the other corners. It was like a protective canopy, and protectiveness is what it symbolised, but it also gave an almost regal feel to the entrance, making the woman feel like a princess. Ali smiled at Farah as he walked past; she smiled back, and the melody and lyrics of the traditional *mehndi* song flowed into her ears.

> The night of the *mehndi* has arrived, the night of the
>   *mehndi* has arrived
> Look at the hands of the beautiful bride
> Full of colour, and fragrantly adorned
> She hides the dreams of her beloved in her heart.

Farah's mind drifted as she reflected on the lyrics; she thought about the hopes and dreams that a bride-to-be carries on this important evening, just days away from her wedding day, when she will utter those all-important words in her *nikah*: *kabool hai*. Just those two words, 'I consent', will seal the Islamic marriage contract and change her life forever. Seeing these formalities and celebrations played out here in Pakistan really brought home to Farah the value of culture, traditions and religion, of how they all play an integral part in bringing together this union in the most beautiful way possible. And then her mind turned to her return to England; she was looking forward to seeing her parents, for she had missed them dearly, but she also had to face going back to the office.

And then a strange feeling overcame her; as soon as she thought about the office, something started to niggle away at her, although she couldn't say what it was exactly.

*

That night, Ali was sound asleep in his bed when his mobile phone rang. There were six or seven rings before he slowly opened his eyes. He looked at the phone; it was Farah. And it was 3.30 a.m.

'Hello,' he said groggily.

'Ali!' she replied loudly.

'Do you know what time it is?'

'Yes, of course I know what time it is!'

'I only got to sleep a short while ago. And I only dropped you off a couple of hours ago. What's wrong?'

'Ali, I've got it!' Farah almost shouted.

'Got what?' Ali asked, as he rubbed his eyes, and stifled a yawn.

'I've worked it out. I know where it is.'

'Where what is?'

'I know where the evidence is – with a *friend*, stored away *safely.*'

'Are you talking about Zaheer? What are you thinking, Farah? Don't do anything rash!' said Ali, now totally focused on the conversation.

'I'm catching the morning flight back home; it leaves at six a.m. I need to get back to London to sort this out.'

'What? You can't go alone; I will come with you.'

'I appreciate your offering to do that, but think about it. You accompanying me will look suspicious and draw attention to what I'm doing. If I go alone, it will just look like I'm returning home,' said Farah.

'But it's so sudden,' said Ali.

'I know it's sudden; I'm sorry. I will phone you once it's all sorted.'

'But you haven't actually told me what you are going to sort. You're not making much sense.'

'It will make sense; I promise. Now I need to finish packing quickly and get to the airport.'

'Wait, I'll drive you.'

'No, it's fine, the hotel has arranged a car for me, and as I said before, it's best if I keep a low profile with this. I'm going to be out of here shortly.'

'Oh, I see.'

'Take care, Ali.'

'But—'

Farah cut off the call before Ali could finish his sentence. He flopped back onto his bed and rubbed his forehead as he tried to work out what the conversation had been all about. He wasn't happy about her going alone; he couldn't help but worry about her safety considering the sort of people she was dealing with. And it would help if he knew what she was planning on doing; he wondered why she didn't trust him enough to tell him. But putting all those things aside, he had expected to spend a few more days with Farah yet, and Ali knew deep down that he was going to miss her.

42

Paul Drake finished his telephone call, placed the telephone receiver gently back on the handset and walked over to his grey metal filing cabinet to pull out the correspondence file on a fraud case that he had been meaning to get around to looking at all week. It was a biggie, a case involving millions, and there were literally thousands of pages to get through. The documents were stored in black folders in boxes stacked on the floor at the side of his desk; boxes the paralegal would be trawling through in the days ahead.

He sat back at his desk, opened the file, and then his phone buzzed.

'Yes?' he asked his secretary rather grumpily.

'Mr Drake, just to let you know, Farah is back in the office, and there are three gentlemen here to see you.'

'Thanks for letting me know. I will catch up with Farah shortly. As for the three men, I don't recall any appointments for this morning. In fact, I remember blocking out the diary specifically because I wanted to look at this fraud case,' he said, a little annoyed at having been disturbed before he had barely opened the file.

'No, they don't have an appointment, Mr Drake,' she replied.

'Then why are you bothering me? You know I don't see anyone unless they have booked an appointment.'

'Yes, I know, Mr Drake. But these gentlemen are with Farah, and they're not clients.'

'Oh?'

'No, Mr Drake, they're police officers. They say they need to see you right now. Immediately.'

Paul fell silent for a few seconds.

'OK, show them through.'

Paul opened his office door to see Farah accompanied by a tall, dark, plain-clothes policeman, who entered with a shorter Asian-looking man, also in plain clothes. Behind him was an officer in uniform.

'Hello, Paul,' said Farah.

'Good morning, Farah,' he replied, and then looked at the police officers.

'I'm Detective Chief Inspector Leon. This is Detective Constable Sandeep, and this is Police Constable Smith,' announced the policeman. The men did not shake hands.

Paul didn't know what any of this was about, but clearly it was something serious. He glanced at Farah, who stood silently and gave nothing away.

'How can I help you?' asked Paul.

'We have a search warrant for these premises,' DCI Leon told him, and handed the papers to Paul, who glanced briefly at the warrant; a cursory look was sufficient for him to be satisfied that the warrant was in order.

'What on earth for?' asked Paul.

'We believe you have files or papers for a Mr Zaheer Mansur. Is that correct?' asked DCI Leon.

'Also perhaps for his wife, Aneela Mansur?' added DC Sandeep.

'No, I don't. Look here, can you just tell me what all this is about? You can't just stroll in here and search this office without even an explanation,' Paul said.

'Mr Drake, you of all people, being an experienced lawyer, should know how this works. Now, if you have nothing to hand over to us, we will begin our search,' said DCI Leon.

The three policemen went over to the cabinet and started taking out and looking at the files, one by one, discarding each file on the floor haphazardly, before moving on to the next one.

Farah walked up to Paul.

'Don't you think it's best that you just co-operate? You know they'll turn this place upside down if you don't.'

Paul didn't respond. He rubbed his hand along the back of his neck as he thought for a moment.

'Wait,' said Paul, infuriated by the intrusion of the police officers and the feeling that Farah was back to her meddling. 'I've just remembered; Zaheer gave me an envelope to keep in

322

the office safe. He told me it was just some personal papers; their wills, I think. I haven't opened it, so I can't confirm what's in there.'

'Lead the way,' said DCI Leon.

Paul took the safe key from the top drawer of his desk and headed towards a small room at the end of the corridor, followed by Farah and the police officers. The room was so tiny that only Paul and DCI Leon could squeeze in.

Paul was becoming increasingly irritated with Farah; she had turned up at her own offices with three policemen in tow, ready to effectively raid the place, and wouldn't even so much as hint at what it was all about. As soon as Paul had heard Zaheer's name, he knew it didn't bode well, and he wasn't happy that Zaheer might have put him in an awkward position.

Paul inserted the long silver key, turned the handle and opened the large, old, speckled grey safe, which was bolted to the floor. After rummaging towards the back, he took out a brown A4-sized envelope and handed it to DCI Leon.

Farah watched DCI Leon emerge from the room, followed by Paul; he opened the envelope and looked at the contents. Paul's face was now flushed; he shot a glance at Farah, but her eyes were fixed on DCI Leon as she waited eagerly for him to reveal the contents. Everyone stood close by. Farah watched for some change in the expression on the police officer's face; he was studying the papers very closely, but he didn't say anything. He read as much as he needed to and quietly placed the documents back in the envelope.

'Thank you for your co-operation, Mr Drake,' said DCI Leon. 'This will do for now, but we may come back again, either to carry out further searches or to question you if relevant. I can tell you that Mr Mansur is under investigation for very some serious offences. Please do not contact him or inform him in any way about this visit, or about our taking the documents. I should tell you that you will be implicated if you do contact him or tip him off in any way, as you probably well know.'

Farah allowed a small inner smile to branch out on to her lips, and let out a hitherto suppressed breath of relief.

'Right,' replied Paul. Farah thought he looked dazed. She had never seen him like this before; he was always slick, and together, no matter what the circumstances may be. Despite seeing tough challenges in the office and in the courtroom, Paul always had a cool demeanour, and this had slipped today. Although Farah wasn't sorry if evidence had been found against Zaheer, she did feel a bit sorry for Paul, as no doubt Zaheer would have reeled him in just like all the others.

'Please, let me show you out,' said Farah, and she accompanied the three police officers out of the building. She was glad that there might now be some closure to this whole mess. As they left, she took out her mobile phone; she had promised to phone Ali and update him. However, when she did call, there was no answer.

*

Mr Amin showed Farah into his office at the High Commission.

'I believe you have some news? I have heard about some of the developments, but I would like to hear the full story from you,' he said.

They sat down facing one another across the desk. His secretary walked in with a tea tray, and left, closing the door behind her.

'Yes. I do have news for you. You will be pleased to hear that Zaheer Mansur was arrested in Islamabad a few hours ago; and I doubt that even his slick, expensive lawyers will be able to get him out of this one.'

'I did hear about his arrest, but I don't know any of the details as of yet. What happened?' Mr Amin enquired.

Farah wondered how he might take the news she was about to deliver about someone who was until recently his right-hand man.

'It seems that Mr Mansur has been a very bad man, in more ways than one,' said Farah sombrely.

Mr Amin listened quietly.

'It turned out that some very important documents had been stored at Drake's. I don't think Paul knew anything about the contents of the envelope, and that is the official police line. In fact, I think he feels like a bit of a mug. This giving business to the firm, and taking a modest kickback, it was all just a cover to gain Paul's trust, and then make sure he was compromised if the authorities got wind of anything suspicious. The money Zaheer got from Drake's was insignificant. He just needed Paul to store papers for him in his safe, no questions asked.'

'So, what did the police find?' Mr Amin asked.

'They found enough evidence to land him in real trouble, the consequences of which I'm sure he won't be able to wriggle out of. It turns out that poor Razia overheard a very important conversation; she may not have known the significance at the time, but it was enough to rattle Zaheer. It seems certain that he had her, shall we say, disposed of to make sure she didn't say anything, even by accident. The police in Pakistan are now aware of the letter that she wrote in prison and are going to investigate Razia's death, and if they can possibly do it, then they will add murder to the other charges.'

'OK, so Razia's death aside, what are they charging him with?' Mr Amin asked.

Farah sipped her tea. Mr Amin took a *nan khatai* biscuit and placed it on his saucer whilst he waited for Farah to continue.

'In the envelope that was stored in the safe, there was an agreement.'

'What kind of an agreement?'

'A bribery agreement.'

'Really?'

Farah could see that this revelation hit Mr Amin harder than she had anticipated.

'A bribery agreement,' he repeated, and placed his cup and saucer back on the desk.

'Yes. It seems that Zaheer had used his official position to connect with an arms dealer to supply weapons to Pakistan. The bribery agreement stated that for the introduction and successful sale of the military equipment, Zaheer would be paid over a million dollars and it also listed the prices for the various arms and machinery to be artificially inflated, allowing further kickbacks to be paid along the supply network.'

'What a complete disregard of all his duties not only as someone working in a position of power and trust, but as a citizen of his own country. How could he even think of being such a traitor, of betraying his Motherland in such a heinous way? What happened with this deal? Did he manage to conclude it?' asked Mr Amin.

'Luckily, it hadn't gone through yet. It would appear that I, without realising it, was the one who inadvertently put a stop to it. Zaheer was very close to concluding the deal. But then I raised the alarm about Razia, which meant he had to return to Pakistan. As he was suspended from his post, and was under investigation, it all had to go on the back burner.'

'Unbelievable,' commented Mr Amin.

'I will always deeply regret not being able to piece it all together in time,' Farah said, with a shudder. 'If I had spotted something sooner, Razia might still be alive; as it is, a whole family has been torn apart.'

'Do not reproach yourself, *beti*. He managed to deceive just about everyone, including me. I was his superior, remember, and I had no idea whatsoever about what he was up to. You at least raised the alarm about his mistreatment of Razia, but I was clueless about that as well as everything else. If I'd had even an inkling, I would have taken action immediately. I must also be allowed to have my own regrets; I should have been more aware of the sort of man he was, and what he was capable of.'

'Well, there's nothing more we can do about this case. I couldn't help Razia in time, but that doesn't mean I can't help others like her who are suffering in the world today. Modern-day slavery is an insidious evil, and someone has to do something.'

Farah got up to leave.

'There is just one more thing. I've had a request. From Aneela,' said Mr Amin.

'Really? What kind of a request?'

'A request to meet with you. She's back in London, and she really wants to see you.'

Farah thought back to the last time she had seen Aneela; she could picture her now, stood over her, threatening her, telling her to stop meddling.

'Why would I want to see her? She should be locked up alongside her husband. She's just as guilty as him.'

'I don't blame you for not wanting to see her . . .'

'I detect a "but",' remarked Farah.

'She cannot harm you. If nothing else, you can give her a piece of your mind and bring some closure to the whole sorry affair.'

'I suppose so,' Farah murmured, but her mind was already drifting.

As Farah left the office, she thought about Razia once again; how despite having a voice, she had been voiceless. Farah couldn't dispel the thoughts of how alone and helpless Razia must have felt, and she promised herself that she would make it her mission to help others like Razia and try to ease their suffering.

43

Aneela answered the door. She wore a plain navy blue *salwar* suit today. She had very little make-up on and looked about ten years younger for it. Her hair was scrunched up into a simple ponytail, and her nails were naked today.

She showed Farah into the lounge, which was now almost bare of all its fancy showpieces, paintings and ornaments. The sofas were still there. How the mighty have fallen; perhaps a bit of a cliché, but Farah couldn't think of a better phrase.

Farah sat down in the single seater.

'Would you like tea or coffee?' Aneela asked.

'Nothing, thank you. I'm fine.'

Farah was taken aback by the hospitality shown by Aneela, especially when she thought back to her earlier hostility.

Aneela walked over to the mantelpiece and picked something up.

'Your earring,' she said, as she handed it to Farah.

Farah couldn't believe it; she had given up all hope of ever seeing it again.

'I found it in the pantry,' Aneela added.

The pantry, thought Farah; the place where she had secretly first set eyes on Razia. She couldn't think about that moment without a mix of grief and anger bubbling up inside her, although she told herself that she needed to try and stay calm.

'Can I fetch you a cold drink, perhaps?' asked Aneela.

'I'm good.' Farah let out a pent-up sigh. 'This isn't really a social call. I probably wouldn't have come had it not been for Mr Amin. Anyway, I'm here now, and perhaps we can get this over and done with.'

Aneela sat down slowly.

'You must think it strange my asking you to come here.'

'It did cross my mind.'

'I— I wanted to explain,' said Aneela hesitantly.

Farah rolled her eyes; she could feel the fury towards Aneela simmering inside her, and she wondered if she would be able to restrain herself from launching a full-on attack.

'Explain, huh? I don't think you could say anything that would ever "explain" what you and that rotten husband of yours did to poor Razia. You beat her, imprisoned her, starved her, and ultimately you killed her.'

Farah could see that her words had wounded Aneela, who fought back the tears and then inhaled a few sharp breaths.

'It is not how it seems.'

'Really?' asked Farah; just like her husband, Aneela was refusing to take any responsibility for her actions. 'I saw you; I heard you. The evening of the dinner party, I was watching you both from the pantry, listening to your abusive tirade against poor Razia, who was crouched over in the kitchen. You were threatening her!'

'What exactly did you see and hear? Did you see me hit Razia, or even threaten to? No! What you actually saw was me pulling my husband away before he could make contact with Razia. Yow saw me intervening and stopping him from hurting her. I always tried to whenever I could. It wasn't always possible. How do you think Razia got that scar on her face? That happened on one of those days when I couldn't stop him.'

Farah held her breath for just a moment and thought back to the scene in the kitchen.

'I know you *think* you have possession of all the facts, but believe me, you don't,' said Aneela. She joined her hands in her lap and interlocked her fingers.

'I am actually Zaheer's second wife; or should I say, much younger second wife. Did you know that?'

'No, I didn't.' This really was news to Farah. Aneela had agreed to be a second wife; something Farah herself had refused to do for Tahir.

'I am twenty-one years younger than him. His first wife lives permanently in the family *haveli* in Pakistan; I am the one who stays with him wherever he is; his full-time wife, if you like. I travel and stay with him wherever he goes, and I see to his every need, if you know what I mean.'

Farah was genuinely surprised to hear this. She had noticed that Aneela looked younger than Zaheer but had never guessed the age gap to be so vast. She must have been very young when she married him, thought Farah – in which case, would she have had much say in the matter?

'He and his first wife, they have three children; all boys. The youngest is in his early teens now,' said Aneela, although Farah noticed that her voice choked up a little as she did so.

Farah thought back to her visit to the Mansur mansion. The teenage boy who she saw fleetingly in the hallway, and the woman who addressed her and Ali briefly, before she disappeared as well. It all suddenly made sense now.

'I think I might have seen him when we went to the *haveli*. And his mother too. Of course, I didn't know who they were.'

'She is the traditional, plain, stay-at-home, run-the-house, see-to-the-children wife. I am the younger, prettier, glamourous one. The one who travels around the world with him, who goes to all the parties with him, who entertains all the guests for him; the one who looks good on his arm. I am the trophy wife.'

'Oh, I see,' said Farah. She thought about the glitzy life Aneela had obviously led, and what a contrast this was to the life of the plain, traditional wife she had seen back in Pakistan. She doubted very much if the life of glamour had been any hardship for Aneela.

'Me and Razia were never all that different, you know,' Aneela continued. 'We were both slaves.'

Hearing this comparison really rattled Farah; she was tempted to give Aneela a piece of her mind, but somehow held her tongue and allowed her to continue.

'The only difference is that I'm still alive and she is dead. But there were many times when I wished that I was dead.'

Aneela cleared her throat before continuing.

'I come from a middle-class family in Lahore that fell upon hard times. My mother used to be a teacher, and my father was the principal at the same school. They also taught local children privately. I only have one sibling; a brother who is younger than me, and severely disabled, mentally and physically. But we lived comfortably in a small apartment in the city. My parents always managed to provide for his needs and to see to my education.'

Farah thought about how tough it must have been to have a severely disabled child, especially in Pakistan, where the healthcare facilities were nowhere near as good as in Britain.

'That is, until our lives turned on their heads, when my father died suddenly of a heart attack, and my mother's health deteriorated very quickly. Her diabetes was out of control, and with my father gone, we struggled to pay the bills and to feed ourselves, let alone pay for much-needed medicines and treatment for my mum and brother. I finished university and started to look for a job. Our savings had dwindled away, and we were certain to lose our home because of our mounting debts. The apartment itself was in desperate need of repairs.'

Farah tried to imagine what this must have been like. She had never experienced any such difficulties; she'd had amazing support from her parents throughout her studies and during her training before she qualified. She couldn't imagine doing all that and being responsible for looking after others as well.

'Then suddenly, out of nowhere, a marriage proposal came from Zaheer. He had seen me at my university when he had come to make some presentations at an awards ceremony, and apparently, he was smitten. He enquired after me and someone mentioned my circumstances; he didn't waste any time. He saw and seized the opportunity. He pounced on my vulnerable situation.'

After getting to know Zaheer so well, after seeing for herself the predatory nature of his character, Farah could have some idea of Aneela's situation.

'He asked my mother for my hand in marriage, and in return he said he would move my mum and brother to better accommodation and see to all my family's expenses. I would never say that my mother forced me into the marriage, but I didn't really have much choice. We were crippled financially, and about to become homeless.'

Farah could only conjecture as to the sort of pressure that Aneela must have felt at the time to agree to the proposal. She could feel some sympathy in this regard, but at the same time, it did not excuse Aneela's complicity with Zaheer's treatment of Razia. In fact, in some ways it made it worse.

'Even if I had found a job straight away, I would never have had a salary that would be able to meet the medical needs of my family,' continued Aneela. 'So I agreed to the proposal. We got married. And to this day, my mother and brother want for nothing. They, and Zaheer, all had everything they needed; the only one who lost out was me.'

'What do you want from me? Do you want me to feel sorry for you? You stood by and let your husband beat an innocent young girl,' said Farah.

'I too was trapped; my family's welfare depended upon my staying in this marriage. But it was more than that. I was petrified of what he would do if I ever left him; to me, to my family. I'm not like you. I was never brave enough. I wasn't even brave enough to fight for my children.'

Farah could see that Aneela's face was troubled, as though she was trying to push away something too painful to talk about.

'Your children? I thought you didn't have any kids.'

'I became pregnant twice. I was so happy. The only thing that could have made my existence tolerable, pleasurable even, was to have a child or children of my own. But you see, the scans showed that I was expecting girls. And Zaheer did not want any girls. I had to have them aborted; both of them. My beautiful girls. The older one would have been seven this year, and the younger one five.'

Farah didn't know what to say. She looked closely at Aneela and tried to visualise the horrors that this woman had been through. Farah knew she could never stand in her shoes, but she could imagine the abuse that Zaheer had inflicted on her, on both her body and her mind. Her thoughts flashed back to the day that Mr Mansur Senior had simply held his hand up to silence her; she could only imagine the way that Zaheer and his family must have treated Aneela.

'Because of the complications of the second abortion, I have been told that I will never be able to have children.'

Aneela's façade cracked, and tears began to trickle down her face.

'I'm so sorry,' said Farah. 'I had absolutely no idea. You looked so in control, so self-assured. I would never have guessed.'

'Why would you? You saw the glamorous, all smiling, all cheerful, devoted wife. But I was dead inside. I did try to caution you. You mistook my warnings as utterances of blind loyalty towards my husband. I was trying to warn you not interfere in the affairs of this man, for your own sake, and for Razia's. I knew, more than anyone else, what he was capable of.'

Farah put her hand to her mouth in dismay, unable to say anything. She remembered how insistent Aneela had been, desperate even, that evening when she had gone to their apartment with Mr Amin. Farah recalled how she had tried her level best to get Farah to put a stop to it all; it had been her way of warning her.

'I'm not saying this to make you feel guilty,' Aneela added quickly. 'I don't blame anyone, except for him.'

Aneela shifted her weight forward and leaned closer to Farah.

'I asked you to come here not so that you would feel sorry for me. It's because I wanted to thank you.'

'Thank me?'

'Of course I am desperately sad that Razia is dead; you must believe that. But if it wasn't for you, I would never have been able to escape him. It's thanks to you that he is behind bars, and from what I have been told, he is likely to remain there for a very long time, hopefully until the day he dies.'

Farah undertook the journey back home feeling confounded and astonished; just when she had thought she couldn't hear any more wickedness about Zaheer, here she was, reeling on the tube journey back to her apartment at the thought of what he had inflicted upon Aneela. And she reeled even more at the fact that she had got it all so terribly wrong; she had assumed Aneela to be complicit, because she was Zaheer's wife and enjoyed the high life with him. In all of the mayhem, she had completely missed the clues that pointed to her being another silent victim.

44

Farah's second day back at work was almost over, and she had found it hard to concentrate. Thoughts of Aneela had tumbled around in her mind, and she wondered to what extent Paul had known about Aneela's sad life, about the way she had also suffered at the hands of his best friend. She concluded that he had probably not known a great deal; Zaheer had managed to pull the wool over his eyes on just about everything else, so probably this too.

She had tried to contact Ali many times since she had got back to London, but he hadn't picked up or returned any of her calls or replied to her messages. She was anxious to bring him up to speed, to tell him about what she had discovered about Aneela. She really wanted to talk to him, not only about this latest development, but more generally about the aftermath of the whole affair, and about what, if anything, she could do, for she felt she must do something.

Farah came out of the offices at the end of the day and started her walk to the tube station. When she turned the corner, she nearly fell over with shock. There was Ali, leaning against the wall.

'Hi!' he said and pulled out a box of *mitai* from behind his back. 'For you!'

'Oh my God! What are you doing here? When did you come? Why on earth didn't you—'

'Forget all that, we can discuss it later,' he butted in. 'I saw a really nice halal Chinese place around the corner. What say you?'

Farah let out a loud sigh, smiled at him, nodded her head, thinking how food always came first with Ali, and they walked to the restaurant.

Ali took a long time to order, and he wasn't his quite his usual chatty self, which Farah found strange. They hadn't really had a proper conversation yet, and Farah had so many questions she needed answering.

'Ali. What's going on? How come you are in London?' she asked him.

'Well, it's nice to see you too,' he remarked, but his words faded away quietly towards the end of the sentence.

'I'm sorry. I didn't mean it like that,' Farah replied. 'It's really good to see you.'

Ali remained quiet. Farah looked at him, but he didn't make much eye contact. He checked his phone briefly before looking up.

'Great news about Zaheer; my mate in the police filled me in,' said Ali.

'I've been trying to get hold of you. I wanted you to hear it from me first,' Farah said. She really had wanted to be the one to tell him what had happened.

'I did see the missed calls, but I was busy trying to sort my flight and then I thought we may as well speak when I got here.'

'He is behind bars still, isn't he?' asked Farah, still fearing Zaheer might wriggle out of it.

'Treason is effectively what he's guilty of by abusing his position to try to act against Pakistan's best interests. And with the charge of murder in addition, I don't think he will be going anywhere anytime soon.'

'Good! I hope they lock him up and throw away the key. He should rot in there until the day he dies!' she replied.

After this short burst of chatter, Ali went quiet again. His being awkwardly silent was not something Farah was familiar with; nor was his avoiding eye contact.

'What's the matter?' she asked him.

'What do you mean?'

'You're quiet, which is unusual for you at the best of times, let alone when you have just hopped off a plane and turned up outside my work so randomly, without a word of warning. And you're fidgety.'

Ali put his mobile phone down. His face, although not unhappy, was strained. For the first time since they had sat down together, he looked directly at Farah.

'You must know?' Ali said softly.

'Know what?'

'You must realise why I am here. You must know why I am sat before you just three days before my sister's big day, why I have travelled nearly five thousand miles to speak to you only to fly back in time for the wedding.'

With everything that had been going on, Farah had forgotten how close his sister's wedding was. She looked at him, and wondered why he had actually come; she wanted to believe her gut feeling, but she couldn't be sure. She didn't want to make a fool of herself. She couldn't put herself through that.

'I'm not a mind reader. Why don't you tell me why you are sat in London three days before your sister's wedding?'

He went quiet again but continued to look at her.

'If you have something to say, Ali – then please, just say it. What is it that I must know?' Farah asked softly.

'You must know . . . you must know that since you left Pakistan, I have missed you.'

Farah let out a tiny sigh.

'I've missed you too,' she replied, and smiled at him.

'No, I mean I have *really* missed you,' Ali said.

Farah looked down for a few seconds; she wanted to be honest with him. She took a soft breath in.

'Maybe . . . maybe I've *really* missed you as well—'

'Then let's not be apart any more,' Ali said.

'What do you mean by that?' Farah asked, as she took her elbows off the table and sat back in her chair.

'Come back to Pakistan,' Ali responded.

Farah thought about this impulsive statement of his; it was madness.

'I can't do that. My life is in England – my family, my career. What is there to keep me in Pakistan?'

Ali reached out across the table for her hands; she leaned forward and slowly placed her hands in his. He squeezed them, gently.

'Us,' Ali said.

Farah didn't respond. She thought about them both; together, as a couple. How would it be?

'I know we haven't known each other for very long,' continued Ali, 'but we just fit. We make each other happy. We make each other laugh. We can talk about anything. We understand each other. How often does that happen?'

Farah slowly let out the deep breath that she had been holding without having realised it.

'You must feel it?' he asked.

'Yes, I do. I do feel it. I don't think I have ever felt this comfortable with another man. I love talking to you. I love being with you, I love spending time with you.'

'Then why don't we build on that, and maybe have a future together?' Ali asked.

Farah couldn't help but smile.

'Why, Mr Ali Omar, what exactly are you saying?'

He smiled back.

'I really, really like you. Perhaps I love you. I definitely hate being without you. And I sense you feel the same?'

'Yes. I do,' confirmed Farah. She had tried her best not to pay too much attention to the feelings she was having for Ali. But now here he was, right in front of her, telling her how he felt, and she could no longer deny her own feelings for him. She had fallen for him; quietly, happily, naturally.

'Then let's do this, let's be together – in England, Pakistan, both, wherever. We will work it out. What do you say?' Ali asked, as he squeezed Farah's hands.

Farah smiled at him, but her cheery mood suddenly changed when she thought about an obstacle that perhaps Ali couldn't foresee.

'I say that there is one big problem,' she replied.

'What's that?'

Farah's mind floated back to Pakistan, and she cringed as she remembered the conversation.

'Your dad. He hates my guts. He said as much to me at the *mehndi*. And I gave back as good as I got. You could say I burned my bridges with him that evening, if there had been any bridges there in the first place. I don't think he would accept me as his daughter-in-law.'

'My dad lives on another planet. To be perfectly frank with you, I don't really care what he thinks. I'm way past that now. My mum and sister adore you; he'll be out in the cold on his own on this one. He's my father, and he's my problem. I will deal with him.'

Their hands were still sealed together. Farah smiled.

'So, what do you say?' Ali asked again.

'I say . . . I need to make a phone call.'

'What? We are in the middle of a romantic conversation and you need to ring someone?' he protested.

Farah just smiled as she dialled the number on her phone. Ali looked on in bewilderment.

'Mum. It's me. OK, yes, before we talk about me coming home to visit you and Dad, there is something else I need to discuss with you first. I've got some really good news for you.'

Farah looked into Ali's eyes, and continued, 'I've found myself a really nice Pakistani boy!'

EPILOGUE

Ali sat on the front row of the large assembly room, which was completely full. The ceremony was about to come to a close. Extraordinary people and important dignitaries from all corners of the globe had gathered together at the United Nations in New York to recognise and celebrate the achievements of people from around the world; selfless, inspirational people who had made an outstanding impact in improving the lives of others.

The host took to the stage for the penultimate recognition.

'This final award is in acknowledgement of the remarkable accomplishments of a young woman who has made great strides in helping others, even though she is herself only twenty years of age. She has carried on the work that was first started by her parents, and has taken it to new heights, opening a further two refuges in the United Kingdom as places of safety for those caught up or trafficked into modern-day slavery, and she has done much to achieve better working conditions for those trapped in bonded slavery in Pakistan. The charity has done an enormous amount to help many to escape bonded slavery, and what is more, it has given those people the tools to start afresh, free from the fetters of slavery. Her incessant campaigning has ensured the passage of a law in Pakistan requiring the feudal landlords to provide free education for the children of all their workers, and to give the families basic rights to free healthcare. The final award today goes to none other than Razia Farah Omar.'

A loud round of applause erupted from the audience, and people took to their feet to show their appreciation of the winner. Razia made her way onto the stage; the way she walked and carried herself was so much like her mother, thought Ali.

She shook hands with the speaker and received her award gratefully. She went and stood in front of the microphone.

'Thank you, everyone. Thank you.'

The people in the audience slowly stopped clapping and sat back down in their seats.

'It is a great honour and absolute privilege to receive this accolade today, and to be acknowledged in this way. I know this room is full of so many deserving men and women who are all making a massive difference to our world. And, whilst I am grateful for this recognition, I cannot in all honesty take all the credit for this award. I must thank three other people, for they have all played their role, and without them I would not be stood here before you. I was named after a young woman called Razia.'

Ali could see in his mind's eye, as though it was yesterday, the first time he and Farah had visited Razia in jail. He remembered how good Farah had been with her; warm, comforting, engaging. Those qualities were innate in Farah, part of her DNA.

'My mother had insisted, years before I was born, that if she ever had a girl, then she would name her Razia, after the young woman whom she had tried to help, a young woman who had inadvertently introduced her to the unjust world of modern-day slavery in all its ugly colours. The meaning of Razia, as I understand it, is one who is satisfied, pleased and contented, and perhaps we can all learn to be more content with what we have and strive to do more for those who do not have.'

The name could not have been given to a more fitting person; the Razia he and Farah had known had suffered so much and had complained about so little.

'My middle name, Farah, has been given to me in honour of my mother. My late mother.'

Ali held his breath a little, as he pictured himself and Farah in the Chinese restaurant in London; holding hands, cementing the beginning of their beautiful relationship.

'I did not know my mother. I never saw her. She died whilst giving birth to me. She passed away minutes after I was born. She never held me. She left this world before I even let out my first cry. But my mother's legacy lives on. She started the Razia Foundation before I was born; an organisation that helps slaves all around the world, and which continues to go from strength to strength in its mission to fight for the freedom of modern-day slaves.'

Ali remembered the exact day when he and Farah signed on the dotted line and established the foundation; he thought back to them smiling as they opened the doors to their first office in Islamabad together, when they opened their first refuge in Birmingham, followed by the second one in Lahore, together, and when they held their first fundraiser in London together.

'I could not be prouder of the charity, and everything it stands for. Finally, there is one more person that I must thank and give a fair portion of the credit to. He is the most wonder-ful man in my life: my father, Ali. Without him, without his guidance and his watchful eye, I would not be the person I am today. Despite enduring the tragedy of his life, when he lost the woman he loved just a few years after marrying her, he bravely continued my mother's work with the Razia Founda-tion, and I owe him everything; he is the reason that I stand before you. Thanks, Dad. This is for you.'

Ali watched from the front row with pride, as she held the award high and pointed it towards him. When Razia left the stage, Ali walked over to her. He drew her close to him with a warm embrace, and then he kissed his daughter on her head, twice.

'Thanks, Dad!' said Razia, 'but you're so funny; you always kiss me twice!'

A tear escaped Ali's eye as he remembered Farah's last words to him; he was holding his wife in his arms, and as he cried, just before she drew her final breath, she said:

'Always show her that you love her, and every time you do, give her my share of the love, too.'

Unbound is the world's first crowdfunding publisher, established in 2011.

We believe that wonderful things can happen when you clear a path for people who share a passion. That's why we've built a platform that brings together readers and authors to crowdfund books they believe in – and give fresh ideas that don't fit the traditional mould the chance they deserve.

This book is in your hands because readers made it possible. Everyone who pledged their support is listed below. Join them by visiting unbound.com and supporting a book today.

Tamanna Abdul-Karim

Mediah Ahmed

Perveen Ahmed

Mashy Ahmer

Shamim Akhtar

Asna Zohra Akram

Rita Arafa

Claire Armitstead

Sandra Armor

Max Aslam

Seema Aslam

Aniez Atlas

Karen Attwood

Ess Aye

Kathryn Azarpay

Amy Bailey

Kerry Bailey

Marian Baldwin

George Merchant Ballentyne

Brooke Banks

Margaret Bassett

Meera Betab

Safia Boot

Mark Bowsher

Richard W H Bray

Jackie Breen

Andrew Budden

Sofia Buncy

Lauren Burns

Claire Chambers

Abbi Chishty

Rachel Clewley

Kerry Clifford

Anne Cockitt

Jane Commane

Tamsen Courtenay

Sajda Currah

Daniel Dalton MEP

Jonathan Davidson

Aaron Dosanjh

Jessica Duchen

Michael Durante

Hafsa Ebrahim

Amanda Elliott

Lisa Elsing-Holden

Clare England

GP Evans

Jean-Michel Ferrieux

Peter Flack

Rosie Garthwaite

Michael Gough

David Green

John Griffiths

Rehana Hanif

Rabiha Hannan

Ken Hawkins

Carolyn E Heath

Emily Holzhausen

Asaf Hussain

Sajad Hussain

Sally Insley

A Iqbal

Jesse Kaur

Abda Khan

Amina Khan

Cass Khan

Ibrahim Khan

Imran Khan

Rizwana Khan

Sabra Khan

Tanveer Khan

Kanwal Khokhar

Shahzad Khokhar

Dan Kieran

Julian Knight MP

Jakob Kveder

Catherine Langson
Frances Lasok
Tracey Lindsay
Marianthi Makra
Asma Malik
Bushra Malik
Rukhsana Masood
Emmeline May
Seema McArdle
Aminah Mehboob
Hajrah Mehboob
Yusuf and Musa Mehboob
Robyna Mian
Philip Middleton
Anita Mir
John Mitchinson
Valdemar Moller
Nick Morgan
Judy Munday
Iram Nadeem
Arifa Nasim
Fozia Nasim
Carlo Navato
Petro Nicolaides
Kate Oprava
Tahira Parveen
Nadee Patel

Anita Pati
Anne-Marie Pearman
Justin Pollard
Kathryn Prescott
Lauren Price
Gwynn Price Rowlands
Holly Pritchard
Wazma Qais
Nasreen Qamar
Nicky Quint
Shaheen Qureshi
Zahra Qureshi
Amarjit Rai
Balvinder Rai
Jenny Ramsden
Sanna Rashid
Jane Richardson
Frances Robinson
Kathleen Rogan-Pearman
Usha Rowan
Waleed Saeed
Saba Sahar
Ioanna Schuppert
Carla Seet
Shubha Sharma
Nerinder Sira
Allan Smith

Henriette B. Stavis

Cathryn Steele

Pauline Subenko

Chris Sudworth

Kate Walker

Emma Wilde

Peter Williams

David Woollcombe

Linda Youdelis

Shannaz Zahoor